As the twentieth century draws to a close, people are driving solar-powered cars—and the air is cleaner. They're eating tasty "left-side" food—and living longer. And they're reading TV's electronic newspaper—and saving trees.

There's a woman in the White House to advise the country, and Dr. Love on TV's Love Channel to advise the lovelorn. Businesses grant new fathers paternity leave, while babies are pampered with Velcro diapers and climate-controlled cribs.

It is a time of wonder—as technology advances the quality of our lives.

It is a time of dreams—as we look to the future of the world we leave our children.

It is the time of Lucy Beckwith and Jim Kazan.

Dear Reader,

Our nostalgic journey through the twentieth century draws to a close with popular author Judith Arnold's *A > LOVERBOY*, a look at love in the future—1998, to be exact!

We hope you've enjoyed traveling through time with us. It seems that no matter the time or the place, romance is always in our hearts.

All the authors in the A Century of American Romance series had their own special reasons for waxing nostalgic—maybe it was to relive the years of their youth or to recreate those of their parents. Maybe it was to remember again and again that special moment when they fell in love. Be sure you have read each and every one of their stories. Consult the listing of all the A Century of American Romance titles at the back of this book.

From all the authors and all of us here at Harlequin, here's hoping A Century of American Romance has become part of your most cherished memories....

Sincerely,

Debra Matteucci

Senior Editor & Editorial Coordinator
Harlequin Books
300 East 42nd St., Sixth Floor
New York, NY 10017

JUDITH ARNOLD

1990s
A>
LOVERBOY

Harlequin Books

TORONTO • NEW YORK • LONDON
AMSTERDAM • PARIS • SYDNEY • HAMBURG
STOCKHOLM • ATHENS • TOKYO • MILAN

To Ted,
who keeps my computer (and me)
on-line and humming.

Published May 1991

ISBN 0-373-16389-4

A>LOVERBOY

Prologue

So this is the Great Plains, Dara-Lyn thought as she gazed out the window at the flat earth gliding silently past. She'd go along with the plain part, but not the great.

Maybe it would look better if she weren't staring through a specially tinted pane of UV-reducing glass, or if she weren't whizzing by at three hundred miles an hour. She'd never been on a magnetic-levitation train before yesterday evening, when she'd boarded the overnighter in Los Angeles. She'd wanted to stay awake, but the train, carried along on pulsing magnetic waves like a surfboard on a breaking ocean curl, had traveled so smoothly and silently, she'd been lulled into a deep sleep that lasted all the way to Dallas-Ft. Worth. The recliner seat had been comfortable and the excitement of the trip had drained her of energy. She'd needed the rest; she just regretted having dozed through her very first maglev ride.

She was awake now, alert and anxious. And hungry, but that was a permanent condition for Dara-Lyn. Like her mother, she was short and slim, but unlike her mother, she never had to watch her diet—probably because she preferred left-side food to all that rich, fatty stuff her mother used to adore. Her mother had grown up in a different era. "I was weaned on French fries and chocolate shakes," she used to lament whenever Dara-Lyn prevailed upon her to increase her greens-and-beans consumption. "There are times, Dara-Lyn, when I honestly believe a Snickers bar would be worth risking a few major arteries over."

Dara-Lyn's mother hadn't lived long enough to clog her arteries. The Big One they'd been predicting for so long had finally hit two years ago, and Dulcie Pennybopper had been among the 30,349 Angelinos who'd perished.

A blade of grief sliced through Dara-Lyn and she closed her eyes against the pain. She felt so alone, so alone. It wasn't fair for anyone to have lost so much when she was only fifteen years old. Dara-Lyn had lost her mother. She'd lost her home—some guy in a uniform told her the house had been "structurally compromised" and would have to be wrecker-balled. She'd lost friends not just to the earthquake but to distance; their entire neighborhood had been decimated and the survivors had been shipped off to safer areas for resettlement. Dara-Lyn had been moved to a youth shelter out in San Bernardino and enrolled in a high school full of zit-faced wizards.

They were nice—not just the folks who ran the shelter but also her new classmates. They weren't *it*, but of course, nobody who lived in San Bern could possibly be as *it* as anyone from Los Angeles. What they were was smart. They knew computers: they knew the latest games and how to hack and how to do really legitimate things with their machines, too. For the first six months after the Big One, when telephone service was all fouled up, three of Dara-Lyn's classmates hacked into the temporary long-distance lines, and Dara-Lyn made friends with some spacey wizard in New York City who said if she ever visited his part of the world, he'd show her a good time.

If she had her life to do all over again, maybe she'd become a wizard, too. Everything was computers these days, and she knew only the fundamentals, which made her feel kind of illiterate. And given that her father was arguably the ultimate wizard of the century...

Her father.

For the zillionth time, she pulled the large brown envelope from her backpack and slid out the clippings. Most of the photos were more than a decade old; for all Dara-Lyn knew, he might not be anywhere near as wow-looking today as he was then. He'd been just a few years older than Dara-Lyn was now when the media had crowned him America's most dangerous hacker, and in the pictures, the resemblance between him and Dara-Lyn was uncanny.

Her mother had never told her who her father was. Whenever Dara-Lyn had asked, her mother had said, "I have no idea. The Mensa Sperm Bank refused to reveal the identities of its donors. All I know is that he had to have an IQ of over one hundred fifty to be allowed to make a deposit. You were conceived with prime sperm, Dara-Lyn."

But after the Big One, when the authorities had let Dara-Lyn salvage some personal belongings from her house before it was razed, she'd found among her mother's things the mysterious brown envelope filled with aged clippings: the numerous newspaper reports about how he'd broken the Pentagon's top-secret codes, the article from a women's magazine about how readers had voted him the sexiest felon of 1988, the issue of *Newsweek* for which he'd been the cover story.

And the item carried by the wire services a few years after his arrest, in which he was quoted as saying, "I'm tired of reporters asking me if I'm really as smart as everyone says I am. That's a judgment call. All I can say is, I earned a Ph.D. from Stanford at the age of twenty-four. I broke a supposedly unbreakable security system in the Pentagon's computer network. I even paid a call at the Mensa Sperm Bank of Palo Alto in 1982. What other evidence do you want?"

Nineteen eighty-two. One year before Dara-Lyn was born.

It was only a matter of hours before she would arrive in Horizon, Kansas. Only a matter of hours before her journey ended, before she found the man responsible for half the genes in her body—"the smart half," her mother had always insisted.

Only a matter of time before Dara-Lyn wrapped her arms around James Kazan, world-renowned hacker, computer genius, blond-haired blue-eyed Wizard Supreme, and said, "Hi, Dad."

Chapter One

A > I crave your body.

Lucy Beckwith closed her eyes, inhaled deeply and counted to ten. Then she let out her breath and reassured herself that hallucinating weird messages on one's monitor was not necessarily a sign of madness.

She had spent too much time at the computer today. The current OSHA guidelines decreed that people whose work entailed viewing computer-display terminals had to be allowed to take a ten-minute break for every hour spent staring at the monitor. But while Lucy was concerned about protecting her vision, she wasn't going to turn off the machine and give her eyes a rest when she was on a roll, when she had momentum and the ideas were flowing. A ten-minute breather might cost her hours in backtracking, stalling and waiting for inspiration to return.

So she hadn't taken a break since she'd gotten back to her office nearly three hours ago, and now, at the end of a long workday, her eyesight was shot. At the bottom of a screen filled with projections for the accuracy of the barometric-pressure prediction program on the Smart-Town energy system she was designing, the letters and numbers had blurred and twisted until she thought they said something totally preposterous.

That was all it was. She would rest with her eyes closed for another minute, take a few more deep breaths, then view the monitor and read the projections she'd called up from the data bank.

A minute passed. She opened her eyes. The sentence was still there.

She pressed the monitor's toggle switch and the screen went blank. Then she pressed it again and uniform rows of kelly-green letters and numbers materialized against a dark gray background. At the bottom of the screen, immediately above the blinking cursor, she read: *A > I crave your body.*

It must be a joke, someone's attempt at risqué graffiti. It was easy enough to tap into Access's central network and leave messages. Either someone had planted a public note as a cute little pick-me-up for anyone who might be tapping into the net during the dreary late-afternoon hours, or someone was sending a personal message to someone else and had somehow connected with Lucy's computer by mistake.

It *had* to be a mistake. No one would ever send Lucy a message like that. But she still found it pretty funny.

Frank had always accused her of having an underdeveloped sense of humor. She supposed he was right, at least when it came to the kind of rib-nudging back-slapping punch-line humor he'd favored. She preferred to think of her sense of humor as warped. She would come home from work chuckling over some incident—like the time her R&D group had been working on a navigational system for the Coast Guard and someone had rewired Eddie's computer so that every time he typed a *P* a *T* would appear. Oblivious to the tampering, he'd printed up an official memo in which he'd used the word *ship* at least a dozen times, and he'd blithely posted the memo all over the building.

Eddie had learned an important lesson about proofreading his memos before he made them public, and everyone had had a good laugh. When Lucy had related the episode to Frank over dinner that evening, his reaction had been a bewildered stare.

Less than a year later, she'd quit her job in Boston and moved to Horizon to take a position as a systems designer at Access Computer Systems, Inc. A year after that, the final papers were signed—"A divorce made in heaven," Frank had called it. And one year later, she apparently still had an underdeveloped and/or warped sense of humor, if she could be amused by the notion of Access employees sending each other mash notes through the net.

Ignoring the projection figures on the screen, she focused on the message at the bottom of her screen. Then she typed:

A > Sorry, wrong number.

She watched the blinking cursor and pretended she wasn't hoping for a response. Within thirty seconds, one appeared:

A > I'm trying to reach Lucinda Beckwith.

Who would try to reach her with such a message? She pushed her chair back from her computer table and glanced at her body, as if to see if it had miraculously transformed into something worth craving. No, it was the same old body she'd always had: five feet ten inches long, with a sedate arrangement of wavy black hair dropping below her shoulders at one end and a pair of size-nine-and-a-half-double-A feet at the other. In between were long legs—her best feature—boyish hips that did nothing to enhance a waistline that was at least an inch too big, breasts the size of lemons, as Frank had never hesitated to point out, and shoulders so broad and horizontal, she

looked as if she were wearing shoulder pads even when she
wasn't.

She scooted in her chair back to the computer keyboard
and typed:

A > Sorry, wrong body.

A > Whose body have you got?

She burst out laughing, then clamped her mouth shut
and glanced around sheepishly, as if afraid someone might
have overheard. Her door was closed, thank goodness, and
the small office was relatively soundproof. She was all by
herself, shut up in her cozy, familiar bailiwick. To her right
was her tidy white-laminate desk; behind her were her
matching white built-in shelves and two file cabinets; along
the windowsill were her potted cacti; and below her on the
floor was a Plexiglas sheet so the casters of her chair
wouldn't get jammed on the nubby gray carpet.

In front of her was her trusty computer. She typed:

A > Who are you?

A > Loverboy.

She guffawed, then pressed her hand to her mouth to
silence herself.

A > Who is Loverboy?

A > The man who craves your body.

A > Circular definitions will get you nowhere.

A > Then I will avoid them. I want to get somewhere.

A > Where?

A > Into your bed. Into your pants. Into your—

She turned off the computer before he could finish the
sentence. Her cheeks burned with color. Fun was fun, but
this was getting obscene. Whoever had sent the messages
was undoubtedly having a laugh at her expense. She suddenly felt irritated.

It wasn't her first irritation of the day. Just after lunch,
Emilio had waylaid her on her way back to her office. As

of that morning, Emilio's wife was nine and a half months pregnant; everyone in the department was awaiting the "honey, this is it" telephone call as anxiously as the expectant father himself. When Emilio waved her into his office, Lucy assumed the call must have come. She followed him inside, thrilled for him and also, just a bit, for herself. Emilio had already informed his staff that he would be taking his full four-month paternity leave, and he'd hinted to Lucy that while he was gone, she would be in charge of the Smart-Town project.

She was startled, upon entering, to find Jim Kazan in the office, lounging in a chair, smiling that insufferably cocky smile of his and looking for all the world as if he, and not Emilio, was the executive project manager.

Lucy didn't like Jim. She'd heard of him during her senior year at MIT, where the "Wild and Crazy Hacker" of Stanford had developed a cult following for having achieved the impossible. He'd broken an unbreakable code, entered an impregnable defense computer network at the Pentagon and injected the message "Kazan Was Here" into all sorts of programs that were supposed to have been top-secret. He'd been arrested and convicted, which only added to his legendary status. A federal judge had sentenced him to provide free security consultation to the Pentagon for the rest of his life.

He should have been sent to prison, Lucy thought, once she'd gotten to know him. A few years behind bars might have done something to shrink his mammoth ego. Instead, the sentence he'd received served as proof that he was a hero, a wunderkind, much too marvelous to have to do time in jail like an ordinary felon.

Despite her reservations about his flouting the law, Lucy had reluctantly counted herself among his admirers. That he worked at Access lent the Kansas Valley-based software design company a certain panache.

But then Lucy had met him and it was loathe at first sight.

She'd been put off by all that wild blond hair of his, shaggy and scruffy and almost as long as Lucy's in back. And those baby-blue eyes, twinkling with mischief, and those damnable dimples, the effectiveness of which he seemed much too keenly aware. He was always smiling, always wise-cracking. Always flirting. He strutted around the research building like a god who'd descended from Olympus to grace the mortals with his exalted presence. When the mood struck him, he would swoop down on one project or another, offer two or three clever suggestions and then waltz off, already bored with the project but not too bored to boast about how he'd rescued it or come up with just the solution the designers were desperate for.

His attitude seemed to be, "I broke the Pentagon code, and I can do whatever the hell I want." For all his reputed brilliance, he seemed like nothing more than a supremely conceited creep to Lucy, and she'd spent her two years at Access maneuvering to have as little as possible to do with him.

Finding him in her boss's office automatically made her wary. He stood as she entered and she acknowledged him with a polite nod. He responded with a wink, making her even more wary.

She turned back to Emilio. "Any word from Dolores?"

Moving to his seat behind the desk, Emilio sighed and rolled his eyes. "Her back hurts, her feet are puffy, she's got hemorrhoids. You don't want to know the words I've been getting from her. Ten years ago, they would have induced labor by now. But they've got this new theory about how the baby lets us know when it's ready to come out, and it's the parents' duty to listen and obey. I'll tell you right now, I'm obeying this kid only until the moment we cut the cord. From then on, it's going to obey me."

"Famous last words," Lucy joked, then grew serious. "I'm kind of busy, Emilio—" she cast a disdainful look at Jim, as if to imply that she was much busier than he was "—so if we can get down to business . . ."

Emilio gestured toward one of the two chairs facing his desk, and Lucy took a seat. As he resumed his seat beside her, Jim gave her legs a blatant inspection, and as soon as she was settled, she yanked her skirt down over her knees and shot him another look, this one lethal. He arched his eyebrows in feigned innocence and she scowled and twisted away.

"I wanted to let you know," Emilio said, "that Jim has been assigned to your project."

"What!"

"He's asked to be put on it."

"For how long?" she asked wryly. "The last project he was on—wasn't it the rocket timer? He lasted all of a week."

"They had a glitch and I fixed it," Jim said in his own defense. "I'm a trouble-shooter, Lucy."

"Well, the Smart-Town project doesn't have any trouble for you to shoot. We're doing fine without you."

"Lucy," Emilio said, his tone placating. "Jim is very talented, and I think he could contribute a great deal to the project."

"Talented?" she grumbled, just to be contrary. "He has a talent for getting publicity for himself—"

"Hey, I haven't made the cover of *Newsweek* in years," he protested with a grin.

"Not for lack of trying. You managed to get coverage for spending your last vacation cleaning up Laguna Beach."

Jim's grin expanded. "It was Venice, not Laguna."

"Thousands of people have done California since the quake, you know. Thousands of people have gone and cleaned the beaches, or helped to rebuild homes and roads, or repainted the rides at Disneyland. But when James Kazan goes to clean rubble from the beach, *USA Today* runs a story on it."

"They thought it might encourage more volunteers to do California," he rationalized. "It was a public service-type thing. If James Kazan can haul chunks of concrete off the sand during his vacation, why can't you?"

"Oh, you're so noble," she muttered.

Emilio held up his hand to halt the argument. "What's the real problem, Lucy?"

"The real problem is..." She paused and sorted her thoughts. The real problem was that the chemistry between her and Jim Kazan was lousy and she didn't want to have to work with him on her precious project. It was the first major system she'd worked on since coming to Access: a centralized computer programmed to do for planned communities and existing municipal clusters what simpler computers did for individual buildings—read the environment and adjust the buildings' atmospheric conditions to maximize efficiency and minimize energy consumption. Ideally, whole towns could be linked to the computer. During the winter months, the computer could increase the heat in rooms facing north, and during the summer it could increase the air-conditioning to rooms facing south. Awnings and tinted windows could be programmed to adjust to the sun's position, and entire blocks of buildings could be fitted with gutters to shunt rain-water into flexible ducts that would direct it into local reservoirs.

Access had been batting around the Smart-Town idea for years, but Lucy had been the one to create a plausible software design. She wasn't going to let a showboater like Jim Kazan sweep in, make a few trivial suggestions and then steal all the credit.

Before she could come up with a diplomatic way of explaining to Emilio that she neither needed nor trusted Jim, the phone rang. They all flinched in unison, and Emilio grabbed the receiver before it could ring a second time. "Yes?" he said breathlessly. "Hello? Delores?" He sprang to his feet as he listened, and Jim vaulted across the room to yank Emilio's sun-jacket from the hook on the back of the door. Abruptly, Emilio deflated and sank back into his chair, sending Lucy and Jim a glum look and shaking his head. "No, it's okay. If the rugs don't match, we'll send them back." Another quick look dismissed Lucy and Jim, and they left Emilio's office so he could discuss home decor with his wife in privacy.

Lucy had always resented being so tall, but as she entered the hallway with Jim she was grateful for every inch of her height, which enabled her to stand almost eye to eye with the egotistical boy wonder. His eyes sparkled in the light from the halogen lamps overhead, and his hair shimmered with streaks of platinum. His perpetual dimples drew her attention to his thin lips and white teeth, his hard jaw and the gold Whole-Earth amulet he wore on a chain around his neck. She wished he were shorter; she wished the gray and khaki linens he wore, the oversize shirts and pleated slacks and his defiantly unfashionable green canvas sneakers didn't make him seem even taller and lankier than he was. She wished she could look down at him.

"What?" he goaded her, clearly able to discern her annoyance. "What is it with you? All I did was ask Emilio to put me on the project."

"What for? Why couldn't you stay on the rocket-timer project?"

"I did everything I could for that project. I know I can contribute a lot to yours."

She was slightly mollified by his acknowledgment that the Smart-Town project was hers. Still, the prospect of having to work with him on a daily basis unsettled her. His splashy style would never mesh with her own quiet, scholarly approach to systems design. "I'm sorry," she said impassively. "I'm very protective of the project, and—"

"And what? You think I'm going to destroy it? You think I'm going to steal it and sell it to a competitor?"

"You do have a criminal record," she reminded him.

"Ah, yes," he said, sighing melodramatically, although his eyes twinkled with humor. "I pointed out the flaws in the Pentagon system before some terrorist could stumble on to them. I'm such a naughty boy."

Lucy glowered. A naughty boy—that said it all. "Look, Jim, if we've got to work together, we've got to. But I don't have to like it."

Still grinning, he gazed at her, deliberately tilting his head to emphasize the three-inch discrepancy in their heights. "Has anyone ever told you, Lucy Dearest, that you've got a significant personality problem?"

She could think of one person who had: her ex-husband. Evidently, Jim shared Frank's opinion of her. She saw that as proof that in his own way, professionally if not personally, he was bound to cause her as much grief as Frank had.

She wished she could strike back at him with a perfectly clever rejoinder, but she had never excelled at the art of verbal jousting. When it came to computers, she was a whiz; her brain would go turbo and her fingers would fly across the keyboard, entering ideas at breakneck speed. But when it came to people—especially male people—her wits failed her. "You'd rather sleep with your lap top than with me," Frank used to accuse her, and after a while, she'd found herself agreeing.

"Look," she addressed Jim with what she considered laudable reasonability. "I don't like you, and you don't like me—"

"Who says I don't like you? I happen to think you've got all the warmth of road slush in February, but that doesn't mean I don't like you."

Again she struggled for a suitable riposte, but Jim's mocking smile stifled her. Not until she'd pivoted on her heel and stalked furiously down the hall to her own office did she think of what she could have said: that she wasn't surprised someone like him found road slush likable; that she was glad he liked her because she assumed he'd be happy to take orders from someone he liked; that she wished him premature baldness and an allergic reaction to Minoxidil.

Instead, she shut her office door with a hinge-rattling slam, which proved only moderately cathartic, and remained inside, blinding herself by staring at her monitor for hours without a break, working feverishly to convince Access, if not the entire world, that her project didn't need James Kazan's input to succeed.

Over the marathon course of the afternoon, she'd come up with some good ideas. But as she locked up her computer for the day, as she stuffed her purse into her backpack, slipped her sun-jacket on and pulled her keys from one of the pockets, she found herself unable to remember any of those ideas. What her mind kept clinging to was *I crave your body.*

She wasn't as vexed now as she'd been when she'd silenced her computer pen pal by shutting off the machine. Embarrassed, yes, but not angry. It was just a gag, nothing worth taking seriously. Probably a junior programmer had been behind it, one of the fresh-out-of-college kids who worked over in the south wing. They were always playing pranks. The guys had probably sent lewd notes through the computer to every woman working at Access, and the women had sent equally lewd notes to the men.

Lucy would bet Jim Kazan's computer would overload on seductive messages. She'd seen the way every female employee, from Access's happily married fifty-eight-year-old president on down, fawned over him. She'd seen the way Access's women preened whenever he approached, and the way they gave him moony smiles whenever he favored them with a casual greeting. She'd seen the way secretaries queued up for the privilege of typing his letters and notes, the way the servers in the dining room always gave him heaping portions of food, and the way the younger programmers gravitated to him, batting their eyes coquettishly, asking if he'd mind helping them resolve some snafu. "I know you can fix it, Jim," they'd purr, and he'd flash his dimples and wink, put his arm around their shoulders and murmur, "Of course I can fix it. If I could break the Pentagon code, I can fix anything."

After locking her office, she walked down the hallway to the stairs and descended, called a greeting to the security guard posted at the door and zippered her sun-jacket. It was a new one, a soft, lightweight white fabric that breathed a lot more effectively than her last sun-jacket. Here in the Kansas Valley, a person had to wear some sort of protection against the sun's UV rays in the summer. Even though the ozone layer had been stabilized, thanks to the international agreements drawn up at the first World Environmental Conference three years ago, the risk of skin cancer still existed. But with the newer fabrics, people could wear their sun-jackets even on the hottest days of the year and not sweat.

The parking lot outside Access was divided into two sections. The bicycle section, where Lucy headed once she was outside, was canopied, but the superlight vehicles section was open to the sky so the solar cells on the mopeds and cars could absorb energy throughout the day. Lucy had owned an early model superlight in Boston, but the power on it hadn't been reliable and she'd wound up using public transit more often than her own wheels. Once she'd moved out to Kansas Valley, she'd sold the superlight and bought a state-of-the-art bicycle instead. The land was so flat and clear, she had to pump only a few times on the pedals and she would practically coast the whole way home.

There was no valley in Kansas Valley. This was one of her first shocks upon moving to Horizon. The Kansas River had carved a narrow swath through the flat countryside, but it wasn't truly a valley. The region northwest of Topeka began grooming itself as the new center of high-tech research, partly due to predictions, ultimately unrealized, about coastal flooding during the polar-cap crisis a few years ago, partly because the high-tech corridor around Boston had yet to recover from the financial woes that had beset the entire state since the late eighties, and partly because the high-tech industries located south of San Francisco lost their appeal as dire predictions of the Big One became almost a daily occurrence. That the Great California Quake had its epicenter in Los Angeles rather than San Francisco did nothing to dispel people's fears, and engineers, computer scientists and their families flocked to Kansas without looking back. It was the immigrants from California who had dubbed the region Kansas Valley, in memory of Silicon Valley.

The parking lot was filling with workers leaving Access for the day. Lucy complimented Bill Harper on his new bike, which was parked next to hers, and he complimented her on her new sun-jacket. As she unlocked her bike and lifted it out of its slot, she asked him how the rocket-timer project was progressing.

"It's doing great," Bill told her. "Ever since Kazan reprogrammed the heat sensors, we've been back on track. That guy's a genius."

Behind a forced smile, Lucy gnashed her teeth. She said goodbye to Bill, straddled her bike, arranged her skirt discreetly over her knees and coasted through the lot. Cruising past the building, she spotted Emilio. "How's Dolores?" she shouted.

"Swollen ankles," he shouted back. "Stretch marks. You don't want to know."

With a wave, Lucy rode out of the lot.

As planned communities went, Horizon was one of the better ones. The main artery through town was clearly divided into lanes for bikers, pedestrians and superlights—fossil-fuel vehicles were banned in Horizon proper and had to be stored in lots and garages outside the town limits. The main road paralleled the Kansas River for half a mile and then veered off into an attractively landscaped boulevard that arched past Access and half a dozen other high-tech firms, the Horizon Health Services building, all four of the town schools, which shared a single sprawling campus, and the community center. A right turn at the major intersection led to the town's municipal offices, a few houses of worship and the community garden. Riding straight through the intersection would bring one to the Horizon Mall.

Lucy rode straight through. She needed to return some videos she'd rented. She was also low on food, and while she was happy to make some purchases through the consumer network on her computer at home, she never felt comfortable ordering food without seeing it first. Once, when she'd had the flu, she'd done her shopping through the home-consumer net. When the delivery arrived a couple of hours later, one of the tomatoes was squashed, the bananas were bruised, and the ice cream had been packed in an obnoxious insulation bag with the ice cream's fat and calorie content printed in bright red numbers and letters all over it.

If Lucy was going to eat ice cream, she didn't want to be nagged about how unhealthy it was. She wanted to forget about cholesterol and enjoy herself.

As usual, the lot surrounding the mall was crowded. All the shaded bike slots were occupied, so she parked in the sun and walked to the huge three-story dome-shaped structure that housed just about every retail establishment in Horizon. Most of the food shops were on the first floor, but Lucy walked directly to the main escalator and glided up to the third floor. The marquis of the Horizon Art Theater greeted her: *Lawrence of Arabia* was still playing. Nowadays, since just about every home contained a wide-screen high-resolution TV and a VCR, movie theaters devoted themselves to the showing of special films that for one reason or another didn't lend themselves to home viewing. Lucy had seen *Lawrence of Arabia* with Frank at a theater in Boston a few years ago. She'd found it boring, but she could understand that its panoramic splendor would have been lost on a home screen.

Next door to the movie theater was one of the mall's six restaurants, and next to it was the video shop. Lucy went in to return the two videos she'd rented on Friday. "How'd you like them?" the clerk asked.

Lucy shrugged. "*Back To The Future Part IV* was one part too many," she critiqued. "The other one, *Rain Man*, I liked."

"Now that one's a classic," the clerk remarked. "It won the Oscar for best picture back in eighty-nine."

"It did?" She'd been in graduate school the year it had come out and she hadn't had much time for movie going back then—or, for that matter, for sitting up till midnight on Oscar night to learn which picture had won. But she'd truly enjoyed the movie, especially the autistic character. For reasons she thought it best not to analyze too deeply, she'd found herself empathizing with him.

After paying for two new videos, she left. Riding down the stairs, she spotted a teenage girl standing near the second-story landing, staring at her.

Teenagers were not exactly a rarity at the mall, particularly during the summer months. Even those who had jobs or were involved in the National Volunteer Service liked to hang out at the mall. The community center was fine for organized dances and concerts, but the mall was *it*, as they would say. Teenagers swarmed in and out of stores, ate snacks, sized each other up and paraded through the main arcade, giving their hormones a well-needed airing. For the most part, they ignored the adults and the adults ignored them.

The girl on the second floor was definitely not ignoring Lucy.

She looked rather typical, Lucy decided as the escalator carried her closer and closer to the girl. Her hair was a light golden color and she wore it in the hatchet-cut style that was unfortunately very popular among people under twenty. Her clothes were similarly adolescent—a garish flowered shirt, baggy bleached-muslin jeans and sandals, that struck Lucy as an open invitation to UV overexposure on her feet.

As always, kids thought they were indestructible. They shunned sun-jackets and hats and walked around risking skin cancer. Some actually went out of their way to cultivate tans. During Lucy's high school years, kids not only spent hours soaking up the rays but also smoked cigarettes, courting cancer inside and out. Not Lucy, of course—she'd always been one of the pale, nerdy egghead types, what they currently called "wizards." Nowadays, though, to be a wizard was respectable, and nobody smoked cigarettes. Whenever an adult complained about today's teenagers in her presence, she was quick to point out that the new generation was an improvement on her own.

The escalator reached the second level and Lucy stepped off. Uncomfortable beneath the girl's piercing blue-eyed stare, she moved directly to the first-floor escalator. Before she could get to it, the girl reached out and snagged her arm.

"'Scuse me," she said.

Lucy didn't want to be rude. She eased her arm out of the girl's grip, taking note of the lightning bolt on the nail of her index finger and of the jangling chain bracelets circling her slender wrist.

The girl's gaze flitted from Lucy's face to her sun-jacket, to the cream-colored blouse underneath it, with her Access badge still hooked onto the pocket, and then down to her matching skirt. Her eyes lingered for a moment on Lucy's chest before rising to her face. "Hi. My name's Dara-Lyn," she announced.

Lucy waited for her to say something more.

"I'm—uh—I'm collecting money to finance repairs on the Watts Towers."

"The Watts Towers," Lucy repeated, bemused.

"Yeah, you know, in Watts. Los Angeles. They were these towers made out of trash, you know? And they were really *it* but they collapsed during the Big One, and I'm helping to raise money to repair them. Rebuild them, actually. You know?"

Lucy sighed. It wasn't that she was indifferent to the plight of Southern California. She'd spent her last vacation at the Mount Palomar Observatory, applying her technical knowledge to the repair of some of the damaged equipment. Not that *USA Today* had considered her volunteer effort worthy of coverage as they had Jim Kazan's.

But towers built of trash somehow didn't seem quite necessary. "Wouldn't it make more sense to collect money for a library or a museum?" she asked, unable to filter her disapproval from her tone.

"Yeah, well, but the Watts Towers are *it*, you know? They're a mess, and you know what the president says— Messes Cost Money."

One thing Lucy could do without was listening to some teenage kid quote the president in an effort to raise funds for trash towers. "I'm sorry, I can't help you," she said, turning away and trying not to feel guilty. If she gave money to everyone who was raising funds for some worthwhile project, she'd be flat broke in no time.

"I see you work at Access," Dara-Lyn remarked, gesturing toward Lucy's ID badge. "I've heard that's a really socially responsible company."

Lucy made a big, unsubtle production of checking her wristwatch.

"So, you think they'd maybe let me come and raise funds?"

"Where? At Access?"

Dara-Lyn nodded.

"I have no idea," said Lucy. If Dara-Lyn were collecting money to rebuild a playground or a housing project, Lucy would not only have given her a few dollars but also would have put her in touch with the company's social-concerns director. But she couldn't see wasting the company's time and resources on Watts Towers. "I'm sorry," she repeated, "but I can't help you."

"You could if you wanted to," Dara-Lyn called after Lucy as she stepped onto the escalator.

Lucy exhaled and tried to stave off her reflexive remorse at not stuffing a dollar bill into Dara-Lyn's hand. But it was more than just the triviality of the girl's cause that prompted Lucy to walk away. It was her eerie, unshakable suspicion that towers of trash had nothing to do with why the girl had chosen Lucy, out of all the hundreds of shoppers meandering through the mall, to ask for help.

Chapter Two

As far as he could tell, she had it right. He pressed a combination of keys to get back to the start of the file and scrolled through the program one more time. Sure, there were gaps and holes; the project was by no means complete. But the work Lucinda Beckwith, Ph.D., had done on the Smart-Town system was basically brilliant.

Jim leaned back in his chair, propped one sneakered foot up on his computer table, tapped the eraser end of a pencil against his chin and scrutinized the figures before him. And tried to decide how he felt about the fact that the number-one shrew of R&D didn't need his help.

He'd fought valiantly to be assigned to her project. He'd pleaded with Emilio, and when that hadn't worked, he'd resorted to bribery. He'd promised to program Emilio's home computer to play Laser Go, and—worse—he'd promised to behave himself with Lucy. "If you just want to give her a hard time, I'm keeping you off the project," Emilio had said. "She's prickly, she's territorial and she's doing a fantastic job. I don't want you fouling her up."

"Fouling her up?" Jim had objected, striking a pose of supreme indignation. "Me?"

"The project is progressing beautifully. And it's her baby. You're a senior scientist here, Jim—that puts you one level above her. If I let you in on Smart-Town and you pull rank on her, she's going to balk.''

"I wouldn't dream of pulling rank," Jim had sworn.

"What kind of dreams are we talking about, then?"

Jim had thought it best to offer a tactful and essentially dishonest answer about his burning desire to explore new applications for the system. The truth was, if he were allowed to join the project, he would probably devote most of his dreams to Lucy Beckwith's legs.

Twenty-first-century men weren't supposed to admit to such sentiments, and in most circumstances, Jim was an impeccably twenty-first-century man. But from the moment he'd caught a glimpse of Lucy's incredible legs, those long, gracefully muscled calves and smooth shins and flawless oval knees... Well, so, he'd regressed a little. Certain impulses simply couldn't be programmed out of the male psyche.

In his dreams, his imagination could venture where his eyes had never been. He dreamed about her thighs. Her hips. Her small, lovely breasts. Her throat. Her soft, expressive lips.

Her brain.

Of all the things about Lucy Beckwith that turned him on, her intellect provoked the strongest response. That she tended to use her intelligence as a shield against his every friendly overture didn't faze him. He'd seen her at meetings and presentations. He'd booted up her files and reviewed her work. He'd read the papers she'd published as a graduate student, during her years at Wang and then at that tiny Charlestown firm that consulted for the Coast Guard. The lady was smart.

Staring at the monitor as he called up her final file on Smart-Town, he felt a distinctly unintellectual tension in his groin. Nothing—not even legs as glorious as hers—excited him the way a fertile female mind did. To him, gazing at Lucy's calculations was as arousing as gazing at a *Playboy* centerfold might have been to a less cerebral man in a less enlightened era.

Well, almost as arousing.

He couldn't stay in his office all night fantasizing about Lucy's data. He was hungry, he needed a workout and he wanted to plan his strategy for the following day—his first full day working on Smart-Town. Kicking away from the table, he clicked off the computer, permitted himself one quick game on his pinball machine—an antique Spider-Man model, circa 1972, with double flippers and a quirky tilt mechanism—and then grabbed his sun-jacket and left the office. It was well past six-thirty and the sun was low enough that he didn't bother with his hood and visor as he climbed into his convertible-top superlight. The lot was nearly devoid of cars at this hour. Access was organized around flex time, and most employees preferred to arrive and leave early. Jim tended to keep his own erratic hours— sometimes he put in six-hour days and sometimes twelve-hour days. But he got plenty of good work done, so no one ever complained.

He cruised onto the boulevard and picked up speed. The balmy June wind dusted across his cheeks and tousled his hair, and the neatly planted birch and apple trees cast long shadows across the roadway. To his right stretched the river and beyond it the flat, verdant acreage of farmland. His friends had warned him that after the excitement of the Bay Area he'd find Kansas Valley boring, but after almost five years, he still hadn't gotten sick of it. Half the population of Kansas Valley was made up of transplanted Californians, anyway. And Jim always found a way of making his own excitement, wherever he was.

In spite of his celebrity status, his home was a modest six-room modular in a meticulously planned subdivision overlooking the river. Celebrity and wealth weren't synonymous, and while Jim received a generous salary from Access, all his consulting work for the Pentagon was done gratis. Not that his financial situation bothered him. He had never been the sort to consider money *it;* if he had more, he'd probably just wind up pouring it into Home-Ties.

He pulled into the garage, climbed out of the superlight and entered the attractive stucco house. It was supposed to be tornado proof, although the preponderance of glass on the river side of the building caused Jim to doubt the builder's claim. Striding through the mudroom to the kitchen, he unzipped his sun-jacket. He tossed it over a wall peg, clicked on his private answering machine and nudged the foot pedal on his refrigerator. As he scanned the refrigerator's contents, he listened to his calls: someone trying to sell him a video subscription to the Topeka daily, which he already subscribed to; someone named Kristin reminding him that they'd met at a party a few weeks ago and asking him if he'd like to go out for dinner; and his sister informing him of a new sunscreen on the market, specially designed for blondes, that she'd read about in *Health Weekly*. "I worry about you, Jim," she reproached. "You always spent too much time at the beach when we were kids, and they keep saying those excesses come back to haunt you."

"They," he muttered with a grin. *"They* keep saying. Who the hell are *they,* anyhow?" He pulled out a container of vegetable lasagna and slid it into the microwave for a five-minute zap. Then he turned off his private answering machine and turned on the one for Home-Ties,

which operated off a separate phone line. While it was re-winding, he got himself a beer.

"Hello...?" came a tentative voice over the machine. "My name is Alice Coker, and I'm calling because I've heard about Home-Ties. We've got no children here, and we have the room and—well, I guess you should just call me back and we'll talk." She recited her phone number and mumbled a goodbye.

A whispery woman's voice emerged from the microwave, announcing that his meal was ready. "Thanks, Bambi," Jim responded. He called all female voice synthesizers Bambi—it was such a vacuously sexy name—and all male voice synthesizers Burt. Talking to his equipment didn't do much to humanize the stuff, but Jim figured that if they were going to be jabbering at him all day, nagging him to take his food out of the microwave, fasten his seat belt and remove his card from the ready-cash machine, he was fully within his rights to jabber right back at them.

He carried his steaming entrée to the computer table, took a sip of beer and dialed the number Alice Coker had provided. While he waited for it to ring, he turned on the computer and booted up the Home-Ties program.

"Hello?"

"Ms. Coker? This is Mr. James from Home-Ties." He never used his real name when he was conducting Home-Ties business; he didn't want his fame—or infamy—to detract from the project. "I got your message. Is now a good time to talk?"

"Oh, it certainly is," she said, sounding a bit less hesitant.

"Why don't you tell me a little about yourself?"

"Well... My name is Alice Coker, as I said on your machine, and my husband is Dennis Coker. We own a small farm in southern Minnesota and we turn a profit on it—not much, but we don't go hungry. We're in our late forties. We're decent folks, Mr. James, and we'd like to share what we've got with a child who needs it.''

"That's very generous of you," he said. "You said you were childless, Ms. Coker?"

"No, we raised a daughter, but she's all grown up now, going to college at the state university. We're mighty proud of her. She did two years in the National Volunteer Service before college, Mr. James, and I know we did a good job raising her, and..." Alice's voice drifted off for a moment, then she laughed nervously. "You must think I'm a braggart."

"Not at all," he assured her. "Now, what exactly are you looking for?"

She hesitated before answering. "Well, I hate to be picky when there are so many children who need help, but...if it isn't asking too much, we'd like someone twelve years old or younger. Is that all right?"

"Of course, it's all right." The fact was, his organization had the names of many preteens who'd lost their homes and families in the Big One, orphans who two years after the quake were still living in group houses and temporary shelters. Any family willing to take in a child of any age earned his whole-hearted approval.

"It's just...I'm just not sure I could handle a teenager right off. I mean, if we had a few years to get to know her, then we could sort of slide into those difficult years gradually."

"I understand." He tapped a few keys on his computer, entering bits and pieces of what Alice Coker had revealed about herself. "You want a girl?"

"Oh, no, girl or boy, we aren't particular."

"You did say 'get to know *her,*'" he noted.

"Oh, well ... I guess maybe I do sort of lean toward a girl. But then Dennis leans toward a boy. Whatever. Really. It's just like giving birth, Mr. James—you take what you get and count your blessings."

Jim smiled. He liked this woman; she was going to make a fine mother for some Big One orphan. "Can you handle medical problems?"

"Well ..." She sighed. "I'll be frank with you, Mr. James—we live a good half hour from the nearest medical center. So if it's someone with chronic problems, you know, something that needs daily trips to the doctor or something, well, that would be hard. But a handicap—we could deal with that. Our house is a ranch and we could put in ramps if we had to. I know, so many of those beautiful children got hurt. But we've got lots of fresh air here, lots of room and lots of love. So you just find us a child who could use those things and we'll be all set."

"It sounds great," Jim said, forgetting his cooling dinner in his enthusiasm. "What I need from you now, Ms. Coker, is some basic information. I'll pass along your number to one of our staff social workers in your area and she'll set up an appointment for a visit. You understand we've got to have an on-site inspection and several in-depth interviews before we match you up with a child."

"Absolutely," Alice concurred. "You don't want to send children someplace where it might not work out."

He ran through the list of questions on his program and promised the woman she'd be hearing in several days from a staff volunteer. Then he thanked her and she thanked him, and they said goodbye. Smiling, he turned off the computer and took another swig of beer.

He'd set up Home-Ties shortly after the quake, when his parents first told him about the enormous number of refugees pouring into Berkeley and other parts of Northern California. His parents had taken in two homeless women, and their neighbors had taken in others, but still, the need for homes was desperate. Especially for the children. "You're a wizard," his father reminded him. "Do something."

What Jim did was establish a network of volunteer social workers throughout the country and set up a computer bank of homeless children and willing families. Designing a program to match families with children had been a snap. Jim's only expenditures were for adding a second phone line to his home and for publicizing Home-Ties—although many of the newspapers in which he advertised wound up donating free space in their pages.

Truth to tell, finding homes for children via the computer and the telephone was a hell of a lot easier than cleaning rubble from the beaches of Venice. If all he'd cared about was doing his good deed for the victims of the Big One, his efforts in creating and running Home-Ties would surely have been enough.

But his sister was right: from the day he was born, he'd been addicted to the three *S*'s—sun, sand and surf. In moments of acute honesty, he acknowledged that one reason he'd taken the position at Access was to get him away from those dangerous temptations. He *was* blond and he *did* have to protect himself from the UVs, and rays were particularly potent at beaches.

He really hated thinking about health. He looked at his tepid lasagna and found himself longing for the real thing, with chunks of sausage and eggy ricotta and a thick slab of buttery garlic bread on the side. Thank God the medical establishment had ultimately reached the unanimous conclusion that, consumed in moderation, beer was a healthy drink. Even if they hadn't, though, he'd indulge in a cold brew every once in a while. There were limits to how healthy a person could be.

He carried his dinner back to the microwave and zapped it for another minute, thanked Bambi and carried the dish and his drink to the living room. In his parents' house, it would have been called the family room, but architects had finally come to the realization that what used to be called the living room in most houses was in fact the room where very little living was done, whereas the place designated as the family room was where most of the living was done. The new house designs generally included a tiny formal room archaically dubbed the "parlor" and used primarily for visits by people the homeowner didn't like. The living room was now a big, comfortable space situated in close proximity to the food supply and furnished with abundant seating, exercise equipment and the entertainment center.

Jim's living room overlooked the river, but as dusk gave way to night, the spectacular view faded into shadow. He closed the insulating shades and switched on a lamp, then flopped onto the down-filled sectional and turned on his TV with the remote switch. He'd missed the network news and he wasn't in the mood to read the electronic newspaper on the Cable Press station. Flipping through the channels, he paused at the Video-Kix station, watched for less than a minute and then kept flipping. Whenever he watched Video-Kix, with its pastiche of pop music, racy cartoons, comedy skits and commercials for spring-soled sneakers, he wound up feeling incredibly old.

He paused at the Love Channel. "At eight o'clock tonight," gushed the off-screen announcer, "*Lovestyles of the Wealthy and Wonderful* visits Canadian rock sensations Shershay La Fem, who will share with viewers some startling insights into the many uses of feathers. Coming up next on *Dr. Love*—'Tongue Training—Godsend or Hoax?'"

Jim laughed out loud. He still had trouble believing the Love Channel was the most popular channel on TV, unless the millions of people tuning in did so for the same reason he did—because its broadcasts were hilariously stupid. According to the viewer surveys, however, most people watched the channel because they actually enjoyed viewing shows about sex.

Not Jim. If he wanted to be titillated, he turned off the television and turned on his mind. He had no interest in what other people did behind closed doors.

Except for one particular woman. Shutting his eyes, he envisioned her as she'd looked standing beside him in the hall outside Emilio's office earlier that afternoon. He pictured her eyes, dark and distrustful, and her wide mouth, her thick black hair and her slim, lissome body. He pictured her creamy complexion and her stubborn chin, her small bosom and high waist and—God, but it was amazing to think that all the rest of her was leg. When Jim was in the mood for titillation, all he had to do was imagine the wonders lurking beneath her clothing and the even greater wonders lurking behind her eyes.

It was crazy. Lucy Beckwith had become an obsession with him. He used to date a lot, even after she first arrived at Access, but his sex life had dwindled practically to zilch in the two years he'd known her. He liked women, flirted with them, socialized with them—but his body couldn't make love to a woman when his mind was lusting after Lucy.

He'd tried to strike up a friendship with her. When she'd been new in town, he'd asked her out, but she'd told him she was married and he'd promptly backed off. Eventually, curiosity got the better of him and he'd hacked into the personnel records. According to her file, she was two years younger than Jim, earned eight thousand dollars less, was exactly five-feet, ten-inches tall and weighed one hundred forty pounds, had graduated summa from MIT before going on for a Ph.D. at the same school, had accumulated glowing references and was legally separated from her husband, who had remained in Boston when she'd moved to Horizon.

Months passed, and he'd heard through the grapevine that she'd obtained a divorce. So he'd asked her out again. Her answer had been a resounding "No."

Maybe she had a boyfriend, although she was certainly secretive about her social life. Jim kept his antennae tuned to Access gossip, and he'd never heard anyone say they'd spotted Lucy in the company of a man.

Maybe she went to Topeka to get her thrills. Maybe she got her thrills watching the Love Channel. Maybe she was asexual.

And maybe, given her obvious dislike of him, she wasn't worth the time he spent thinking about her.

He pressed the remote control to summon the Movie Library, which he'd just started subscribing to a few months ago. It was more expensive than renting videos at the mall, but it was also more convenient, and he never had to worry about someone else's having rented the movie he wanted to see. With the Movie Library, he could select any film in the collection for his viewing, regardless of whether anyone else was watching it.

He ran through the list—new releases, oldies, classics, classic oldies. He wanted to see something light, something frothy, something starring someone clever and talented and gorgeous enough to drive Lucy Beckwith out of his thoughts for a while.

He ended up selecting *2001: A Space Odyssey*. Hardly light and frothy, and it lost much of its impact on his home screen. The notion that back in the late sixties, a movie director would envision so sterile and space-oriented a future perplexed him. But the music resonating through his stereo speakers was great, the special effects were fun, and he'd always had a soft spot for the early scenes in which dozens of cute chimpanzees played with bones. And the scene just before the intermission, in which HAL the computer read the lips of the two astronauts while they conferred in the pod, had to be one of the pinnacles in the history of cinema.

HAL the computer. Now there was a clever, talented, gorgeous starring character. Unfortunately, HAL didn't distract Jim from his thoughts of Lucy. Quite the contrary—HAL made Jim think about how adroit Lucy was with computers. HAL made him wonder how Lucy would fit into each scene in the film, whether she'd take charge, whether she'd eat the funny-looking paste the movie presented as food of the future, whether she'd walk upside down in her astronaut whites. Whether, when HAL burst into his famous rendition of "Daisy, daisy," Lucy would sing along.

One thing Jim knew for sure, though: given her choice of a lover, Lucy would pick HAL over him any day.

Chapter Three

A > Good morning, gorgeous.

Lucy had arrived at Access ten minutes ago and settled at her desk with a mug of herbal tea, prepared to review the program she'd been working on the previous day. She had to get some work done—lots of work. Tons of work. Enough work to prove to Jim Kazan that his input into Smart-Town was totally unnecessary.

But instead of her program, her monitor was welcoming her with a polite and indisputably flattering greeting. This must be what they meant by user friendly, she thought as a slow smile spread across her face.

A > Good morning, she entered into the computer.

A > Today we have a surprise quiz. Please clear your desk.

She laughed.

A > Are you ready?

A > Yes, she typed.

A > How high is the sky?

She panicked for a minute. The question wasn't unanswerable—she could put down something about light diffusion through the stratosphere or some such thing. But a technical answer wasn't what was needed here. She had to be clever. Whoever her secret pen pal was, he was funny, and Lucy doubted she could equal him in wit.

She took a deep breath and entered: *A > High enough so I don't bump my head on it when I'm standing.*

A > Correct, appeared on the screen, and she experienced an unreasonable rush of elation. This was absurd. She had a job to do, a project demanding her attention, and here she was, beaming like a goofy little girl at the praise of some anonymous entity armed with a computer.

A > How many wizards does it take to change a light bulb?

A > None. The light bulb changes due to energy flow. Electrical current alters the filament matter.

A > Very good! Who's the smartest person in Kansas?

A > You.

A > Why?

A > Because you crave my body, she entered, then closed her eyes and shook her head in amazement. How could she have written that? Whatever had possessed her to type such a cheeky response? *Obviously a sign of intelligence,* she added, figuring that since she'd already gone too far, she had nothing to lose by going a little farther.

A > Do you smoke after sex?

She recognized the question; it had been a trademark joke of some old-time blond bombshell. Madonna? No, too recent. Bette Midler, maybe?

Lucy struggled in vain to remember the punch line. The computer hummed. The cursor blinked. The answer lurked just beyond her reach.

She had to write something. Not to write something might mean failing the quiz—whatever that was worth. *A > No,* she typed, *smoking isn't healthy.*

A > And sex is. Very good!

A > Who are you?

A > Loverboy.
A > Who is Loverboy?
A > Wouldn't you like to know.

Gazing at the monitor, Lucy considered his rhetorical question. Maybe she *wouldn't* like to know. If she knew to whom she was sending such audacious messages, she would become painfully inhibited. She would be too embarrassed to face her correspondent at meetings or outside Access, at the mall or the community center. What if he was married? What if he was a pervert? What if he was a twenty-year-old intern toying with an older woman's fragile ego? What if he was someone she detested?

Shaken, she turned off her computer. She stared at the blank screen for a moment, trying to muster the courage to turn it back on and boot up Smart-Town. If she turned the machine on, Loverboy might barge in again. She wasn't sure how to handle him if he did.

She suffered an unexpected pang of regret. She had been pleased to receive a message from him the moment she'd turned on her computer. She'd been cheered and flattered by the glowing green words on her screen. She'd enjoyed stepping out of her reserved character for a few giddy minutes, throwing off her innate modesty and exchanging bawdy transmissions with a safely invisible spirit. In the four years she'd spent with Frank, she could not recall a single time they'd talked about sex in anything but the most clinical of terms.

No matter how pointless it was, no matter how risky, she liked talking sexy with a mystery man on the computer. She didn't want him to become real, someone she knew, someone she actually had to interact with. The moment she found out who he was, the fun would end.

Of course, Loverboy knew who she was—except that on the computer, she could be someone else. In person, she would never be able to joke about sex with a man. Through the computer... Through the computer, it was different.

Before she could turn her machine back on, Emilio's voice emerged through her desk intercom. "Lucy?" He sounded breathless and addled. "Lucy, Dolores just called and—oh, Lord, this is it! I'm going to be a daddy!"

Lucy let out a cheer and raced to the door. Emilio's secretary was already pacing the hallway, heralding the news like a town crier. Doors flew open; Victor, the resident curmudgeon of the systems-design department, grumbled about the inconvenience of parental-leave regulations and Patricia, the department's efficient budget director, announced that anyone wishing to contribute toward a gift for the new child should drop by at her desk and leave a donation.

"The baby isn't even born yet!" Lucy protested.

"It's important to plan ahead," Patricia explained.

Emilio bolted out of his office, his fingers trembling on the zipper of his sun-jacket. Lucy hurried over to him and closed the jacket for him. "Do you want someone to drive you home?" she asked.

"No, no, I'm fine. Oh, Lord, I can't believe it! When I left the house this morning, nothing was happening. By the time I got here, her water had broken. I can't believe it! I was gone for less than a half hour—"

"It doesn't take a half hour for water to break," Patricia pointed out.

"She's having contractions. She said one of our neighbors was going to take her to the medical center and I should meet her there. This is unbelievable!"

"It's very believable," Lucy murmured, patting his shoulder and ushering him to the elevator when he seemed too shocked to walk down the hall by himself.

"I'm forty-four years old, Lucy. Maybe I'm too old to be a first-time father."

"You aren't too old. Lots of people have children in their forties," she reassured him.

"At least Dolores is a few years younger than me. She'll have more energy. She'll be a good mother."

"She'll be a terrific mother," Lucy insisted, practically shoving him into the elevator when it arrived. "And you'll be a terrific father. Now go coach her through labor."

He nodded. "Take care of Smart-Town, Lucy. I've got to coach Dolores. That's what I'll do. I've got to help her with her breathing," he mumbled just before the door slid shut.

"Somebody ought to help him with his breathing," came an amused voice behind Lucy.

Spinning around, she discovered Jim Kazan slouching against the wall opposite the elevator door, his hands in the pockets of his loose-fitting linen slacks and his cheeks scored with dimples as he grinned. She raised her dark eyes to his unnervingly beautiful blue ones and then lifted her gaze higher, to the shaggy corn-colored mane crowning his head. "Are you volunteering?" she asked, annoyed that he should have such striking blond hair, such calculatingly seductive eyes. "You could follow him to the medical center and make sure he gets there in one piece."

He shrugged indolently. "I'm not into babies," he said. "They secrete too much. And all that mushy-gushy affection . . . it's not my style."

No, Lucy thought archly. Jim's style of affection without a doubt ran more to hanky-panky than to mushy-gushy.

"What?" he challenged, evidently reading condemnation in her gaze. "Don't tell me you think babies are *it?*"

In truth, Lucy's sentiments about babies were extremely complicated. She worshiped babies, adored them, thought they were the world's most precious gifts. Yet she doubted she would ever have a baby of her own. She wasn't an effusive person; she didn't feel comfortable revealing her emotions to others. She related more easily to computers than to human beings. Children mystified her.

If she were truly desperate to have a child, her single status wouldn't be a major hurdle. She could be artificially inseminated, or she could adopt. Access provided excellent on-site child care, so she could have a child without jeopardizing her career.

She could have a child and be an anxious, insecure mother. She could have a child and pray that Andie and Roland at the Access Children's Center offered her child all the mothering and fathering that Lucy was constitutionally unable to provide.

That didn't seem like the right way to go about creating a new life. And it certainly didn't seem like anything she wished to discuss with Jim Kazan.

"If you'll excuse me..." she muttered, turning toward her office.

"As a matter of fact, I won't." He clamped his hand over her shoulder, immobilizing her. "You and I need to talk."

Although he wasn't holding her tightly, she couldn't ignore the inherent force of his grip, the understated power in his long fingers as they curled around her shoulder. Her mind conjured an unwelcome vision of him hoisting boulder-size chunks of debris from a littered beach in Venice, California. She pictured his muscles flexing, his back arching as he hurled the heavy rubble into the rear of a dump truck for removal to a recycling center.

She was used to being surrounded by desk-bound wizards like herself. They rode bikes and did aerobics, but they weren't the sort of people one thought of as *strong*. Jim was strong, and for some inexplicable reason, that bothered her.

"What do we need to talk about?" she asked in a deceptively calm voice.

"Smart-Town."

She cursed under her breath. She actually had to work with Jim—and Emilio was gone and would remain gone for his full four-month paternity leave. He wouldn't be available to run interference.

Her spirits rose slightly as she recalled Emilio's parting words *Take care of Smart-Town, Lucy.* Jim had been standing behind her at the elevator; Emilio had to have seen him, but he'd specified that Lucy should take care of the project. Perhaps he'd issued that final order just to make sure Jim understood who was in charge.

And she had every intention of exercising her authority. "I'm sorry," she said crisply. "I haven't got time to talk right now."

"When will you have time?"

"I don't know."

"Can we have lunch together?"

His hand was still on her shoulder. She wondered why he hadn't removed it, why she hadn't asked him to. It wasn't a flirtatious gesture. He had no personal motive for asking her to join him for lunch. He'd come on to her once or twice in the past and she'd rejected him. She didn't think he'd waste his charms on her at this point.

Just to be sure, she said, "Lunch is out of the question."

He let his arm drop. "All right, Dr. Beckwith," he said, his smile taking on an ominous quality. "You name the time."

She couldn't avoid him forever. If she tried, he'd interpret it as a sign of weakness. "Four o'clock," she suggested. "We can meet in the dining room for coffee."

His grin transformed from threatening to inexplicably triumphant. "Four o'clock. I'll be counting the minutes, sweet beets." He winked, then pivoted and jogged down the hall, his garish green sneakers padding noiselessly along the carpeted floor.

As she rubbed the place on her shoulder where his hand had been, Lucy acknowledged that she would be counting the minutes, too. But not with gleeful anticipation. Not with joy. The prospect of having to collaborate with Jim filled her with dread.

So did the possibility that he'd put his hand on her again.

DARA-LYN WOLFED DOWN two oat rolls, a bowl of yogurt drizzled with honey and a glass of citrus-blend. The food at the Horizon Youth Hostel wasn't as good as the food at the group home in San Bernardino, but it was healthy and filling and she wasn't going to complain.

The hostel was smaller than she'd expected—but then, Horizon itself was smaller than she'd expected. The whole town was maybe twelve square miles. A person could easily bike from one end to the other.

Once she was straightened out with her father, she had every intention of exploring the entire town, getting a feel for the place and making herself at home. James Kazan would buy her a super bike. He'd deluge her with presents. She was his long-lost daughter, after all. She was fifteen and he was famous and they were blood. What more reason would he need to give her everything her heart desired?

In the meantime, she would live here at the hostel and collect money for Watts Towers. The towers weren't an official National Volunteer Service project, but a private group had been trying for nearly a year to raise money to rebuild them, and Dara-Lyn figured, why not raise some dollars for a good cause? She was too young to join the NVS, anyway. You had to be at least sixteen.

Eight other teenagers were currently living at the hostel, a converted farmhouse on the northern end of town. The manager seemed stricter than the manager of the group home back in San Bern, but Dara-Lyn was willing to abide by the rules: clean her room, perform two household chores a day and observe a 9:00 p.m. weeknight curfew, ten on weekends because she was high school age. Given that the nation's hostels were tax-supported, the kids who made use of them couldn't crab about having to do the dishes or sweep the floors every now and then.

A sensational-looking guy carrying a bowl of wheat-flake crunch and a glass of citrus-blend wandered out of the kitchen and motioned toward a seat across the table from her. "Anyone sitting here?" he asked, beaming her the hottest smile she'd ever seen.

This guy was *wow*. He was tall and pale and his eyes were magnetic, and he had to be college age at least. She swallowed and tried to act unruffled, even though his smile made her feel tingly all over. "You can sit there if you want."

"My name's Bobby," he said as he lowered himself into the chair. "What's yours?"

"Dara-Lyn."

He took a sip of his juice, then smiled again. "What brings you to Horizon?"

"Watts Towers," she told him. "I'm collecting money to rebuild them."

He nodded and dug into his cereal. "You're with the NVS?"

"Uh-uh." She wasn't about to admit that she'd been too young to join, so she told him, "They're doing the Towers with private financing."

Bobby nodded again. "I wish I had something to give you," he said. "I'm kind of broke, though. College bills and all."

He *was* college age. And he was talking to her. He could have sat at two other tables in the small dining room, but he'd sat at hers. This was just too *it*.

"Where do you go to school?" she asked.

"Antioch."

She didn't know where that was—probably someplace back East. "So what are you doing here? NVS?"

He nodded. "Infrastructure. I'm with a crew doing repairs on I-70. Everyone else on the crew is staying at the hostel in Topeka, but they ran out of beds over there, so here I am."

"I bet you wish you were in Topeka," Dara-Lyn guessed. "It's kinda boring here, you know?"

Bobby shrugged. "Where are you from?"

"I live in a group home in San Bernardino."

His smile faded and he got that awful look of pity Dara-Lyn so often saw in people's eyes when they encountered victims of the Big One. She didn't want Bobby's pity. She wanted his love, his undying devotion, his arm to hang on to for a date at the mall or something. She wanted to have this hottest-looking male offering her his heart and soul. "Oh, Dara-Lyn," she wanted to hear him say, "I've spent my whole life looking for a girl to love, and you're *it*."

What he said, however, was, "I've heard some of those group homes are pretty bad."

"Mine's okay," she told him. "Better food than here, too. And the home's not too crowded. I share my room with only one other girl."

He ate. She listened to the muffled rhythm of his molars grinding the cereal and thought it sounded super.

"Who told you the group homes are bad?" she asked.

"My adopted sister." He took a swig of juice to wash down the cereal, then elaborated. "My family adopted a Big One orphan about a year ago. She was living in a group home in Riverside. She said the place was jammed."

"Yeah, well, a year ago, things were kinda crowded." The group home at San Bern had been packed at first, but in the past year, a lot of the younger residents had been placed with families out of state. Dara-Lyn had heard rumors that many of them had been legally adopted, but she tended not to think too much about it because the idea of adoption depressed her. It meant your folks were really and totally gone for good. It forced you to cut ties with the past, and that was just too sad.

Apparently no one wanted to adopt her. She figured she was older than what most people wanted. But that was okay; she couldn't be adopted, anyway. She had lost her mother, but her father was still alive—and close by. Soon, she would have her own family, a real family.

None of this good-deed adoption stuff for her. She was going to have herself a genuine dad.

And in the meantime, maybe she could get Bobby to take her out to the mall tonight.

AT A QUARTER TO FOUR, Lucy set up her computer to print a hard copy of her data, then left her office for the printer room next door. She turned on the plotter, checked the paper supply and returned to her desk. She was surprised to discover that her data occupied only the upper half of the monitor screen. On the lower half, a window had been opened, displaying one word: *A > Peekaboo!*

She gnawed her lip. She had to get her material printed out and then go downstairs to talk to Jim. She'd love to defer the meeting and exchange bits and bytes with Loverboy, but that would be irresponsible. Jim Kazan was supposed to be the irresponsible one, not Lucy.

Sighing, she entered instructions for the computer to transmit her data to the printer next door. Through the open door of her office she heard the purr and click of the plotter churning out her hard copy. Her eyes, however, never strayed from the lower window.

After a minute, the plotter shut off and another message appeared: *A > You light up my world.*

She didn't want to be unfriendly, but she couldn't get herself into the proper mood for Loverboy's brand of repartee when she was trying to psyche herself for her impending confrontation with Jim, a meeting during which he was bound to do something repugnant—like wink and call her sweet beets—or to attempt to finesse her project out from under her.

A > I can't talk now, she wrote, feeling silly about her reflexive courtesy. *I'm going to turn you off.*

A > No! You're going to turn me on.

A > I've got work to do.

A > If you turn me off, you'll break my heart.

She groaned. They were just words on a screen, for crying out loud. Just some joker fencing with her. Why was she personalizing the situation?

A > It isn't fair that you can just turn me off, he wrote when several seconds elapsed without a response from her.

A > It isn't fair that you know who I am and I don't know who you are, she countered.

A pause. She glanced at her watch: five minutes to four. She'd give him one minute, and then she'd have to head downstairs.

A > No names, love. Ask me something else, and maybe I can help you out.

She had to leave. She had to face off with Jim.

Unable to stop herself, she settled more comfortably in her chair and wrote, *A > Do you work for Access?*

A > I work for myself.

A > At Access?

A > Sometimes.

He must be a consultant. Were any consultants currently working for Access? She couldn't think of any.

Maybe he'd tapped into her computer from outside. If he did frequent consulting for the company, he would know the computer system well enough to enter from any compatible machine.

A > Are you in Horizon?

A > At the moment.

Not a permanent resident, then. Someone who came and went, working for himself. Sometimes.

Unless he was lying.

A > Do I know you?

A > No.

So much for racking her brains in an attempt to remember every consultant she'd ever met at Access. She'd never met this one.

A > Are you telling the truth?

A > It would break my heart to lie to you.

Two minutes past four. Still, she was reluctant to end the conversation. She asked, *A > How can you crave my body if we don't know each other?*

A > You don't know me, but I know you.

She frowned. This mystery wasn't worth solving; his identity couldn't be so important. *A > Prove that you know me,* she wrote in spite of herself.

He took his time answering. *A > You are tall,* he finally wrote. *At night, I dream of having your long, lovely legs wrapped around my waist, holding me deep inside—*

She turned off the machine with a resounding snap of the switch. Then she swiveled away from the monitor, as if by refusing to look at it, she could also refuse to think about the erotic message that had appeared on it. But the potent words burned through her body, flushing her skin and searing her in other, more intimate places. Her respiration grew shallow, her throat tensed, her heart raced. Her legs—those long, lovely legs Loverboy claimed to want wrapped around his waist—pressed tightly together, as if she could smother the warm sensation blossoming within her hips.

Who the hell was he, to write such a message? And what was wrong with her that she could react so crazily to what amounted to nothing more than an arrangement of electronic impulses on a screen?

It was only a wisecrack, a variation on "I crave your body." That a simple description could leave her breathless and blushing was a result of her lack of sophistication, nothing more.

She filled her lungs with air, emptied them and inhaled again. Her pulse began to slow, her muscles to unclench. Another minute, and her skin cooled off. If she was going to present herself to Jim as the acting project leader of Smart-Town, she had to appear composed and in control. She couldn't let him see her in this ridiculous feverish state.

One more minute. She stood, smoothed her hair back from her face, straightened her beige skirt and strolled out of the office. Perhaps her tardiness wasn't such a bad thing. Let Jim wait for her. Let him cool his heels. Let him develop a little humility.

A few people were relaxing in the attractively decorated main dining room, enjoying an afternoon snack and watching a talk show on the six-foot television screen along the far wall. As usual, the TV was tuned to the Love Channel, broadcasting a talk show. The three glamorous guests were discussing the benefits of navel surgery. "Let's face it—a belly-button is a scar," one of the guests observed. "No one thinks anything about having plastic surgery done on other scars. So why not have it done on the very first scar in your life?"

"You may not believe this," another guest gushed, "but once I had my belly-button altered, I found it much easier to achieve multiple orgasms."

Ordinarily, Lucy would have roared with laughter at such a remark. After her recent dialogue with Loverboy, however, she found it disconcerting.

Doing her best to ignore the broadcast, she ventured into the dining room. The clock above the kitchen door read 4:12. Approaching the coffee machine, she scanned the room in search of Jim.

He was nowhere in sight.

HE'D RUNG UP 210,000 POINTS when the machine decided to register Tilt. The lights blinked off, the bells fell silent and the heavy silver marble rolled listlessly past inert bumpers and unresponsive flippers until it vanished into the hole at the bottom.

Jim snorted. The same left-wrist maneuver that had resulted in a tilt today had earned him an extra ball yesterday.

It was nearly four-fifteen, and he shut off the pinball machine. He was feeling loose and lively, fully prepared to dazzle the shrew with his ideas about unveiling Smart-Town at the second World Environmental Conference, which was scheduled for October in Geneva. Dr. Iceberg Beckwith might have the science down, but she didn't know the first thing about publicity.

Jim knew the first, second and thousandth thing about it. He was going to make himself indispensable to the project, and she was going to have to stop looking down her out-of-joint nose at him.

Exiting his office, he jogged down the hall to the stairs and descended. His long-legged strides carried him swiftly to the dining room. He spotted Lucy standing near the coffee machine, her arms folded across her chest and her face screwed in a radioactive scowl.

Yes, indeed. She was the sort of woman to give a guy fifty demerits for every minute he was late.

He started across the room, rehearsing an apology in his head. Before he could reach her, Sasha Benson from personnel reached up and caught his sleeve. "Hey, Jim," she said, pulling him to a stop at the table where she was sitting with two other women. "Didn't I hear something about you buying a new superlight?"

Jim had gone out with Sasha a few times back in '96. She was married now, but Jim wasn't above appreciating her lush auburn hair and smooth skin. She'd been a looker when they'd dated, and she was a looker now. But she'd been in the market for marriage and Jim hadn't been.

"Something tells me if I did you'd want me to give you a ride in it," he teased, refusing to respond to the impatient frown Lucy was firing at him from across the room.

"You bet."

"Well," he said, with exaggerated sorrow, "there's no truth to the rumor. As long as my old superlight has life in it, I'm not about to trade it in."

"I bet you could afford new wheels every year," one of the other women murmured.

He steered his smile to her. "I don't even know your name, and you're betting on my finances!"

"This is Alix Fairchild," Sasha said in introduction. "She just joined the personnel department a couple of weeks ago."

"Alix Fairchild." He gave her a courtly bow, then whispered, "Don't bet on me. I'm a confirmed contrarian, and you should never bet on a contrarian. Especially a confirmed one."

"A contrarian? What's that, some kind of cult or something?" she asked, batting her eyes furiously at him.

"A contrarian," he confided, "is someone with the strength of Atlas, the intelligence of Einstein, and the prowess of Casanova."

"Get out of here!" Sasha shrieked, swatting at him and erupting in laughter.

Jim estimated that Lucy's scant store of patience might be just about exhausted by now. He straightened up, bade the women farewell and turned with deliberate slowness until his eyes met Lucy's. "Sorry I'm late," he said as he ambled over to the coffee machine.

"I can see how sorry you are."

Her voice was cool and constrained. That, of course, was one of the things that intrigued him about Lucy Beckwith—her refusal, even when she was obviously seething with rage, to let her emotions flare out into the open. If she'd berated him for his tardiness, he would have laughed. But he knew how easily she could be rattled if he put his mind to rattling her, and the fact that she was struggling so hard to maintain her poise impressed him.

"I really am sorry," he said, this time meaning it. "Let me pay for the coffee."

She gave him a skeptical look. "I'll have decaf."

He pulled his cash-card from his wallet, inserted it into the slot, slid a cup below the spout and pressed the decaf button. Then he ordered a cup of regular for himself. After registering the purchases, the machine expelled his card.

"Do you mind if we go into the no-TV lounge?" she asked. "If I have to listen to another minute of talk about how vertical navels lead to better sex, I'll scream."

"I'd love to hear you scream," Jim remarked as he led her toward the soundproof door to the no-TV lounge. "Is that true, about vertical navels?"

"How should I know?" she retorted, her cheeks turning a dark pink as she stepped through the doorway.

He shouldn't tease, but she provided such an irresistible target. "You don't have a vertical navel, I take it."

"My navel is none of your business."

"I thought you were doing navel research back in Boston," he punned.

"It was for the Coast Guard, not the navy. And your spelling is atrocious, if you don't know that one *navel* has an *E* and one has an *A*."

"Being unable to spell is a sign of genius, you know." He closed the lounge door, shutting out the inane babble on the television. They took seats on one of the semicircular couches. "I have an innie, myself. How about you? Innie or outie?"

She gave him a withering look, then sipped her coffee. "Well? What did you want to talk to me about?"

"WEC-II," he said.

"What about it?"

"I think it would be the perfect place to unveil Smart-Town."

She appeared startled. "WEC-II? That's supposed to take place this fall."

"Right."

"Smart-Town won't be ready to go public in four months."

"Parts of it will. There won't be another World Environmental Conference for another three years. If we don't introduce the system at this one, we'll lose an invaluable opportunity."

"Jim, the project won't be ready," she said firmly. "And we aren't going to introduce anything before it's ready."

"But the publicity—"

"I know you love publicity. You've built your entire life around pulling outrageous stunts for the publicity."

"Just one outrageous stunt," he objected.

Undeterred, she continued, "I'm not going to present Smart-Town when it's not far enough along. We'll get publicity for it some other way, when the time is right."

Jim shook his head. He should have guessed she'd opt for caution. "I think we should discuss this with Artie Bauman over in business development."

"Did you mention it to Emilio?"

"I only just thought of it ten minutes ago," Jim confessed.

A line creased the narrow bridge of her nose. "You asked for this meeting this morning. What if I'd said yes to lunch? What would you have told me at lunchtime if you didn't even have this inspiration until ten minutes ago?"

"I always get my inspirations ten minutes ago," Jim explained, offering a winsome smile that failed to thaw her.

"Speaking of which, have you heard from Emilio? Any news about the baby?"

"Nothing yet." She looked as if she were trying hard not to be concerned—and failing.

"Hey, seven hours isn't so long. It's their first child. The first labor is usually a long one."

"How would you know? You don't like babies. They secrete too much."

"They do," he insisted. His sister's two children had secreted all over him during their infancies. "I know about labor," he said, "because I know everything, sweet beets."

She bristled visibly. "My name is Lucy. You can call me Dr. Beckwith."

"How can a person named Lucy be so unloose?" he asked, then plowed ahead before she could scold him further. "I think Artie Bauman is going to love my idea. As far as the project's not being ready, well, you can make it ready if you streamline it a bit. You don't have to have every ounce of hardware cast in plastic, you know. Just get the basic concept into shape and we'll roll with it."

"If you want Access to send you to Geneva for the conference, you'll have to find another project to ride on," she said. "I won't have you sacrificing Smart-Town so you can make a big splash in the media."

"Big splashes lead to big bonuses," he reminded her. When she appeared unmoved, he added, "Public enthusiasm leads to bigger research budgets. If we can get the Department of Energy excited about Smart-Town, they'll pressure Access to devote more resources to getting the work done. It's not going to hurt, Lucy."

She eyed him dubiously, but he sensed that he'd struck a chord. A bonus wouldn't motivate her, but a bigger research budget would. She was a true-blue wizard, a dedicated, unmaterialistic scholar, just the sort of woman who set his mind to dreaming. And she had such wide, expressive eyes, as dark as the coffee in his cup. Such delicately sculpted cheeks, such enticingly firm breasts, such lean hips.

And a soul the temperature of which usually seemed to hover somewhere in the vicinity of absolute zero.

It had taken Jim over a year to crack the Pentagon's computer system. Apparently, Lucy Beckwith's heart was more securely shielded than the Department of Defense. In two years of intermittent effort, he still hadn't figured out how to decode her.

One of these days he was going to break in. He was going to gain access. He was going to establish a positive interface with her.

He'd broken into the Pentagon system for the thrill of doing it. But that thrill would pale to insignificance beside the thrill of breaking into Lucy.

Chapter Four

A > Really, Lucy, nothing much has changed. The hunger for love is a constant. People needed love in 2000 B.C. And they'll need love in 2000 A.D. It's a part of human nature.

A > I'm not so sure about that. In 2000 B.C., love was a luxury. People mated for practical reasons. Love had nothing to do with it.

A > Love has everything to do with everything. It's the same today as it was then and as it will be forever more. Granted, in 2000 B.C., love wasn't expressed in pop songs and pink heart-shaped boxes of carob crackers. But the hunger was there.

A > That hunger wasn't love, Loverboy. It was purely physical.

A > Maybe, maybe not. Maybe humans don't break down into distinct physical and emotional parts. Maybe one hunger feeds the other.

A > People mated for survival, nothing more. For reproduction and protection. Whatever affection they might have felt for each other was never put to the test of time— they died young.

A > Maybe they died young because they didn't get enough love.

A > You're a romantic.

A > And proud of it.

A > Then why are you sending messages to a nonromantic like me?

A > Because I believe that deep in your heart of hearts, you're a romantic, too.

A > How can you possibly know what's in my heart of hearts? You don't know me well, and I don't know you at all.

A > I know what I see. I know what I sense.

A > You sense that I'm a romantic?

A > I sense that you could be one if the right man came along.

A > That is a retro sentiment. You must be what they used to call a sexist pig.

A > Oink, oink.

Lucy's lips curved in a smile. Whoever Loverboy was, he had an uncanny ability to plumb her depths and win her trust, to engage her in the most profound philosophical dialogues—and then, when things risked becoming too intense, to leaven the discussion with humor.

For four days in a row now, Lucy had turned on her computer each morning to a cheery greeting from Loverboy. Throughout the course of the day, Loverboy would contact her, sometimes just to say hello, and sometimes to engage her in a longer conversation. Wednesday afternoon, they'd had a spirited debate about exercise, comparing the relative merits of Loverboy's rowing machine and exercycle to those of Lucy's cross-country-ski machine. Thursday morning, they'd wandered into the treacherous terrain of politics and discovered that their opinions coincided on just about every issue: that the federal government ought to add an even higher surtax to the cost of fossil fuels; that WEC-I had succeeded in developing a global environmental consciousness far more than either of them had anticipated; that one of the senators from Kansas seemed much more intelligent than the other; that the establishment of limits on campaign financing at all levels had done a great deal to redeem politics in America.

They talked, as well, about love. They talked about Platonic ideals and the commercialism of Valentine's Day, about the conflicting human yearnings for company and privacy, connection and solitude.

And then there were other discussions, heated, passionate, crazy discussions that Lucy couldn't believe she was participating in, let alone enjoying. On one occasion, Loverboy had broken into her doodles on the barometric-pressure prediction system to ask whether she wore a bra. Instead of taking offense, as she might have under other circumstances, she'd rejoined, *A > Do you wear a jockstrap?*

A > I wish I did, he'd written. *Whenever I think of you, my body gives me away. A jockstrap might help keep me under control.*

A > Something tells me nothing could keep you under control, she'd entered, to which he'd responded, *A > Not when it comes to you, Lucy B. Someday, you and I are going to meet, and when we do all control will fly out the window. Well, not all control,* he'd amended. *When we finally get naked, I will be a gentleman the likes of which you've never known before. I will make absolutely certain that you lose control before I do.*

In a person-to-person conversation, such a bold statement would have flustered Lucy beyond salvation. But conversing through the protective barrier of her computer liberated her. Somehow, even the most intimate topics didn't seem so dangerous when the element of human confrontation was removed.

So, instead of retreating, she'd typed, *A > Don't be so certain. I happen to be a very controlled person.*

A > I intend to change that, he'd boasted. When she'd asked how, he'd answered, cryptically, *A > By being myself, Lucy love. By being myself.*

Yesterday afternoon, as she was about to shut her computer for the day, a poem had suddenly materialized on her screen:

> *A > Last night I dreamed you were in my bed.*
> *Visions of ecstasy in my head.*
> *I dreamed we were loving, and nothing could hinder*
> *The passionate cries of my dearest Lucinda.*

No one had ever sent her a love poem before. Even though this particular love poem was of borderline taste, she'd been moved by it. She'd jotted it down on a slip of paper, folded it tightly and tucked it into her pocket for safekeeping. Later, when she'd climbed into bed, she'd read it one last time—and visions of ecstasy had swirled through her head throughout a dream-filled night.

She used to look forward to work for the pleasure of the work itself. She'd looked forward to coming to her office and turning on her computer and her brain. But ever since Loverboy had invaded her monitor and her life, she'd discovered herself looking forward to work for a completely different sort of turn-on.

She was baffled and more than a little concerned. She worried about the way her concentration kept slipping, about how, even as she labored over Smart-Town, one small part of her mind focused stubbornly on the blank space at the bottom of her monitor. She worried about her simmering frustration over Loverboy's anonymity, about her fear that if they ever did meet, the reality of him would never measure up to her fantasies.

The only reason she could relate to him was that he was in her computer. That understanding frightened her—but she wasn't willing to bring their electronic friendship to a halt. Not yet. Not when it made her so happy.

She stared at the *A > oink, oink* on the screen for a moment longer, then chuckled and shook her head. *A > I've got to get to work,* she typed, aware that she'd arrived at her office half an hour ago and still hadn't done any of the things Access was paying her a generous salary to do.

A > Killjoy. Give me one more minute—I've got a surprise set up here, but it's going to take time to boot it through to you.

Against her better judgment, she smiled, sat back and gave him his minute.

The monitor went black. Then a small red star appeared in the lower righthand corner of the screen. As it expanded, a blue star appeared in the lower lefthand corner. Then an amber one, a white one, pink and green and lemon yellow and turquoise stars blinked to life on the screen, each brightening and expanding and abruptly bursting in a stunning display of fireworks.

Lucy was so transfixed by the beautiful graphics, she barely heard the knock on her door. More stars shot like comets across the screen, magenta and royal blue, orange and silver gray, exploding and trailing shimmering streamers. She gazed at the spellbinding visuals, trying to blink away the tears that unexpectedly sprang to her eyes.

Another sharp knock on the door. "Just a minute," she murmured, refusing to budge until the last streaks of color had faded and the monitor returned to vacant blackness. She sighed, warm with joy and excitement and an unfathomable serenity. No man had ever gone to such an effort to thrill her.

The third knock was impatiently loud. Issuing another shaky sigh, Lucy turned off her computer and stood on weak legs. If she looked as enraptured as she felt, she was going to shock whoever was on the other side of the door. She swept her fingers through her hair and cleared her throat as she went to the door and opened it.

Finding Jim Kazan on the threshold ought to have put a damper on her mood. There he stood, all six feet plus of him, with those broad shoulders and rangy legs and trim hips, those tantalizing blue eyes and that eye-catching Whole Earth amulet glinting against his upper chest where the top two buttons of his shirt fell open. His hands were hidden in his pockets, but even though she couldn't see them, she found herself remembering the inherent strength in his fingers when he'd clasped her shoulder.

For some inexplicable reason, Jim's presence seemed to add fuel to the smoldering coals inside her. The sight of this tall, ruggedly built man with a smile as radiant as the light show she'd just witnessed on her monitor caused her legs to sway beneath her and her eyes to burn with fresh tears.

Mortified, she averted her face and fell back a step. "Yes?" she said, embarrassed by the unnaturally low, husky quality of her voice.

"Are you okay?" he asked as he entered her office.

"Of course, I'm okay."

"You look kind of zonked."

She raised her eyes and gazed steadily at him. If she was zonked, it was none of his business. Loverboy was welcome to get personal with her, but Jim wasn't.

"What do you want?" she asked brusquely.

His smile widened, creasing his cheeks with dimples. "Ah, now that's the charming sweet beets I know," he taunted. "As cold as the driven snow."

"I believe the expression is, 'As pure as the driven snow.'"

"Hey, you're over thirty years old and divorced. How pure can you be?"

She shot him a reproving look. "What do you want?" she repeated in a clipped voice, resenting him as much for dousing the lingering embers of her passion as for having inadvertently reignited them a moment ago.

"I'm so glad you asked," he said as he shut the door and circled the office, scanning her shelves and appraising the dryness of the potting soil surrounding her cacti before he settled his hips against her desk. His smile grew mocking. "You're so godawful neat."

"Forgive me," she muttered.

"Hey, no—I respect neatness," he swore, pressing his hand to his heart. "I mean it, Lucy—I happen to think neatness is the epitome of something, although I haven't yet figured out what."

"What do you want?"

"What do you think I want? To talk about Smart-Town."

"Fine," she said, exerting herself to maintain a calm facade. "What about it?"

"Well, I mentioned my publicity idea to Artie Bauman in business development—"

"You talked to Artie Bauman? Why wasn't I included in this meeting?"

"It wasn't anything formal, Lucy. I ran into him in the men's room and we got to talking."

Fury shot through her. She could withstand personal teasing but not professional duplicity. Trying to collect herself before she spoke, she marched around the room and took deep breaths. Whenever her pacing brought her within a few feet of Jim, she switched direction, refusing to get close enough for him to grab her shoulder as he had before. Refusing to get close enough to smell his clean, bracing aroma or glimpse his roguish dimples.

"In other words," she said when she trusted her voice not to tremble with rage, "you went behind my back. You cut me out. You snuck around—"

"It was the *men's* room, Lucy. I couldn't very well bring you with me."

"Of course," she snapped. "I can imagine what it's like when you guys gather round the urinals and talk shop."

To her dismay, he started chuckling. "Yep, that's how it was. First we compared sizes, and then we held a contest to see who had better aim, and then we discussed the marketing of the Smart-Town system."

She didn't want to be amused, but a reluctant smile tugged at the corners of her mouth. Why fight it? If she wanted to defend her project against Jim's machinations, she'd have to learn to get along with him—and much as it galled her to admit it, he could be funny on occasion. "Who had better aim?" she asked, her attempt at an apology.

His eyes danced with laughter. "Are you sure you wouldn't rather know which one of us was bigger?"

"Believe me, Jim, that's the last thing I want to know. What did Artie say?"

"He said if we could put something decent together this summer, a preview at WEC-II in October would definitely be in order. The question is, can we put something decent together? As things now stand, you're not far enough along in the design, and the reason is, you're trying to design too many levels of the system at one time. What

I thought was, let's streamline it a bit. Cut out the frills and get the basic concept into shape. We'll put together a simple prototype, something for show-and-tell. We can add all the auxiliary stuff later.''

"What auxiliary stuff? Every component of the system is essential."

"Essential to making the system work, yes," he agreed. "But not essential to making a big splash at WEC-II." His gaze circled the room, and then he shoved away from the desk and dropped onto her swivel chair. Before she could stop him, he turned her computer on and booted up her first file. "Let me show you what I mean," he said enthusiastically. "For the sake of argument, let's forget the water system, forget the moving solar panels—"

She stared with growing uneasiness as her monitor warmed up and began to fill with data. When her computer was on, Loverboy could tap into it. If he sent her one of his love notes while Jim was seated in front of the screen, she'd die.

"I'm not going to forget the water system," she said as she inched toward the machine, positioning herself so she'd be able to shut it off instantly if a message from Loverboy appeared. "The water system is very important."

"In the final analysis, it is," Jim agreed, punching in some data. "But as far as streamlining... Watch what I'm doing here." He pressed a few keys, calling up some graphics. "Just stick with me for a minute, Lucy. I'm on to something good here."

You're on to my private communication system, she thought apprehensively.

"The trick is to keep it simple. Wow the politicos. They're not going to understand any of this, anyway. All we've got to do is dazzle them...."

He continued entering data, describing, explaining. Lucy sometimes nodded her head, sometimes shook it as she tried to absorb what he was saying. She kept her tone light and steady as her hands clenched into fists at her sides, as her stomach twisted into knots. One word from Loverboy, one joke, one question, one shooting star and she'd never hear the end of it. Jim would ride her mercilessly for the rest of her tenure at Access. She wouldn't be able to face him, let alone retain her grip on Smart-Town.

None of Jim's suggestions was particularly complicated, but she could scarcely follow his rapid-fire concepts. She felt like an imbecile, repeating his comments and saying "I see," when all she could see was the rectangular void at the bottom of the screen.

"If we can perfect the temperature-control transmissions and show how the central program can coordinate everything," Jim said, "we'll have the whole world lining up to place their orders. The central program, Lucy—that's the heart of the system."

"The heart," she echoed, her voice catching.

"Are you with me on this?"

"Uh-huh."

He swiveled in the chair and glanced up at her, his expression doubtful. "What did I just say?"

She stared at the screen, listened to the purr of the computer motor, grew queasy with the fear that Loverboy would accidentally humiliate her in front of Jim. "The heart of the system," she managed.

"What about it?"

"I don't know," she groaned, then reached around him and shut off the machine, unable to bear the suspense anymore. "I can't read this stuff over your shoulder, Jim! You're changing things and scribbling things, and I'm standing here getting a stiff neck trying to see past the glare on the screen!"

He seemed nonplussed by her outburst. "Are you okay?" he said for the second time.

Oh, Lord. She was doing a wonderful job of humiliating herself without any help from Loverboy. "I'm fine," she said quietly, turning away and gulping in a deep breath. As long as the computer was off, she was safe. Her best strategy would be to get Jim out of her office before he had a chance to turn it on again.

"If I seem a bit distracted," she said, forcing the exasperation out of her voice, "it's because you barged in here while I was working on something else." She was a terrible liar. But what she said was the truth, and she had a good chance of convincing him. "My mind was focused on an entirely different subject. I just can't switch channels that easily. What I think you should do is print up some hard copy and let me go over it when I've got the time, and—"

Rising from the chair, Jim continued to scrutinize her, his eyes probing her with the deft precision of blue lasers. "I want to *talk* to you about this," he said. "I don't want us passing notes back and forth. We need give and take. We need each other's input. We'll get a lot more done if we talk than if we shut ourselves up in our separate cells and print things on paper."

"All right," she conceded, her tension leaving her too drained to argue. "You want to talk? We'll talk. But not now, not when I'm in the middle of something else."

"How about tonight?" he asked, continuing quickly so she couldn't object. "I've got meetings all day today, and I don't want to put this off until Monday. We can go to the mall for dinner after work and bounce ideas off each other. Okay?"

"Sure," she said, just to be rid of him. He wasn't flirting with her or coming on to her. Spending an hour or two with him that evening would be strictly business; she could live with it. "The mall for dinner. I was planning to go there anyway, to pick up something for Isabella."

"Isabella? Is that what they named her?"

Lucy nodded. The baby had been born late Tuesday night, a healthy eight-and-a-half pounder. According to Emilio, mother and daughter were doing splendidly. "She is the most beautiful girl in the entire universe," Emilio had declared when he'd phoned Lucy Wednesday with the news.

"Isabella was Emilio's grandmother's name," Lucy told Jim.

"Isabella Montega," he murmured. "That's really pretty."

Her eagerness to clear him out of her office abated. That he could wax sentimental over a mushy-gushy baby's name struck her as curious—and also rather appealing. "It is pretty, isn't it," she concurred.

"Well," he said, "why don't we meet out in the parking lot at five o'clock?"

"All right."

He moved to the door, opened it and turned back to her. "We can call it our first date," he teased, then winked and closed the door, denying her the opportunity to correct him.

HE STROLLED DOWN THE HALL to his own office, shut the door and let out an exuberant whoop. He had her, he had her for sure. She was hooked, bewitched, caught in his trap, trapped in his spell.

"Kazan, you're brilliant," he exulted as he crossed the room to his computer and turned it off. Then he proceeded to his pinball machine, regarded it for a moment and moved on to his Velcro dart board. He yanked off the three Ping-Pong size balls, backed up against the opposite wall and threw the balls at the target, scoring one bull's-eye and two complete misses. "You, old boy, have outsmarted her, outwizarded her, dazzled her beyond words," he continued, unable to sit still. "She doesn't know what hit her, but, oh, man, she's been hit."

He gathered the two errant balls from the floor, stuck them to the dart board, roamed to his portable CD player and inserted *Graceland.* The Paul Simon album was one of his favorite oldies; it had come out just about the time he got arrested, and listening to it had kept him sane and confident during the several bleak months when he'd found himself in very real trouble, before his lawyer had worked out the deal with the Pentagon.

As the first song's syncopated intro settled into a driving bass line, Jim lifted the genuine metal Slinky his sister had unearthed in an antique shop and sent to him for his last birthday. He played with the metal coil, sang along with Paul Simon about miracles and wonder, and tried to work out a strategy for his dinner with Lucy. What if she was all stiff and stuffy? What if she spent the entire meal doing her road-slush impersonation? How could he transform her back into the adorably muddled, rosy-cheeked, glassy-eyed, love-struck woman she'd been when he'd stormed her office ten minutes ago? How could he turn the dinner conversation from Smart-Town to sweet talk?

It would be easy enough to zap her computer just before they were scheduled to meet. He couldn't repeat the fireworks—he'd spent over an hour last night programming that gig—nor could he concoct another poem on such short notice. A simple note, though, something short and potent . . .

No. If he contacted her just before dinner, her rosy cheeks and glassy eyes wouldn't be for him. They'd be for Loverboy.

Chastened, he set down the Slinky, turned off the CD player, and slumped onto the floor, resting his back against the five-foot-long stuffed whale doll propped up against a wall. He closed his eyes and thought about what he'd done, concluding that at this point, his situation more closely resembled the two Velcro dart board balls that had missed the target than the one that had scored a bull's-eye.

He'd gotten through to Lucy, yes—but not as himself. The sensual glow that had illuminated her face when she'd opened her office door had been put there not by Jim but by Loverboy's fireworks display. If she'd seemed momentarily electrified by Jim's presence, it was certainly not because she was thrilled to see Jim. What he'd discerned in her eyes, in the softness of her lips and the rise and fall of her breasts had been merely the lingering effects of Loverboy's computerized seduction.

Jim hadn't trapped her in his spell. Loverboy had.

He tried to predict what would happen if he revealed Loverboy's true identity over dinner tonight—and he didn't like what he envisioned. Lucy would in all likelihood thrash him and trash him. She already viewed him as a prankster, a joker. Loverboy, she would fume, was just his latest and most outrageous stunt.

All right, then: no true confessions tonight. No coming clean. He'd play this thing out a bit longer.

In time, he hoped, Lucy would acknowledge her romantic side, not just to some disembodied intelligence in her computer, but to the world at large. Loverboy would erode her armor until she was more receptive to real flesh-

and-blood people—like Jim. Loverboy would thaw her out, and then Jim would take over.

If he worked it right, she might never have to find out the truth.

Chapter Five

Tommy was playing at the Horizon Art Theater. "Well, they finally got rid of *Lawrence of Arabia*," Lucy observed as she and Jim stepped off the escalator onto the third floor of the mall.

"You didn't like *Lawrence of Arabia?*" he asked.

"I thought it was plodding and violent."

"Ah, but all that sand!" He shot her a quick smile. "I can't help it—I'm addicted to sand. If I can't have it between my toes, I'll take it on a theater screen."

Lucy returned his smile.

She'd been on edge all day, her emotions soaring and sinking to such extremes that she might well have developed a spiritual case of the bends. Her communication with Loverboy that morning had captivated her. Then she'd been so fretful when Jim had commandeered her computer, she'd stupidly agreed to have dinner with him— which he'd implied was a date. And then she'd heard nothing from Loverboy for the rest of the day.

Worst of all, she was actually enjoying Jim's company. He kept saying things that shouldn't have made her smile, and she kept smiling. Clearly something was wrong with her.

He'd been waiting for her in the bicycle-parking area when she'd emerged from the building at five o'clock. He'd even wheeled her bike over to his superlight and strapped it into the narrow storage space. An aerodynamic convertible, his vehicle was a few years old but sporty looking and beautifully maintained. In an unexpected display of chivalry, he'd helped her into her seat before taking his place behind the wheel.

He'd driven at a leisurely pace, the electric engine virtually silent as they cruised along the boulevard, past the schools and the medical center, past the evenly spaced trees and pruned shrubs. Even with her sun-jacket's hood and visor on, she'd been pleasantly buffeted by the hot, dry summer wind that gusted into her face, soothing her, refreshing her, enabling her to laugh at Jim's jokes and to accept his company with equanimity.

She'd collected her wits enough to object when he proposed that they dine at The Court, the mall's most elegant eatery. She didn't see how a restaurant with an ambiance reminiscent of the palace at Versailles would lend itself to shop talk. Nor did she care to spend an astronomical amount of money on her meal. She wasn't going to let Jim pay for her dinner—that would definitely signify that they were on a date.

So they'd settled on the Art House, next door to the theater on the third floor. Riding up the escalator, Lucy had kept her face forward and her eyes on the marquee and tried not to think about Jim standing on the step behind her, so close she could lean back against him if she wanted. Why she'd been so conscious of his nearness was another mystery she preferred not to examine.

Jim held the door to the Art House open for Lucy, and she preceded him into the restaurant. The hostess led them to a table by one of the glass walls overlooking the mall. It was as close to dining alfresco as one could get in Horizon; from their seats they could see the tiled walkways, the potted trees and shrubs, the milling shoppers, the swaggering teenagers and beckoning shop signs. Yet the glass effectively blocked out the din of voices and background music.

"The food isn't as good here as at The Court," Jim commented as he passed Lucy one of the two menus the hostess had left for them.

"I've eaten at The Court once," she said. "I took my father and brother there when they visited me in April. I thought the portions were rather small for the price."

"That's part of the experience," Jim joked. "Feeling ripped off is supposed to make the food taste better."

Chuckling, Lucy opened her menu to the entrée page. She dutifully scanned the left-side offerings: poached salmon with kelp, broiled chicken on a bed of steamed spinach, whole-wheat pasta topped with fresh tomatoes and mushrooms, and on and on, each listing followed by a tally of the dish's calorie, sodium and cholesterol content. The dishes sounded palatable in a grim sort of way, but she couldn't work up much enthusiasm for any of them.

Loverboy's suspicions notwithstanding, in her heart of hearts, Lucy knew she was less a romantic than a right-side food aficionado. Heaven help her, she *liked* red meat and creamy sauces. She liked an occasional sprinkle of salt, an occasional shot of refined sugar. At home, she was generally diligent about consuming a healthy diet, but when she ate out, she liked to indulge in rich cuisine.

She perused the menu's right side: barbecued ribs, roast beef with gravy, scallops broiled in butter and wine. "What are you going to have?" she asked Jim.

He lowered his menu. "I haven't decided yet—although I am going to have a beer. Would you like one?"

A beer. As alcoholic beverages went, beer was currently deemed the healthiest. She wondered whether Jim was a fitness fanatic, whether he would berate her if she ordered her dinner from the menu's right side. He certainly looked awfully healthy. His complexion possessed a natural golden radiance, and he had the clearest eyes she'd ever seen, and all that thick, lush hair, and those strong, powerful hands—

It would be just as well if he turned out to be a leftsider. She'd have a good excuse to revert to disliking him.

"I'll have a glass of burgundy," she decided, aware as soon as she spoke that she ought to have steered clear of liquor altogether. She would have to sip the wine very slowly. She couldn't allow anything to cloud her mind tonight.

A waiter arrived at the table. "A glass of the house burgundy," Jim requested, "and an Anchor Steam, and . . . should we order dinner, too?" he asked Lucy.

"Sure. I'll have the goulash with egg noodles and a house salad with blue-cheese dressing."

A satisfied smile crept across Jim's face as he appraised her over the top of his menu. Then he turned to the waiter. "I'll have the sirloin, rare, sour cream and butter on the potato, and Thousand Island dressing on the salad." He handed the waiter his menu and Lucy's, then beamed his smile at her. "I didn't know you were a rightsider."

"I'm not always," she informed him, wondering why his dimples appealed to her so much more tonight than they usually did. "Every now and then, I splurge."

"Hey, if I ate a steak every day, I'd be sick," he said. "But sometimes you just get a craving. What's your favorite sweet?"

"Ice cream," she confessed.

"Me, too. Let's have sundaes for dessert."

She laughed. "Let's see how we feel after we've eaten our dinners."

He pulled a face. "Sensible in spite of yourself, aren't you?"

"I'm afraid so." She spread her napkin across her lap and studied him. Why, after having managed to ignore his smile for two years, did she suddenly find herself melting in its gentle glow? Why did her cheeks grow warm and her fingers grow cold as he returned her gaze? This was James Kazan, admitted felon, tabloid celebrity, the greatest threat to her first major professional accomplishment at Access. Why should she be so pleased to find herself sitting across a restaurant table from him on a Friday night?

Loverboy—that was why. Loverboy had awakened what little romanticism she had in her, and for some silly reason, she was projecting it onto Jim. If she could have her choice, she'd rather be seated across a restaurant table from Loverboy tonight. But as long as that was impossible, a strikingly good-looking man like Jim made an acceptable stand-in.

The waiter brought their drinks, and Jim raised his mug in a toast. "To you," he said simply.

Lucy had lifted her goblet, but his words took her aback. She had expected him to drink a toast to Smart-Town or Emilio's daughter or to his wonderful self, perhaps. "Thank you," she said nervously before sipping her wine. "This isn't a date, though. Drinking a toast to me doesn't change that."

"Of course not," Jim muttered. "You just keep reminding me every ten minutes or so that we aren't on a date. God knows what might happen if I forget." His grin tempered the sarcasm; Lucy didn't take offense. "So, what do you think you're going to get for Emilio's baby?"

"I don't know. I was hoping to browse through the mall and get inspired."

"How's Emilio doing?"

"I've only spoken to him once since the baby was born," Lucy reported. "He sounded...grave. Not sad, but very solemn. He seems to think babies are a serious business."

"Wait till he changes a few diapers. He'll learn not to take them too seriously."

Lucy recalled what Jim had said about babies' secretions. "Have you changed many diapers?" she asked.

"A few."

She frowned. "You don't have any children, do you?"

"None that I know of," he joked, then drank some beer. "My sister has two kids," he explained, "and I've done my duty as an uncle."

"Does your sister live nearby?"

He shook his head. "Up in Oregon. I visit when I can, though. I was out there for Easter. And if I do California again on my next vacation, I might shoot up the coast on the maglev for a weekend visit."

"Will you be doing California again?" she asked.

"If there's another beach for me to clean. Venice is vastly improved at this point, so I doubt I'd go back there. My first time doing California, I worked in Malibu."

"I take it you limit yourself to beaches?"

"What's wrong in specializing?" He leaned back in his chair, waiting for the waiter to set their salads before them before he continued speaking. "The California beaches are a disaster. They've got not just the damage to the piers and houses, but also a real erosion problem. Cleaning up the beaches doesn't mean just clearing the rubble and grooming the sand. They've had to rebuild wharfs and board-walks, reconstruct seawalls, reinforce the shoreline's integrity..."

"I didn't realize it was so complex," Lucy remarked. "I guess I just sort of pictured people removing the trash from the sand so they could play volleyball."

"Volleyball's important, too," Jim said with a grin. He speared a tomato wedge dripping with salad dressing. "You ought to do California, Lucy. It's quite an experience."

"I *have* done California," Lucy told him.

"Really?"

"*USA Today* didn't consider my efforts worthy of mention," she said dryly, "but yes, I spent my last vacation at the observatory on Mount Palomar, repairing some equipment."

Jim looked impressed. "I didn't know they had damage there. It's not exactly close to the epicenter."

"When a quake registers 9.2, you don't have to be close to the epicenter to suffer damage," Lucy reminded him. "They have such delicate instruments there, and a lot of stuff was damaged. An old school friend of my brother's works there, and I heard they needed technical help, so I went."

"That's noble."

Lucy bristled at his patronizing tone. "I didn't do it to be noble," she snapped. "Or to get my name mentioned in the national media. I did it because—"

"Hey, ease up." Jim reached across the table to pat the back of her hand. "I'm being sincere. I'm hot on doing California because I'm a Californian myself, and the Big One hit close to home, literally. But even with that personal interest, I still wound up doing glamour work—cleaning beaches. You went off somewhere out of the way and made your quiet contribution, and you didn't even get to play in the sand and the surf while you were at it. I mean it, Lucy—it's very noble.''

Her indignation vanished as quickly as it had come. "Well," she said, "it was fun."

Jim's eyebrows shot up. "Fixing broken instruments was fun?"

"For me it was," she said as she nibbled on her salad. She wasn't a cavorting-on-the-beach type. Swimsuits made her look flat chested, and she couldn't keep herself from worrying about overexposure to the sun, and beaches were so...public. So populated. At Mount Palomar, Lucy had been led to a computer lab in which several hard disks had crashed with the resulting loss of volumes of data. Armed with a portable CD player and her knowledge, Lucy had turned on some Bach and set to work repairing the hardware and then reprogramming it. Except for meals, she'd been left to herself, just her and the machinery. She'd had a wonderful time.

Jim's surprise seemed to fade. He regarded her with curiosity and something more—admiration, perhaps. The impish gleam was gone from his eyes, replaced by quiet respect. They were still that unreal Kansas-sky blue, but they were devoid of the teasing humor she usually saw in them. The intensity of his gaze unnerved her.

"We ought to talk about Smart-Town," she said, her voice emerging softer and deeper than normal.

"I suppose we ought to."

The waiter appeared at the table with their entrées— heavy, hearty dishes destined to do catastrophic things to their cardiopulmonary systems. Lucy inhaled the paprika-laden aroma of her goulash, then eyed Jim's juicy steak and his potato with its opulent crown of sour cream. "We ought to talk about it before we both die from heart attacks," she said with a chuckle.

Jim smiled and sliced a chunk of steak. "We can always work off our guilt with some postprandial aerobics," he suggested, then asked her what sort of exercise equipment she preferred.

So much for Smart-Town. As they gorged on their dinners, Lucy described the Nordic-Track built-in in her living room.

"I'll bet you did a lot of skiing in Boston," Jim guessed.

"Downhill more than cross-country," she told him. "And not in Boston proper. The best slopes are in Vermont. My father owns a cabin near Stowe, and ever since my brother and I were kids, we've been wintering up there."

"Kansas must have been quite an adjustment for you—it's so flat here."

She shrugged. "I like it. I spent Christmas up at the cabin last winter, and it was nice. But I like Kansas fine."

"So do I." He ate for a minute. "Can I ask about your mother?"

"What about her?"

"You've mentioned your father and brother several times, but never your mother."

Lucy twirled her fork through the noodles and nodded. "She died in a car accident when I was three. I honestly don't remember her very well, except that she was tall and shy and very beautiful." In truth, Lucy rarely thought about her mother, other than being aware of a certain gap in her life, the lack of a maternal presence. It wasn't so much her own mother as a female sensibility she'd missed, a woman to explain clothing and grooming to her, to teach her about men and love. Instead, Lucy had had to model herself on her father, and she'd wound up becoming a scientist and a loner.

She didn't regret her choice of profession, and she credited her father for inspiring her to aim high and achieve great things. But still, there was something missing in her life. She didn't know what it was, because she'd never really had it, but she was aware of a vacuum inside her, an empty space where something was supposed to be but wasn't. Human warmth, Frank used to say. Wifely arts. Feminine wiles.

Whatever it was, Lucy didn't have it.

She pulled herself out of her wistful thoughts. "We really have to discuss work," she said.

"All right." Without further urging, Jim launched into a cheerful monologue about his ideas for the project, and Lucy was almost sorry she'd steered their conversation back to safe territory. She never talked about her mother; she rarely even thought about her. What was the use of thinking about the voids in her life? Why dwell on what she'd never had? Why complain about it to others?

Even so, she'd been flattered that Jim had cared enough to ask. She wondered if he'd care enough to listen if she ever tried to reveal her feelings.

"I see a major Third World market for the system," he declared exuberantly. "That's where most of the building is going on. In the new residential districts being planned for outside Mexico City, something like Smart-Town could be brought in in the early stages and incorporated into the designs. Same thing with the new residential zones in New Delhi and Cairo and Beijing. If the bureaucrats are going to follow through on their promises to house their citizens, they may as well build housing that includes leading-edge technology. They're halfway through the reconstruction of Beirut, but it isn't too late to add Smart-

Town. And Smart-Town technology can be adapted to existing communities...."

There was something mesmerizing about the way he spoke. She was drawn in not just by his ideas and his abundant knowledge, but by the fervor in his voice, his energy and enthusiasm. He'd make a marvelous professor, she thought. He could probably get anyone excited about any topic.

A college professor, or maybe a preacher.

"So, what do you think? I'm way off base, right?" he asked in conclusion. "You think I'm nuts."

"I think you're nuts, yes, but maybe not so far off base," she answered with a smile. "Smart-Town can be useful in the overpopulated cities. And I agree it should be marketed where most of the building is taking place." She maneuvered the last noodle onto her fork. "I guess I just don't like having to deal with the marketing end of things," she conceded. "I like to do my science and not be bothered with the selling end."

"That's one way to wind up in R&D for the rest of your life."

"I like research and development," she said.

Jim shrugged. "So do I. Truth is, I like it all. And right now—" he glanced around until he spotted the waiter "—I'd like an ice cream. How about you?"

They ordered sundaes—Lucy a hot fudge and Jim a butterscotch. If she had to exercise for an extra hour to undo the damage, so be it. To be able to share an ice cream with a like-minded rightsider was too rare a treat to pass up.

The waiter brought their sundaes in globe-shaped glass bowls. Lucy groaned at the size.

"If my sister saw this," Jim said with a conspiratorial grin, "she'd lecture me from here to tomorrow."

"Does she worry about your diet?"

"My diet, my skin, my hair.... She says this is what happens when you become a mother—you start worrying. If she's right, then I'm glad I'll never become a mother," he remarked before digging into his sundae.

Lucy took a taste, holding the chilly ice cream and warm fudge on her tongue for a luscious moment before she swallowed. Her pleasure ebbed when she realized she was being watched.

More accurately, both she and Jim were being watched, spied on through the glass wall of the restaurant. A petite blond teenager stood on the other side, flagrantly staring at them.

"Oh, no," Lucy muttered. "It's her."

"Who?" Jim glanced around curiously.

"That girl, outside. She's with the NVS or something, collecting money. She accosted me here at the mall on Monday."

Jim shot a quick look at the blond waif loitering in front of the video-rental store in her motley apparel, with her hatchet-cut hair, her chain bracelets and her sandaled feet. "She looks pretty harmless," he noted.

"I'm sure she's harmless. But she's a real pest."

"What's she collecting money for?"

"I don't remember. Something unimportant, though— I do remember that."

"Why do you think she's staring at us?" Jim asked, turning to look out the glass again.

"I have no idea. She should have learned I'm not an easy mark."

Now that Jim was staring at the girl as openly as she was staring at him, she smiled slightly. So did he. It dawned on Lucy that the girl must have recognized his famous face. "Oh, no," Lucy repeated under her breath. She'd been having an unexpectedly lovely time with him, but if he started acting like a star hacker and welcoming the attention of fans, he was going to destroy whatever fragile affinity had taken hold between them this evening. Rightside diner or no, she wasn't going to feel at all friendly toward him if he began to flirt with a groupie.

He wasn't exactly flirting, she allowed. But he wasn't ignoring the girl, either. His eyebrows arched in a question. The girl pointed at herself and then at him. He shrugged. The girl pressed her hands together in a pose of supplication. He shrugged once more, then nodded. The girl gave a jubilant leap, then raced toward the restaurant's entry.

"Why did you invite her in?" Lucy asked, frowning.

"Hey, how can you sit and eat an ice-cream sundae with a kid like that staring at you through the window? I would have choked on it."

"So instead, she's going to stare at us without the barrier of the window."

"Come on, Lucy," he said lightly, his eyes alive with amusement. "Let's just find out what she wants."

Within a minute, the bewildered hostess was ushering the girl to their table. "I'm sorry," the hostess began, "but she—"

"It's all right," Jim assured her, rising to his feet and waving the hostess away. Then he gave the girl a careful inspection. Her hair, Lucy noticed, was the same striking flaxen shade as his. "What?" he asked gently.

The girl gaped at him for a moment. She had to crane her neck to view his face—he stood nearly a foot taller than she. She clutched her hands together in front of her, her fingers clenched tightly. Lucy spotted the lightning bolt enameled onto her fingernail and scowled.

"You're James Kazan," the girl said breathlessly.

Jim pretended to mull over her observation. "So I've been told. Who are you?"

The girl pressed her hands more tightly together, causing her narrow shoulders to rise. She seemed to be struggling to breathe. Her round blue eyes remained riveted to him. Lucy might as well have been invisible. "I can't believe it," the girl whispered. "James Kazan! This is so *it!*"

Jim's smile began to show a strain. "It may be *it* to you," he said with forced patience, "but to me, it's something of an intrusion."

"Oh, yeah, I—I'm sorry," she stammered, acknowledging Lucy with a contrite smile before turning back to Jim. "I'm sorry, it's just—I mean, I've heard of you, and there you are, just sitting there, and you were on the cover of magazines and, like, *wow.*"

"Watts Towers," Lucy suddenly remembered. "You're collecting money to rebuild Watts Towers."

"Yeah, that's right," the girl said. She seemed to be recovering from the shock of having spotted a certified celebrity. "I'm Dara-Lyn Pennybopper, and I'm collecting money for Watts Towers. You know, you shouldn't eat that stuff," she added, waving at their melting sundaes. "It's really bad for you. I mean, really, Mr. Kazan, you're supposed to be a genius. You should know better."

Lucy ground her teeth. Jim laughed and dragged an extra chair over to their table. "Well, I've certainly been put in my place, haven't I," he said, gesturing toward the chair. To Lucy's great annoyance, the girl sat. "Dara-Lyn Pennybopper," he reflected. "It's an odd name."

"Well, actually, my mother changed her name to Pennybopper before I was born. She was an actress, kind of," the girl babbled, as if Lucy and Jim were supposed to care. "Her real name was Doris Penborn, but she changed it to Dulcie Pennybopper because she thought it would stand out more. Being in show business and all, she thought Doris Penborn didn't sound glamorous enough.''

"I can see how she'd think that," Jim concurred. Lucy picked at her sundae and simmered.

"She's dead, now," Dara-Lyn said, and Lucy choked on her ice cream. No matter how pushy and rude the girl was, Lucy couldn't smother an abrupt stab of pity for her.

"That's too bad," Jim said sympathetically.

"She died in the Big One." Dara-Lyn gave Jim a soulful look. "And I haven't got a father. I mean, I do have one, only I haven't exactly connected with him yet, if you know what I mean."

Jim studied her, his eyes bright with compassion. "What can we do for you? Are you hungry? Would you like me to order you something to eat?"

"Uh-uh," Dara-Lyn retorted, shaking her head vehemently. "You won't catch me eating this junk." She gestured contemptuously at their sundaes.

"Then what can we do?" Jim persisted.

She seemed momentarily distracted by something she saw through the glass wall. Lucy peered out and noticed a good-looking young man waving to Dara-Lyn and pointing to his watch.

"That's Bobby," Dara-Lyn said, sounding inexplicably boastful. "He's my ride back to the hostel. I guess I'd better make this quick." She offered Lucy a fleeting smile, then turned back to Jim, evidently able to guess which one of them would be more receptive to her appeal. "Well, like she said, I'm collecting money to rebuild Watts Towers, Mr. Kazan, and what I was wondering was, well, could I come to your company and ask for donations?"

"Come to Access? I don't see why not."

"Jim—it's Watts Towers," Lucy interjected. "Just some abstract outdoor sculptures. This isn't like houses for the homeless or new school supplies or anything important. You can't waste the company's time on this.''

Jim sent Lucy a disapproving look. "She's a quake orphan, Lucy. Ease up.''

Lucy pressed her hand to Dara-Lyn's shoulder, urging her around. "I'm very sorry about your mother,'' she murmured. "Believe me, I know what it's like to lose your mother. But Access prefers to devote its resources to more important projects. If you were collecting for something a bit more significant—''

"Watts Towers are significant,'' Dara-Lyn argued. "Mr. Kazan thinks they are, don't you?'' She twisted back to Jim and gazed into his eyes with sheer adoration. "Don't you?''

"Well...'' He squirmed in his seat. "I can't say I'm really worked up over them, Dara-Lyn. But what the heck. You want to try your line out on our social-concerns director at Access? She'll probably say exactly what Lucy's saying here, but if you want a chance—''

"Oh, I do, I do,'' Dara-Lyn gushed, grabbing his right hand in both of hers and pumping it up and down. "Oh, thank you, Mr. Kazan, thank you. I'd love to come to Access and talk to people and everything.''

He gently eased his hand from hers and reached into his hip pocket for his wallet. "Here's my card,'' he said. "You give me a call next week, and I'll see what I can do for you.''

"Oh, thank you!'' She squealed and pressed the card to her breast, as if it were a priceless treasure. Then she read it. "Oh, is it Dr. Kazan? I'm so sorry, Mr. Kazan—I mean, Dr. Kazan—''

"Jim,'' he corrected her. "Just call me Jim. Now you'd better go catch your ride back to the hostel. I'll talk to you next week.''

With another squeal, Dara-Lyn rose from her chair and bounded out of the restaurant. Outside, she joined up with her friend and waved a gleeful farewell to Jim through the glass wall.

Lucy sank back in her chair. Her sundae had melted into a soupy mess, and she nudged it away. Jim was eyeing her curiously, expectantly.

"I don't trust her," she finally said.

"What's not to trust? She's a kid. An orphan."

"I know," Lucy agreed pensively. She wished there were an obvious character trait she could point to, some rational explanation for her uneasiness about Dara-Lyn. "There's just something about her I don't trust."

"Pennybopper." Jim contemplated the name for a moment. "Why does that sound familiar to me?"

"She said her mother was an actress."

He ruminated some more, then shook his head. "I don't know. It has a certain sound to it."

"Yes. A weird sound."

He might have scolded her for her negative attitude. But he only chuckled. "It's no big thing, Lucy. I'll put her in touch with Sophie Dexter in the Social-Concerns Department, and that'll be the end of it."

Lucy sighed. She wished she could believe him, but she couldn't. She didn't know why, but she couldn't.

HE WAS *IT*. DARA-LYN COULDN'T believe how *it* he was. Compared to him, Bobby was just a nice guy.

James Kazan had what her mother used to call "charisma" and Dara-Lyn called "wow." His eyes were infinite, and his smile sent out turbo waves. She could have just sat there staring at him forever and ever.

And he was her father. That wow man was her father.

She sat next to Bobby in his superlight, fondling the business card her father had given her, tracing her finger along its stiff edges, reading and rereading the dynamic green letters embossed on it, Access Computer Systems, Inc., below the green-and-silver lightning-bolt-logo—a lightning bolt just like the one she'd painted on her fingernail as soon as she'd seen the one at the entrance to Access. At the bottom of the card were the words "James Kazan, Ph.D., Senior Scientist," along with the company's address and telephone number.

Senior Scientist. That sounded so important. Senior Scientist and Ph.D.

A father. A family. A home. She'd found it tonight. She'd touched it. At long last, everything she'd ever wanted was within reach.

Chapter Six

"Giftwrap it, please," said Lucy as she pulled her wallet out of her purse.

Jim stood off to one side, waiting patiently. She'd told him he didn't have to stick around while she shopped for a gift for Emilio's baby; she was willing to get her bike from his superlight so he could go home. But he was in no hurry to say goodbye to her.

The dinner had gone surprisingly well, considering that she supposedly hated his guts. No one would have guessed from her attitude toward him during the evening. She'd been attentive and friendly, and she'd answered his questions without any apparent hostility. More than once, she'd leveled a direct gaze at him, and he'd felt a sharp pang of longing in the pit of his stomach—or, more accurately, below his stomach, deep in his muscles, in his groin, in his soul. Maybe it was one-sided, maybe she didn't feel anything the least bit like it, but one piercing look, one instant of communion between her eyes and his and his libido flared to blazing life.

As he watched her confer with the toy-store clerk, he performed some quick mental calculations. On the plus side: they both ate right-side food; they'd both done California; they hadn't come to blows over Smart-Town. She hadn't picked a fight with him, hadn't iced up on him, hadn't curled her lip at him. Hadn't been sarcastic and hadn't behaved like road slush.

She'd smiled at him more than once. After a brief objection, she'd let him pay for dinner. She'd told him about her mother—not that in doing so she'd revealed any shocking secrets, but Lucinda Beckwith was clearly not the sort of woman who liked to talk about herself or her personal history. That she'd shared a little part of herself with him had to mean something.

On the minus side: her aloofness toward that Big One orphan. Jim racked his brains trying to figure out what it was about Dara-Lyn Pennybopper that had rubbed Lucy the wrong way. Granted, the kid had been pushy, but so what? Granted, her choice of a social project was pretty limp, but big deal. The only explanation Jim could come up with for Lucy's negative reaction to Dara-Lyn was that Lucy resented the way the girl had recognized him, the way she'd gone gaga over him. Lucy resented his fame.

For better or worse, Jim was famous. If Lucy had a problem with that, there wasn't much he could do except prove to her that, fame notwithstanding, he happened to be a great guy.

Another minus, he acknowledged as she handed her card to the sales clerk, was her choice of a gift for Emilio's baby. She'd bypassed all the cute, cuddly dolls and stuffed animals, the whimsical music boxes and frilly sunbonnets, and selected a mobile composed of numbers in arithmetic weight configurations: a big red 2 balanced by a bright green $5 - 3$, a daffodil-yellow 7 balanced by a blue $6 + 1$, a 4×2 balanced by an 8. He would concede that the mobile was visually appealing and that Emilio's baby might enjoy gazing up from her crib at a mobile made up of floating numbers as much as she'd enjoy gazing at one made up of silver stars and moons or pastel ponies.

But he was desperate for a sign from Lucy that she was a softie inside, that beneath her frosty reserve lurked a cute-cuddly-doll-and-frilly-sunbonnet-type woman. He'd discovered reservoirs of warmth in her through the computer; with Loverboy, she wasn't so self-protective, so remote. If only she could relate to Jim the way she related to Loverboy, if only Jim were permitted the privilege of experiencing her humor and spirit, if only he could really tap into her....

Her purchase complete, she turned to him. "All set," she said.

"When are you going to see the baby?" he asked as he escorted her out of the toy store.

"Maybe this weekend. I'll give Emilio a call tomorrow morning and see if the family is up to receiving a visitor."

"Give them my regards," said Jim. He'd chipped in on the flowers and card Patricia had sent on behalf of everyone at work, but unlike Lucy, who'd worked with Emilio for two years, Jim didn't really know Emilio well enough to feel comfortable buying his daughter a special present or paying a personal call.

They rode down the escalator to the first floor, Jim perched on the step behind Lucy. Her hair was nearly a solid black, shot through with just enough brown to soften the shade. It fell in relaxed waves against her shoulders— a classic cut, almost a nonstyle, but it suited her. He wondered if it would feel as silky as it looked. He wondered how it would look splayed out on a pillow.

If he were as smart as he was reputed to be, he would put more distance between Lucy and himself by stepping back onto the riser behind him. But the daredevil in him prevailed, and he inched forward to the edge of his step and let his chin brush lightly against her hair. One dip of his head, a mere twenty-degree tilt, and he could bury his lips in the glossy waves. He was crazy enough to try.

The escalator thwarted him by arriving at the first floor before he had a chance. Apparently unaware of how close she'd come to being kissed, Lucy stepped off and waited for him. When they stood on level ground, the top of her head was even with his eyes. Her lips were within inches of his, and he decided that, as tantalizing as her hair was, there were other parts of her he'd rather kiss.

He casually offered her his arm. She didn't seem to notice, however; she simply started toward the mall's south entry, which opened onto the parking lot where he'd left his superlight. With a sigh, he fell into step next to her.

The sky had darkened during their dinner, transforming into a vast moonless blue-black expanse scattered with stars. "I've lived in Horizon for two years," Lucy remarked as they stepped out into the prairie breezes, "and I'm still amazed at how clear the sky is here. Air pollution seems to have missed Kansas completely. Look at all those stars, Jim!"

Another plus. Perhaps the sign he'd been looking for, the sign that Lucy was as much a romantic as Loverboy had accused her of being. She didn't have to become misty-eyed over stuffed animals as long as she became wide-eyed over the infinite wonder of a star-dappled night sky.

They reached his superlight and drew to a halt. "I enjoyed dinner," he said, trying to keep his tone unassuming.

Lucy glanced at her bike, imprisoned in the storage space, and then returned her gaze to him. He held his breath, awaiting her response. "So did I," she said. "And it was nice of you to pay for my meal. Next time, you'll have to be my guest."

Next time. There would be a next time. She'd said it before he had to, and the mere fact that she had counteracted the minuses in his assessment of their evening.

He smiled. She smiled back. A warm gust of wind tossed her hair back from her face. He leaned toward her and touched his lips to hers.

He heard the thud of her toy-store package hitting the bumper of his superlight. Inching back, he scanned her face. Her skin appeared creamy, her eyes unnaturally luminous. Her lips remained pursed, locked in the shape of the kiss.

She didn't run away, didn't slap him, didn't jam the heel of her sensible flat-soled shoe into his instep. She didn't ask him what on earth he thought he was doing—which meant she knew damned well what on earth he was doing. And she didn't tell him not to do it again.

So he did it again.

This time he lifted his hand to her chin and angled her face to his. He caressed her lips slowly, gently, eroding the surprisingly little resistance he sensed in her. He traced the sharp, graceful line of her jaw with his thumb, sliding it up as far as her earlobe. Her hair was softer than he'd imagined, and he shifted his hand until he could twine his fingers into its lustrous depths.

A sigh escaped her, and her eyelids sank halfway. She whispered his name in what might have been a protest, but the parting of her lips and the tiny motion of her tongue as she enunciated the single syllable inspired him. His hand tightened at the back of her head and he slipped his tongue inside, along her lower lip, along her teeth and then beyond.

She sighed again, a deeper, shakier sigh. She swayed slightly and he brought his other arm around her waist to steady her. "Jim," she whispered again, and he understood how lucky he was to have such a name, the mere uttering of which allowed him to surge deeper, to fill her mouth, to taste the ice cream and wine and sweet, sensuous femininity on her breath, to possess her in some way.

He urged her against him, grateful that neither of them had bothered to zipper their sun-jackets when they'd left the mall. Two fewer layers of material between them, he thought, two fewer barriers between his chest and her small, firm breasts. Her height complemented his; his hips found hers and moved against them, subtly, without aggression, only enough to hint at the sublime pleasures this kiss could lead to if they let it.

"Jim," she said, more forcefully this time. He pulled back and her eyes fluttered open. Her respiration seemed labored, her gaze unfocused and her chin thrust forward at a curiously defiant angle.

She was bringing things to an end. He knew it and he could accept it. But he stubbornly kept his hand in her hair, twining his fingers through the softness, stroking his thumb against the nape of her neck.

Slowly her gaze sharpened on his face; slowly her breathing returned to normal. Slowly the delicate flush that had spread along her cheekbones faded.

"This is not a good idea," she said.

"I think it's the best idea either of us ever had."

"Could you remove my bicycle, please?"

If she'd asked him to remove his trousers, even in this public outdoor location, he would have done it. Removing her bicycle wasn't nearly as thrilling a proposition. It took all his willpower to withdraw his hand from her hair, to take a step back, to refrain from lambasting her for her prudishness. "I like you, Lucy," he said. "I—"

"Don't say anything," she said, cutting him off. She folded her arms protectively across her chest and pivoted to face the superlight.

His mind scrambling for a way to salvage the moment and the mood, he took his time retrieving her bicycle. If he pushed her she'd feel threatened. If he retreated from her, she'd think he had only been experimenting, measuring her potential as an easy conquest.

"Are you free tomorrow?" he asked as nonchalantly as he could.

"No."

"Sunday?"

"No." She lifted her backpack out of the superlight, stuffed the gift-wrapped mobile inside it and swung it onto her back, smoothing the straps over her shoulders. "Thank you for dinner," she said tersely, mounting the bike with a maximum of modesty so that he barely caught a glimpse of one knee before she had her skirt arranged neatly over her legs. "Good night."

"Good night," he murmured, watching as she jerked the handlebars around and rode away, pedaling for her life. Even after she was out of sight, he remained where he was, staring at the space where she'd stood, feeling the air gust in to fill the vacuum her departure had created. He stood where he was, picturing her as she'd looked in the flush of arousal and then afterward, as chilly rationality had reclaimed her. He stood there, appreciating everything that was wonderful about her and cursing everything that wasn't.

It had taken him a long time to break into the Pentagon computer network, he recalled. He'd spent over a year of odd hours, late-night raids and weekend marathons in the basement lab at Stanford, over a year of hastily scribbled ideas, insights jotted into the margins of his notebooks, coded memos stuffed into his shirt pockets and inspirations inked onto his palm when he couldn't find a scrap of paper to write them on.

Over a year of false starts, U-turns, retro analyses and fresh attempts. And then, one Saturday night in October of his twenty-second year, turboed up on caffeine and brainpower, he'd penetrated the first layer.

He'd been nowhere near reaching the core of the system that night. As it had turned out, he'd been months away from tapping into the top-secret stuff and leaving his cheerful electronic calling cards scattered around for the Pentagon brass to choke on. But he'd conquered the first hurdle. He'd gotten inside. He'd experienced, however fleetingly, the taste of victory.

It had been the most exhilarating moment of his life—until now. Until he'd experienced that first faint thrill of victory with Lucy.

Someday, Lucy B., he murmured under his breath, *someday I'm going to tap in. I'm going to imprint myself all over you.*

Smiling, he climbed into the superlight and cruised noiselessly out of the parking lot into the starlit Kansas night.

BY SATURDAY MORNING, HE WAS feeling less optimistic. Two days loomed before him, long and empty. Why wouldn't she see him during the weekend? Why couldn't she recognize that something special might exist between them if they gave it a chance? She'd kissed him, hadn't she? She'd kissed him with a measurable degree of passion. What was she so scared of?

Passion, he answered himself.

Restless and lonely, he distracted himself with some TV. He caught a few minutes of *Come Again,* the Saturday-morning forum on the Love Channel, before calling up the most recent Judy Tenuta comedy from the Movie Library. Settling into his rowing machine, he tried to burn off his frustration on the oars and fill his mind with the comedienne's nasally inflected sneering, but all his sweating and panting and halfhearted smiles at the jokes spilling from the TV screen couldn't unravel the hard, aching knot lodged deep inside him. Calling his sister wasn't much help, either. Hearing her description of the Nostalgia Night disco party she and her husband had attended at their community center made him wish he could take Lucy dancing. He'd even be willing to disco, just for the thrill of holding her in his arms.

Desperate to burn off some tension, he hopped into his superlight and drove to Access after lunch. He let himself into the empty building with his personal key, raced up the stairs on foot, unlocked his lab and turned on his computer. If he couldn't be with Lucy, he could be with her project, fixing it up, slimming it down, making it presentable so that even the technologically illiterate bureaucrats at WEC-II would understand it.

The first place to start streamlining, Jim decided as he scanned the list of Smart-Town files, was the water system. Water conservation was a major facet of Smart-Town, but there was no need to present the project in an overly technical manner at this stage. It took him all of five minutes to figure out Lucy's passkey and unlock her files. He called up the water-system files, ran through Lucy's preliminary work, played a drum solo with two pencils against his knee as he perused the data on the screen and shook his head in admiration at what she'd come up with so far.

Tossing his pencils onto his desk, he hunched forward and attacked the keyboard, commanding the computer to translate Lucy's figures into a graphic rendering. He wondered if there might be a way to route the water directly into storage tanks in each Smart-Town building instead of a central reservoir.

He began to doodle. He experimented, hypothesized, embellished, deleted. The distraction he needed finally came; he plunged into the water system, submerged himself in it, lost track of time, hunger and unfulfilled lust for his long-legged colleague. When a janitor rapped on his door at five o'clock to ask what he was doing, Jim emerged from his wizard trance long enough to accompany the janitor down to the dining room, where he helped himself to a sandwich and a carton of milk from one of the huge industrial refrigerators and left a note and his cash-card number taped to the counter. Then he returned to his office and plugged back in.

His brain went turbo. The hell with streamlining and simplifying. His individual reservoir concept was absolutely brilliant and he decided to take it as far as he could, as fast as he could. He felt invigorated, energized, megacharged. When he got stuck on a part of the design, he danced through a few games of pinball, racking up a quarter of a million points while he figured out a solution. When he blanked out on the auxiliary switches, he stretched out on the floor with his head cushioned by the stuffed whale and dozed for ten minutes to clear his mind.

He left his office at 5:00 a.m. Sunday, drove home, showered and fell into bed for six hours of sleep. Then he ate a belated breakfast and called his Home-Ties social worker in Minneapolis. "Hey, Louise—how's it going?" he asked between guzzles of coffee.

"It's going," Louise replied good-naturedly.

"How's Minneapolis?"

"You really want to know? The Skyway maintenance project is four months behind schedule. It takes an extra fifteen minutes to get from anywhere to anywhere else downtown. Folks around here are getting sick of it, but you know. Gotta cope, right?"

"Gotta cope," Jim agreed. "How's your mother doing?"

"Better. She's started playing the piano again."

"You're kidding. When did she have the joint replacements done? Less than a year ago, right?"

"Eight months. I tell you, these Teflon joints are something. When they first started using them in hip replacements, I thought, that's great for folks who have arthritis in their hips, but what about folks like my mother, with their fingers all gnarled up? Now that they've got the smaller joints perfected...well, she's been reborn. She can write with a pen, dice onions, knit and play the piano. Without any pain. It's amazing."

"That's great," Jim said. Although he'd never met Louise Taylor, he and she had been phoning each other on a regular basis ever since she'd joined the staff of Home-Ties as a volunteer a year and a half ago. Jim had heard all about her mother's arthritis, her agency's successful drive to have all school children in Minneapolis receive the AIDS vaccine before the age of ten, her roommate's botany experiments on the satellite laboratory launched by the New World Space Consortium last August, and her pet dog's propensity for burying his soya biscuits in the upholstery of her living room sofa. "Listen, Louise," he said once she'd exhausted the subject of her mother's new knuckles, "I was wondering if you've got anything for me on Dennis and Alice Coker."

"I was out at their farm yesterday," Louise reported. "Nice place, spacious house. Good people. I want to do at least one surprise drop-in before I fax you anything, but they look really promising."

"I liked the way the woman sounded on the phone," he said.

"My only concern is that they aren't just looking for an extra pair of hands to help them on the farm. I was pleased to see they've got several paid farmhands and don't seem to be hurting for help. The mother said that, of course, she'd expect the child to do chores—cleaning the bedroom, washing the dishes, that sort of thing. But I want to make certain they aren't simply looking for cheap labor."

"That's a good point," said Jim. Home-Ties always had to consider every possible motive adoptive families might be harboring when they offered to take in a Big One orphan. "Alice Coker told me she would prefer a preteen girl. Did she mention any preferences to you?"

Louise laughed. "She told me she'd talked about preteen girls when she spoke to you on the phone, and that after she got off she felt very guilty about it. Said she'll take anyone, any age, and she was sorry if she'd sounded picky."

"I think she's a fine woman," Jim decided.

"I think so, too. I'll have something faxed to you by the end of the week."

"Thanks." Jim said goodbye and hung up the phone. The depressing silence of the house reminded him of his own preference for a particular tall woman with dark, sultry eyes and lips that fit perhaps a bit too perfectly to his. There were so many available women in the world, giddy adolescent groupies and party sophisticates who asked him out on dates, neighbors and friends and that new woman in personnel who didn't know what a confirmed contrarian was....

So he was picky. So, unlike Alice Coker, he wasn't willing to take just anyone. So here he was, all alone with another twenty hours to kill before he'd get to see Lucy again.

Back to the lab. Back to the mind-numbing pleasures of the Smart-Town water system.

This time he had enough foresight to bring along a thermos of coffee and a couple of sandwiches—fresh-ground peanut butter and alfalfa sprouts on whole-grain bread, penance for the steak and ice cream he'd gorged on at the Art House. He let himself into Access's vacant headquarters, went directly to his office and vanquished the eerie silence of the building by putting *Graceland* into his CD player and cranking up the volume.

He toiled hard. He lost himself in sheer brainwork. By two o'clock in the morning, he'd completely overhauled and redesigned the water system.

He was exhausted. He would never make it to work on time the following morning—or later that same morning, he amended as he blearily eyed his watch. Not that it mattered to his superiors, not that he had to punch a clock or anything—but he'd been eager for Monday morning to arrive so he could see Lucy again. The way he felt right now, even if he did come back to Access at nine o'clock that morning, he wouldn't be able to see Lucy—or anything else. He'd be blind with fatigue.

He had to go home, get a solid eight hours' sleep minimum, shave and wash his hair and spend some sweat time on the exercise equipment, giving his body the sort of intensive workout he'd just given his brain. For his own sanity he had to, even if it meant not seeing Lucy until the afternoon.

Rising from his chair, he stretched. His neck and shoulders were stiff and his stomach ached with hunger; he'd polished off the sandwiches hours ago. He turned off the

CD player and moved lethargically to the window. Through the tinted glass he could scarcely discern the stars, but when he squinted he could make out a faint silver arc in the sky, seemingly no thicker than an eyelash.

A new moon had been born and was starting to grow. Just like Emilio's little daughter. Just like the newborn water system of Smart-Town. Just like his relationship with Lucy, he hoped. The skinny sliver of moon was like a first kiss, shimmering with promise, poised to swell into a full, round heavenly sphere.

All the technical busywork in the world couldn't make him stop obsessing about her. One brief, sleepy glimpse out the window and there he was, back in fantasy land, wondering how many kisses it would take to melt road slush into water, to make the water boil, to turn it into torrid plumes of steam.

After an entire weekend away from him, would she still be scared? Or would she be a little more receptive to him, a little less skittish? Would she be ready to experience starbursts and fireworks in her soul instead of on her computer screen?

He had no way of knowing. But it wouldn't hurt to stack the deck a little. It wouldn't hurt to remind her that romance was a grand and wondrous thing. It wouldn't hurt to get her in the right frame of mind so that when he finally did see her again, she wouldn't turn tail and run.

All he needed was a time bomb.

Chapter Seven

"Lucy! Come in!"

Emilio swung the door open and beckoned her into the entry of his farmhouse-style home. As soon as she was inside, he closed the door and sagged against it, as if the mere act of welcoming his visitor had drained him of energy.

A quick appraisal of his grooming—or lack thereof—fortified Lucy's first impression. His salt-and-pepper hair was mussed, his shirt wrinkled, his slacks marked with a damp spot near one knee. The cheerful glow in his eyes was contradicted by the purple shadows circling them.

"You look tired," she said.

"I am," he confessed with a smile. "However, I can think of nothing I'd rather tire myself with than changing Isabella's diaper. Which is exactly what Dolores is doing right now. Come on in."

He ushered Lucy through the entry and up the stairs. In truth, she wasn't particularly interested in witnessing a diaper change. *Babies secrete too much,* she thought, the words whispering through her head in Jim's laugh-filled voice.

Still, she'd come here to pay homage to the new baby and she was determined to be a good sport about it. At the top of the stairs, Emilio led her into a sun-filled nursery, where Dolores stood hunched over a table by the window, babbling incoherently. "Who's my lit-too poopsie?" she gurgled. "Who's my lit-too goochee-poo?" Her gibberish was punctuated by the rasp of Velcro fastenings being torn open. "Mommy's going to make you nice-y dry."

Lucy swallowed her laughter. Dolores was an attorney, a member of the Horizon Planning Board and a regional representative to the Great Plains Resource Council, and here she was chortling and burbling over a dirty diaper.

"She's beautiful," Emilio murmured. Lucy didn't know whether he was referring to his wife or his daughter.

The sound of his voice alerted Dolores to Lucy's arrival. She twisted around and beamed a smile across the nursery. "Lucy! Hello! Come on in, come meet our little precious."

Lucy crossed the room to the table. Dolores looked just as disheveled as Emilio, her hair tousled and her clothing rumpled. Yet her eyes sparkled with the same boundless joy as her husband's as she inched aside and made room for Lucy at the table.

There, squirming and kicking and tangling her little arms and legs in the cloth of her open romper, lay Isabella. Her face was round, her eyes dark, her chin defined by a deep crease below her lower lip. She issued a happy, intermittent hum as she experimented with her left hand, opening and closing her chubby fingers, plucking at her mouth, while her other hand clasped a strand of her mother's hair.

She was absolutely wonderful.

"Look at these Velcro diapers," said Dolores, demonstrating the side fastenings on a clean cloth diaper. "When my sister had her babies ten years ago, everyone was still using the disposables. I nagged her about the environment and she said she didn't care, she wasn't going to put those horrible safety pins next to her little baby's skin. But these Velcro strips are perfect." She slid the clean diaper around Isabella's tiny pink bottom and closed the sides. "There you go, lit-too precious, sweet as right-side food. I could eat you up!"

Lucy opened her mouth to say something rational, something calm and analytical about how pretty Isabella was, how happy Lucy was for Dolores and Emilio. What came out was "Let me hold her."

Dolores closed the baby's romper and handed her to Lucy. "She might spit up on you," Dolores warned, draping a small waterproof cloth over Lucy's shoulder. "I tell you, if they can cure AIDS, they ought to be able to cure spitting up."

"I don't mind," Lucy said, astonishing herself. Isabella was warm and solid; her skin smelled of honey.

Emilio spoke up. "If you get tired of holding her—"

"Not a chance." Lucy passed him the gift-wrapped mobile and snuggled the baby close.

Her arms molded naturally around the tiny child. She gazed about the room, taking in the Plexiglas crib with its built-in two-way intercom, its temperature and respiration monitor, its fabric-trimmed handholds and cushioned rim; the brightly colored waterproof padding covering the floor; the traditional stuffed animals scattered about the room and the new Infant Touch-N-Learn mounted on one wall.

Lucy carried Isabella over to the colorful learning toy and sat on the floor in front of it. "What's this, Isabella?" she asked in an uncharacteristically lilting tone. "Is this your learning center?"

Isabella stopped sucking on Lucy's shoulder, and Lucy turned her to face the Touch-N-Learn. She let out a chirping sound and flailed her uncoordinated limbs at the stimulating array of pictures on the toy's large square buttons.

"Okay," Lucy agreed, reaching out and touching the button featuring a picture of a cow. "Let's try this one."

"Cow," said the simulated voice inside the Touch-N-Learn, followed by a long, loud, "Mooooo!"

Isabella squealed. So did Lucy.

"You think we bought that for her?" Dolores confided, flopping down onto the floor beside Lucy. "I play with it more than she does." She pressed the button featuring a rain cloud with drops of water falling from it.

"Rain," the simulated voice said. The damp, refreshing patter of a downpour filled the room.

Isabella squealed again. Lucy nuzzled her neck.

She would have been content to spend the rest of the weekend seated cross-legged on the floor of the nursery, cuddling Isabella and cooing to her. But Isabella clearly had other ideas. After Emilio opened the mobile Lucy had brought and Isabella tried to stuff the numeral four into her mouth, Dolores declared that it was time for a feeding. Lucy reluctantly handed Isabella over, and a chill shivered through her flesh. Her arms ached with emptiness.

She wound up staying for only an hour. Dolores and Emilio were obviously tired, and when Isabella went down for her nap, her parents appeared all too ready to join her in dreamland. Promising to visit again soon, Lucy took her leave.

Pedaling her bicycle slowly out of the neighborhood, she tried to focus on the plethora of toys and gadgets the Montegas had shown her: a Crawl-Matic to exercise Isabella; a traveling stroller that telescoped into a six-inch cylinder that could be stowed in a backpack; a diaper-wash attachment for the washing machine; remote-control gates at the top and bottom of the stairs; and the "infant environment" in the living room, with its flexible walls, padded bottom and adjustable shape, offering the protection of an old-fashioned playpen without the prisonlike atmosphere.

But as dazzling as all the hardware was, Lucy's mind kept zeroing in on the software—Isabella's soft skin, her soft hair, her soft, throaty voice, her soft little belly. She had the most beautiful belly button, Lucy recalled, already healed, pink and delicate. If anyone ever attempted to perform navel surgery on Isabella, Lucy would personally strangle the surgeon.

She wanted a baby. She wanted a husband with whom to have a baby. She wanted a lover, someone as exciting and unpredictable and tender and funny as Loverboy.

Someone who could kiss like James Kazan.

She was as shaken by that thought as she was by her powerful reaction to Isabella. Why should she be thinking of Jim in such a context? Just because he'd kissed her last night without invitation or provocation...just because she'd enjoyed his kiss much more than she should have....

She couldn't deny what she was feeling. She wanted a baby—but not only a baby. She wanted her baby to have as its father a man Lucy could love.

Her mind conjured the image of a tall man, blond-haired and blue-eyed and dimpled, with a medallion hanging from his neck on a chain. She imagined a man capable of unleashing astounding sensations inside her with his possessive embrace, his heated kiss and the sensual motions of his hips against hers—and a man capable of making her laugh and think and become misty eyed the way only Loverboy could.

She wanted it all: Jim's kisses, Loverboy's romanticism and the sweet exhaustion of motherhood. She was thirty-one years old, and she wanted it all. And somehow, all three of those wants—baby, Loverboy, and Jim—braided together into a single confusing, exquisite strand in Lucy's soul.

"OH, MY GOD." SHE STARED in disbelief at the unfamiliar figures scrolling across her monitor. "What the hell did he do?"

She had been worried about how to behave with Jim on Monday morning, what to say, whether to allude to their crazy, lovely moment of intimacy in the parking lot outside the mall. She had avoided the problem by avoiding his office, using the back stairway to the third floor and forgoing her usual detour to the lounge for a cup of tea. She had ducked into her own office, shut the door, let out her breath and prayed that she wouldn't run into Jim until she was prepared to face him.

Which would probably be in about two centuries, she had thought sullenly as she turned on her computer and waited for a good-morning message from Loverboy to appear.

The computer had issued its soothing hum, the monitor warmed up, and she gazed at the *A >* prompt and the blinking cursor.

Nothing.

Frowning, she had turned off the computer and turned it on again. Ever since he'd entered her life last week, Loverboy had sent her a daily greeting within a minute of her powering up her machine. She hadn't realized how accustomed she'd grown to starting her day with a message from him, but when no message appeared, she felt bereft.

What if he was gone? What if Lucy never received another love poem or starburst display again?

Groaning, she had shoved all thoughts of him to the back of her mind and booted up the Smart-Town file on the water system she'd commenced work on the previous week after she'd polished the barometric predictor.

Now she scrolled through the file from beginning to end and then back to the beginning for a second run-through, shaking her head and blinking her eyes as if the problem lay with her perception of the file. But there was nothing wrong with her eyesight or with her brain's ability to digest the figures on the monitor. Her design for the initial collection of rainwater remained exactly as she'd left it on Friday, but everything else had been altered. She punched in a command for graphics and flinched at the confirming visuals.

Instead of shunting the water into community reservoirs, the design now directed the water into individual water tanks within each building. If one building's water tank filled beyond the requirements of that building, a separate switching mechanism would divert the water to another building's tank. Filters and purifying systems would be installed in each building, along with on-site water-quality gauges.

Jim had done it. She knew no one else would have dared to enter her files without her permission, and then to rearrange and restructure her concept. No one else would have had the nerve.

No one else would have come up with such a brilliant design.

Anger and dismay warred within her. If only his concept had been stupid, she could come down hard on him. She could demand that he be removed from the project and sent back to rocket timers or wherever, and she could steer clear of him. She could return to the safety of despising him.

Instead, she would have to incorporate his ideas into the system. They were simply too ingenious, and she was too dedicated to Smart-Town to let her emotions interfere with her scientific judgment. What Jim had come up with was magnificent, damn him.

He ought to have discussed his ideas with her before he'd invaded her files, though. He'd been the one to say he and Lucy shouldn't shut themselves up in their offices and pass memos back and forth, but should instead get together for give and take. Obviously, the give and take he'd had in mind was of a sexual nature. When it came to work, he'd gladly go off on his own and vandalize her designs.

The return of her self-righteous rage invigorated her. She switched off her computer and stormed out of her office. She wasn't going to avoid Jim—she was going to corner him and collar him and demand that he apologize for trespassing on her files. Then, in her position as head of Smart-Town, she was going to explain to him that while she intended to make use of his ideas, under no circumstances was he to swagger around Access bragging to everyone that he had single-handedly saved the project. She would conclude by telling him that he was never, ever to kiss her again. Or touch her, or smile at her a certain way, or wink at her, or use the term "date" in reference to any meeting he would have with her.

She knocked on his door. When he didn't answer after several seconds, she pounded harder on it.

The door next to Jim's swung open and Victor stuck his head out. "He's not there," Victor muttered.

"Do you know where he is?"

"As far as I know, he didn't come in today. I can't think with all that knocking, so I'll thank you to stop it."

Lucy mumbled an apology and returned to her office. So, he hadn't come in today. Probably he was afraid to face her. He must have realized that between his assault to her nervous system and his assault to her work, it would be prudent for him to lie low for a while, even if that meant he had to miss a day of work.

The bastard—mangling her data and then going into hiding so she couldn't confront him with his crime!

Still enraged, she slammed her office door, slumped into her chair and turned on her computer with the idea of digging through the backup files to see if any of her work had survived his incursion. Before she'd completed typing in a command, a window opened up on the bottom half of her screen. Neat green letters spelled out a message: *A > I'm out of touch but you're not out of mind. You can't talk back, so just sit back . . . and enjoy the show.*

Lucy's anger evanesced. She relaxed, her abdominal muscles unclenching and her hands unfisting. She felt her frown lines melting and her cheeks rising in a smile. Her eyes focused solely on the monitor.

The figure of a man, a silhouette in white with a red valentine occupying one side of his chest, appeared a fraction of an inch from the left border of the window. A split second later, a white silhouette figure of a woman, also with a red valentine occupying her curvacious chest, appeared at the right edge of the window. Slowly the two figures moved toward the center of the window, toward each other, his hand reaching for hers. They met, their hands touched, then finally their fingers overlapped, until their hearts merged into one. The single shared heart began to pulse.

Lucy let out a quiet, blissful sigh. She forgot about Jim, Smart-Town, the water system, everything. Everything but Loverboy.

A > I've saved this for you, he wrote. *You can boot it by entering the command: 2HRT-BT1. My heart is yours with that simple command. 2HRT-BT1.*

The window at the bottom of the screen went blank.

Fighting off her daze, she yanked open a desk drawer, pulled out a pen and scribbled down the command before she forgot it. Then she entered the command into the computer. To her delight, the silhouetted man appeared, and then the silhouetted woman, and then they moved together across the screen, slowly but steadily, until they were touching, blending, united. Two hearts beating as one: *2HRT-BT1.*

Her heart beat in their tempo. Wherever he was, whoever he was, she knew Loverboy's heart was beating with hers, as one.

SHE PROBABLY SHOULDN'T have come, but a kid could only spend so much time hanging around at the mall trying to raise bucks for Watts Towers. It would have been more fun to cruise here with Bobby in his superlight, but he hadn't gotten back to the hostel from his NVS highway work, and even if he had, he would have been zonked, not exactly thrilled by the idea of driving Dara-Lyn all the way across town so she could catch a glimpse of James Kazan. Bobby seemed to have a soft spot for Dara-Lyn, but she didn't want to take advantage of him.

So she'd come to Access herself, riding on one of the bicycles she'd found in the basement of the hostel. The headmistress had said they were there for the use of residents.

She stared for a while at the silver lightning bolt that stood above the driveway leading into Access. The big technical companies in California usually had guardhouses at the entries, and the guards would stop you and demand some sort of ID or something to get in. But in Horizon, people weren't so paranoid.

The Access building itself was a boxy white structure of stucco with lots of tinted glass windows. The main part of the building stood four stories tall, and long two-story wings extended out from it on two sides. The landscaping was attractive: hedges lining the driveway and the outer perimeter of the parking lot, leafy trees and manicured lawns. But it was too midwestern for her tastes. She missed palm trees.

How James Kazan could have left the palm trees of California for this boring Great Plains vegetation was beyond Dara-Lyn. She wondered if she could ever get used to it. She supposed she'd have to. A person could get used to just about anything if it meant having a real home and a real family.

She directed her attention to the broad double doors opening into the parking lot. A steady stream of people poured out, evidently leaving work for the day. If Dara-Lyn had arrived at the building earlier, she might have figured out a way to get inside, but with the workers all heading for home, she would be lucky to find James Kazan as he was leaving. Even that would be worth the trip, though.

The sky was overcast, yet everyone emerging from the building wore sun-jackets. Compared to them, Dara-Lyn felt downright funky in her splashy flowered shirt and mustard-yellow slacks.

A superlight cruised up the driveway, passing her en route to the parking lot. The driver apparently didn't notice her, but she noticed him. With his sun-colored hair blowing wildly in the wind, she couldn't help but notice him.

It didn't make sense that he would just be arriving at work at four-forty-five. Maybe he had already departed for the day, discovered that he'd left something in his office and returned to pick it up.

Dara-Lyn stayed where she was, hovering discreetly near the hedge in the driveway, trying to decide how to approach him. She wasn't even clear on what she wanted from him right now—except maybe to see where he worked, how he fit in, how his colleagues treated him. She wanted to learn how a certified genius like James Kazan spent his days. She wanted to get close to him, to get to know him. Someday soon, they would be living together, and she wanted to be prepared.

He took his time climbing out of his superlight. He seemed tired to Dara-Lyn, sluggish. But incredibly handsome. Every time she realized how handsome he was, she experienced a great surge of pride. Suzette O'Rourke always used to brag about how everybody had crushes on her father—which wasn't surprising, since he was the veejay on *Sizzle-Vids* on the Video-Kix network and was really sensational looking. But being a veejay wasn't so exciting. Anyone with the right looks could do it. It didn't take brains.

Hacking into the Pentagon computer network and making a donation at the Mensa Sperm Bank—now that took brains.

He unzipped his sun-jacket and pulled off his sunglasses as soon as he was out of his superlight. Definitely tired, she realized as she studied his eyes. Even from her distant vantage, she could see the gray shadows underlining them, and the eyelids sagging slightly, diminishing the blue sparkle of his irises. *Why is he so tired?* she wondered. It wasn't late, and even if he'd worked a full day, he shouldn't look as if he were ready to zonk out.

Improper nutrition—that must be it. If the man ate less ice cream and more raw fruit, his energy level would soar. She'd make sure he upped his beans-and-greens consumption once she was living with him and could keep an eye on his diet.

He had been walking toward the building, but he halted at the end of the row in which he'd parked. Dara-Lyn glanced toward the double doors to see what had caused him to freeze in his tracks. She spotted the woman at once.

She couldn't *not* spot the woman, given the woman's unusual height and ramrod-straight posture, the way she held her chin high and her shoulders square, the way her thick, dark hair contrasted with her pale, pampered complexion. Whoever she was, that woman stood out. She'd stood out on the escalator the first time Dara-Lyn had seen her. Dara-Lyn had approached two other Access employees she'd spotted at the mall that evening, but they hadn't made an impression on her like that of the statuesque woman with the lush black hair and the piercing eyes.

Obviously the woman made an impression on James Kazan, as well. He began moving again, slowly and cautiously, his gaze riveted to the woman, who remained on the sidewalk, returning his stare.

What if they were lovers? They'd been having dinner together Friday night, and that was the sort of thing lovers did. Dara-Lyn knew all about such things; her mother had had her share of lovers over the years. She'd dated, gone out to dinner with them, occasionally brought them home for the night. Dara-Lyn had had boyfriends, but her mother had had lovers, and Dara-Lyn had never liked any of them.

She didn't like the tall, dark-haired woman, either. What on earth was James doing with someone like her when he could have married Dara-Lyn's mother? Sure, he hadn't ever met Dulcie Pennybopper, and he still didn't know the particulars of his bond with Dara-Lyn's mother, but if he *had* known, if he'd stayed in California instead of exiling himself to this flat, dull place and getting involved with a grim-lipped Amazon...

Damn. Dara-Lyn had only just found him. She didn't want to have to share him with someone who didn't even think the Watts Towers were worth a donation.

James had reached the woman. He put his hand on the woman's shoulder, and the woman said something to him, words garbled by the wind before they reached Dara-Lyn's ears. She heard the deep-pitched rumble of James's equally garbled response. The woman shrugged his hand from her shoulder and folded her arms forebodingly across her chest. James took a step toward her and she took a step back. Their voices rose and fell in an angry counterpoint.

The realization that they were fighting boosted Dara-Lyn's spirits. It was nasty to take pleasure in their spat, but she truly relished the prospect that her father wasn't irrevocably attached to the woman. Her glee waned when James placed his hand on the woman's shoulder again, then slid it down to her elbow. The woman raised her other hand and hatcheted the air with it, emphasizing some point she was trying to make. He argued back, still holding her elbow, still gazing straight into her eyes.

Abruptly, the woman turned away and shook her head. With little apparent effort, she freed her elbow from James's grip and stalked away. He stared after her, his expression unreadable.

Now what? Dara-Lyn thought disconsolately. If the Amazon had just done him dirty, this would not be the most appropriate time for Dara-Lyn to pedal over on her borrowed bike and say hello. But if she didn't say hello, her trip across town would have been a waste.

What the hell. She and James Kazan were family. She didn't have to hide from him.

Straddling the bike, she coasted up the driveway into the lot, steering straight for James. He was staring after his cranky sweetheart and didn't see Dara-Lyn's approach, so she cleared her throat and shouted, "Hi."

Startled, he spun around. Now that she was only a couple of feet from him, she could see clearly the exhaustion dulling his eyes and tugging at the corners of his mouth. Even so, he managed a weary smile. "Well, hello there."

Her heart fluttered slightly, then slowed back to normal. He looked happier to see her than he'd been to see the Amazon. It would be fun to think he liked her better, but Dara-Lyn didn't dare to let herself be that optimistic. She'd have to try not to judge the woman so harshly. Someday—heaven help them both—she might wind up as Dara-Lyn's stepmother or something.

James Kazan seemed to be waiting for her to speak. "I—uh—I just thought I'd come see where you worked," she said, then decided that sounded stupid. "I mean, you gave me your card and it made me kinda curious."

He continued to scope her, his smile inscrutable and his eyes still a spellbinding blue despite his fatigue. She felt a little weird being the focus of such a stare, and she lowered her eyes to his strong jaw, his shoulders and the gold charm dangling from a chain around his neck. His shirt was open at the collar, and she could see that the charm was a circle with latitude and longitude lines criss-crossing it.

A Whole Earth amulet, she recognized with a silent gasp. The only way you could get a Whole Earth amulet was if you did something so vital to the future of the planet that the president or someone equally up there recommended you. Dara-Lyn wondered what James Kazan had done to merit his amulet. Showing the flaws in the Defense Department's computer security system, maybe.

Or having the warmest, most natural, most wow smile Dara-Lyn had ever seen. Whether or not the president was aware of James Kazan's smile, Dara-Lyn believed that smiling was essential to the future of life on Earth.

"You know, I've been thinking about you," Jim said.

Her heart fluttered again, a quick palpitation that froze the air in her lungs for a second. He'd been thinking about her. He hadn't seen her except for just a few minutes in a restaurant Friday night, and *he'd been thinking of her!*

"Oh?" she said in an ultimate low-key voice.

He stuffed his hands into the pockets of his baggy linen trousers and peered down at her. She wished she had inherited his height along with his coloring and what little intelligence she had. She wished she'd inherited his dimples, too. He was so *it.* It didn't seem fair that Dara-Lyn wound up so average looking.

She wanted to ask him what exactly he'd been thinking about when he'd thought about her, but she didn't have the nerve. Instead, she asked, "Are you going to work now?"

He sighed. "If you want me to introduce you to the Social Concerns Director, I can't do it today," he said. "It's too late. If she hasn't already left for home, she's probably closing up her office right now."

"That's okay," Dara-Lyn assured him. "I mean, I didn't come here for that."

His eyes narrowed on her. "Why did you come?"

"I guess—" she nudged a loose pebble with her toe, refusing to look directly at him when she mumbled "—I guess I was thinking about you, too."

"Oh, yeah?" He sounded amused. "What were you thinking?"

"I don't know. I guess…like, you're so famous and all. And you were so nice the other night." *Unlike your snooty girlfriend,* she added mentally. "What were you thinking about me?" she ventured, figuring that if he could ask her, she could ask him.

"What I was thinking about," he said, "was … well, a few things." He paused, then said, "Pennybopper," pronouncing each syllable distinctly and thoughtfully. "Did your mother ever make any movies or videos? I don't know why, but her name sounds familiar."

"She did a few shows," Dara-Lyn boasted. "She used to appear on Video-Kix a lot. She was very talented and very beautiful."

"I'm sorry that you lost her," James said earnestly.

Dara-Lyn nudged the pebble with her toe some more. His pity embarrassed her; she didn't want it.

"Actually, I was really thinking about some other things," he admitted, giving her a sweeping inspection with his eyes. "Have you got a minute?"

"Sure." For James Kazan, she had all the time in the world.

He held her bike by the handlebars as she dismounted and then propped it up for her against a tree. Then he took her arm—much more graciously than he'd taken the Amazon's arm earlier, Dara-Lyn thought—and ushered her along the walk to a concrete bench. He gestured for her to sit, then took his seat next to her.

He gave her a gentle smile. "Have you ever thought about moving away from California? Not just for a summer at a hostel, but actually moving away for good."

Heavens, yes. Ever since she'd realized that he was her father she'd thought about moving away from California for good. She wasn't thrilled by the prospect—she figured she could always try to talk him into returning to his na-

tive state instead—but if she had to stay in Kansas in order
to live with him, she would. The important thing was to be
with her father. Where they lived was secondary.

"Sure," she said nonchalantly.

"I think...now, I don't want to be presumptuous, Dara-
Lyn. You're mature and you seem pretty self-sufficient,
and California is your home. But you've lost so much
there, and it isn't the same place it used to be."

"I know."

"And I'm sure you miss your family."

"My mother, you mean," she said. How could she miss
the other member of her family when she was sitting right
next to him?

"Are you living with relatives now?"

Dara-Lyn shook her head. "My mother's parents didn't
want anything to do with her after she changed her name
and had me. She was a rebel," Dara-Lyn declared proudly.
"I'd like to think I am, too."

"Even rebels need families," he observed.

Yes, yes, yes. She needed a family—the family her father
could provide.

"Are you living in a group home now?"

"You mean in L.A.? Yeah. I mean, not in L.A.—the
home they moved me to is in San Bernardino."

"Well...if having a family meant leaving California, do
you think you could do it? Not just leave the group home,
but move to another part of the country?"

"I like it here," she said, then bit her lip. Was she being
too obvious, too forward? She really ought to break the
news to him that he was her father before she broached the
subject of her moving in with him.

He smiled in what Dara-Lyn interpreted as approval.
"How would you feel about being adopted?" he asked.

"Adopted?" Her voice squeaked. What was he saying? Was he offering to adopt her? Had he already figured out that he was her father? Was he just circling around the subject until he could find out whether she knew?

Her hands went clammy in her lap. Her eyes strayed to his green sneakers, to his long, athletic legs, to his Whole Earth amulet. Her pulse drummed in her ears. What if he did know? What if he was about to acknowledge their relationship and take responsibility for her? What if her dream was about to come true?

She didn't know what to say, so she didn't say anything at all.

"I'm speaking hypothetically," he explained.

She wasn't sure what that meant. "Do you think someone would want to adopt me?" she asked, her voice still squeaky.

"I'm sure someone would."

You, she thought, lifting her gaze to his face. *You want to adopt me.* From the way he was looking at her, from the honesty and sincerity in his eyes—eyes the same sky-blue color as hers—she understood that he did know and that he wouldn't turn his back on her. Even if sperm-bank donors were under no legal obligation to support their genetic offspring, she knew that James Kazan was too noble to reject his own flesh and blood.

"I'd like that very much," she said, softly but fervently.

His smile illuminated his entire face, brightening his eyes, dimpling his cheeks and erasing the creases from his brow. "Well, then, I'm glad you found me," he said, arching his arm around her and giving her a light hug. "I'll take care of everything." He rose to his feet. "Right now, though, I've got to get inside and hit the old computer."

"Go to work, you mean?" Dara-Lyn asked, standing as well. "It's almost dinnertime."

"Access operates on flex-time," he explained. "Sometimes I work all night and sleep all day. I don't intend to work all night tonight, though—just smooth out some ruffled feathers."

"I can guess *whose* ruffled feathers," Dara-Lyn muttered before she could stop herself. Not that she would have held back the words if she could. She had always spoken her mind to her mother about the lovers in her life, and Dara-Lyn had every intention of maintaining that tradition with her father.

Even so, it wasn't a nice thing to say. She steeled herself for a scolding from James. He only laughed. "Hey, she's the boss," he explained. "Her wish is my command."

"She's your boss? That big, tall lady with the looks-could-kill eyes?"

James shrugged in resignation. "At the moment, that's the way it's shaping up. So, if you'll excuse me, Dara-Lyn, I do have to get to my office. But soon—I promise you—I'm going to make sure you've got yourself a family."

"That would be great," she said, lost in the affectionate glow of his gaze. "I'd like that a lot."

"Your wish is my command, too," he said with a regal bow, then joked, "Lots of commanding women around here, aren't there?" He ruffled his fingers through Dara-Lyn's choppy hair, then waved, pivoted on his heel and jogged into the building.

Commanding women. He thought of her as a *woman*. What a sensational dad he was going to make.

She floated back to her bicycle and coasted out of the lot. Her wish was his command, James Kazan's command. That was just about as *it* as you could get.

KNOWING THAT HE COULD HELP yet another Big One orphan find a family gave Jim a satisfying buzz, but by the time he'd reached his third-floor office, the buzz was gone, replaced by edgy discontentment. It hadn't occurred to him, when he'd played around with Lucy's design for the water system over the weekend, that his suggestions would upset her.

He'd been so happy to see her. He had overslept, not stirring until after four. He'd raced through a shower, thrown on the first clothing he'd come across and sped down the boulevard to Access, hoping to catch Lucy before she left for the day. He'd seen her emerging from the building just as he approached it, and after he'd spent the long weekend haunted by her, the sight of her cut through his drowsiness and made his mind come wonderfully alive. Her pale gray slacks had emphasized the glorious length of her legs, and her slender, graceful body had sent a ripple of hunger through his nervous system. Her eyes were so dark, so intensely lovely—until they'd met his. At that moment, they'd hardened with fury.

One kiss. One little kiss. She couldn't possibly hate him for that, could she?

As it turned out, she'd found something quite different to hate him for. "How dare you sabotage my research?" were the first words out of her mouth.

"Sabotage? What are you talking about?"

"You trampled on my files. You must have come in over the weekend just to stomp all over my work. Those were my designs, Jim, and you stomped all over them. I can't believe—"

"Lucy." He'd reached out to touch her. Just a touch, he'd thought, just a bit of affectionate contact and her anger would dissipate. "I didn't stomp all over it," he'd murmured. "I was fooling around with a few ideas, that's all."

"Fooling around. That's you in a nutshell. Just fooling around." She'd twitched her shoulder, tacitly informing him that she didn't want his hand there. As soon as he removed it, she'd crossed her arms self-protectively in front of her.

He'd understood that when she spoke of "fooling around," she was referring to more than just her research. "I'm not fooling around with you, Lucy."

"No. You're dead serious about trying to take over my project. You'll even try seducing me to get your hands on Smart-Town, won't you? Well, it won't work."

"Cripes! How'd you end up so suspicious?"

"I'm not suspicious, Jim. I'm smart."

"If being smart makes you suspicious, Lucy, then smart people must be fools."

"Fine. I'm a fool. I'll admit it." She'd ducked her head as he'd reached for her once more. He hadn't meant his comment as an insult. He didn't think she was a fool and he had to convince her of that.

He'd cupped his hand around her elbow, urging her back to him. "Don't talk that way, Lucy. I like you, okay? I like you."

"I can't imagine why," she'd said. From her expression, he'd sensed that she was striving for lofty irony, but her voice had actually sounded poignant. "I'm suspicious, I'm foolish and I can't even design a decent water system. Your input was terrific, Jim. Next time, though, don't bury my backup files so deep I have to spend half the afternoon exhuming them. Please let go of me. I'd like to go home."

Watching her stalk away, he suffered an ache of weariness and futility deep in his bones. He was too tired to fig-

ure out how he'd managed to blow things so royally, let
alone how he was going to repair the damage. All he knew
was that he had to repair it somehow.

Because as incensed as Lucy was, as deeply as she
despised him, he wanted to kiss her again. That first kiss
had only whetted his appetite for more, much more. He
wanted her. Angry, insecure, suspicious or whatever—he
wanted her.

Okay, he thought, reviewing their confrontation one
more time. He would concede that he hadn't exactly presented his alterations on the water system as suggestions.
He'd simply tapped into her design, perused it and gotten
a bit overenthusiastic. He hadn't *trampled* on her design,
though. He hadn't *sabotaged* it or *stomped* on it. She
hadn't had to accuse him of such felonious acts.

What had really infuriated her wasn't so much that he'd
stomped on her design but that he'd *improved* it. The system he'd come up with was clever and imaginative and all-
around masterful. She couldn't deny it, and to her credit,
she hadn't.

In other circumstances, on any other project, he would
have been gloating over his success. But right now he felt
far from smug. His intelligence had placed a wedge between them. Lucy was too busy resenting him to allow
herself even an instant's pleasant memory of the passion
they'd ignited in each other on Friday night. If only he'd
been more sensitive to her professional situation, if only
he'd proposed his water-system concepts diplomatically, if
only he'd shared them with her in casual conversation instead of entering them directly into her files...

She'd said she had spent the entire afternoon recovering her backup files. Collapsing into his chair, he turned
on his computer and entered the net, searching for those
files. He was curious to see what she'd done with them—

if she'd saved them, renamed them or deleted them in a mindless rage.

Before he'd finished his search, however, he'd lost interest in the water system. What else had she discovered in her computer today? Had his time bomb gone off?

He went through the manipulations to dig up her other computer operations of the day. There, amid the directions she'd entered to resurrect one of her backup files, he saw the command: *2HRT-BT1*.

Another direction to call up another backup file, and then *2HRT-BT1*. Ten minutes later—he checked the Time Entered column to be sure—*2HRT-BT1*.

Four times. Five. Six...

Well, Loverboy was scoring points with her, at least. Jim might well be positioned at the bottom of her Z list, but Loverboy was certainly making grand progress with Lucy B.

Jim's elation was painfully short-lived. What good was Loverboy when Lucy's loathing of his creator grew by the minute? The more she was drawn to Loverboy, the more she despised Jim. If two hearts were beating as one, it was hers and her imaginary sweetheart's, not hers and Jim's.

Smart people could really be fools, couldn't they?

Chapter Eight

A > *You are a romantic.*

  A > *What makes you so sure?*

  A > *You loved the graphic I created for you.*

He was right about that. Throughout the previous day, whenever she'd felt her temper start to flare over Jim Kazan's desecration of her water-system file, she had booted up Loverboy's graphic and it had cheered her. She'd watched the two silhouetted figures gliding across the monitor until their hands joined, and then their bodies, their hearts, their souls. The imagery had been more poetic than the rhyming stanza Loverboy had composed for her last week, more exciting than the starburst graphic, more erotic than any of his ribald one-liners.

Wherever he'd gone off to on Monday, today he was evidently back on line in Horizon. She had scarcely turned on her computer and arranged her fingers on the keyboard before he barged in and commandeered her monitor with his bold assertion that she was a romantic.

Maybe he was right about that, too. Not in a general sense, but when it came to Loverboy...maybe he was right.

She wondered if a kiss from him would arouse her as powerfully as Jim's kiss had. She wondered if his arms would feel as good around her, if his height would match hers as well, if he was graced with enchanting eyes and an irresistibly dimpled smile like Jim's.

She wondered why she was still harboring thoughts of Jim at all. Surely a cerebral affair with Loverboy was more satisfying than a carnal affair with Jim would ever be.

A > How do you know I loved the graphic? she entered into the computer.

A long pause, and then he wrote: *A > You booted it up seventeen times yesterday.*

Nonplussed, she blinked several times and then reread his answer, digesting its implications. She could think of only one way he could have found out how often she'd used the *2HRT-BT1* command yesterday: he would have had to have tapped into her computer and called up her temp files for review. Yet when would he have had a chance to do that if he was out of touch all day? The graphic and the brief message he'd sent her had presumably been prepared in advance and planted in her computer to appear while he was away. So how had he managed to get into her temp files?

How, for that matter, did he know so much about her? Exactly how much did he know? She stared uneasily at the screen, considering her response.

A > Don't turn me off, he implored when her silence extended beyond a full minute.

She didn't turn him off, but she didn't write anything, either. She didn't know what to write.

A > Are you mad at me?

A > No. She weighed her words carefully before adding, *Sometimes I think you know too much about me.*

A > I don't know enough, he argued. *I wish I knew why you're so afraid to admit you're a romantic.*

A > I'm not afraid.

A > Then admit it.

She wouldn't admit it—it wasn't true. *A > I've got work to do,* she wrote.

A > DON'T TURN ME OFF!

She chewed on her lower lip. She *did* have work to do. Jim had arrived at Access late yesterday afternoon, just as she'd been leaving. Once she'd been gone for the night, he could easily have tampered with other Smart-Town files. This morning, she was determined to inspect them all, examine them for signs of mischief and protect them against further unauthorized incursions from the wunderkind.

Jim was dangerous. He kissed too well and he undermined her work. She ought to be spending her time at Access shoring up her emotional and professional defenses against him, not engaging in idle talk with Loverboy.

This wasn't idle talk, though. No conversation with Loverboy ever was. Lucy felt as if she and he were slowly but inexorably traversing the screen of their lives, inching along on a bridge of electronic impulses, their hands extended toward each other, their hearts pulsing in unison. She had never felt this way about another human being—not that Loverboy was a human being. But he was an intelligence, a point of view, a soul reaching for her, touching her.

A > I'm a failure at love, she typed. *You want to know about me? Then know this: I'm divorced. My marriage was a disaster.*

A > These things happen, he wrote philosophically.

She set her fingers free on the keyboard. The words poured out, unpremeditated and uncensored. She let them flow, let them fill the screen. *A > This thing happened to me because of who I am. I lack what it takes to make a marriage work. A good wife would have put romance into the relationship, and I didn't. I didn't know how to. I wasn't sociable enough. Nowadays they call people like me wizards, but back then I was just a nerd. I'm too shy and too tall. I don't have a sense of humor—*

A > You have a great sense of humor. You laugh at my jokes, don't you?

A > I didn't laugh at his. He was my husband—I should have laughed. I should have tried to understand what was important to him. I should have made an effort to get to know his colleagues better and to be charming at parties and to learn racquetball. I should have been more outgoing and more spirited. I should have spent less time with my computer—

A > Stop it.

Her fingers froze. She stared at his blunt reproach and then perused the woeful litany with which she'd saturated the screen.

What she'd written was true. She had been a lousy wife. If Loverboy hadn't ordered her to stop, she could have gone on listing her shortcomings forever.

Loverboy claimed he didn't know enough about her. Evidently what she was telling him were things he didn't *want* to know.

A > Did your husband find fault with you? he asked.

A > Oh, yes—every chance he got.

A > Did he try to understand what was important to you? Did he get to know your colleagues and pursue your interests? Did he try to be more introspective and reflective? Did he laugh at your jokes?

No, she conceded to herself. Frank hadn't wanted to learn the computer games she had programmed on their home PC, and he hadn't wanted to meet her fellow software designers, and he'd never passed up an opportunity to label her sense of humor underdeveloped. But it hadn't occurred to Lucy to find fault with him. He'd been so gregarious and popular—she'd wished she could be more like him. She'd envied him.

A > Marriage works both ways, Lucy B., Loverboy observed. *Your ex should have been willing to meet you halfway. Don't blame yourself. You don't deserve it.*

Her eyes burned with tears as she absorbed Loverboy's conciliatory message. How she had needed to hear such words when her marriage had been crumbling. How she'd ached for her father to offer her such consolation, or her brother. All they'd said at the time was, "If you haven't got what it takes to be a wife, don't be a wife. If you can't make the marriage work, put an end to it. Face the facts. You aren't a good wife to Frank."

Not once had anyone said, "Frank isn't a good husband to you. Frank hasn't got what it takes. Frank can't make the marriage work." If the people she loved had said that, if they'd said it enough times, perhaps they could have convinced her that she wasn't solely responsible for her divorce.

Now Loverboy was saying what she'd been so desperate to hear two years ago. She wasn't sure she believed him, but she drank in his benevolence like a thirsty wanderer stumbling upon a stream after years in the desert. She savored his words, feeling his tenderness bathe her parched spirit and bring it back to flowering life.

If only Loverboy would become a real person to her, someone she could see and hear, someone she could wrap her arms around...

If he did become real, she would probably wither up again. Frank had insinuated that what little warmth she had inside her was devoted to computers. Amend that to computer-screen pen pals, and he'd be absolutely correct.

A > I have to go, she wrote, depressed by the comprehension that the only entity to whom she could reveal her emotions so candidly—the only entity for whom she could feel such a deep, trustful attachment—didn't even exist in the flesh for her.

A > Promise me you'll never put yourself down again, he wrote.

She smiled sadly. *A > I'm only being honest.*

A > You are wonderful. That's the honest truth, Lucy. You are wonderful.

The monitor went dark.

AT TWELVE O'CLOCK, SHE TURNED off her computer and went downstairs for lunch. She wasn't particularly hungry, but she needed a break to save her eyesight—and her brain. She'd spent the last two and a half hours poring over her Smart-Town files, searching for Jim Kazan's fingerprints on her programs. All the while, her mind kept turning and twisting, at one moment chagrined at the understanding of how much she'd related to Loverboy and at the next moment basking in his generous words: *You are wonderful. That's the honest truth....*

Someday she was going to demand that he step out from behind the computer. She was going to square her shoulders, muster her courage and insist on meeting him. She was going to have to find out, once and for all, whether this guy was for real.

The dining room was crowded. The air carried the muffled hum of voices in conversation, but most of the diners ate in silence, their attention drawn to the huge-screen television beaming down at them from the wall opposite the doorway. It was tuned to the Love Channel.

As Lucy slid her tray along the counter, waiting for the server to prepare the Jarlsburg-and-romaine sandwich on whole-wheat bread she'd ordered, her gaze drifted to the television. The show being broadcast was obviously an extremely dated rerun of a bygone series. The scene Lucy was watching took place on the deck of a cruise ship filled with lounge chairs on which scantily clad women lay charring their flesh beneath the sun.

A number of the diners watching the show snickered at the stupidity of the sunbathers. Lucy focused instead on the exchange between two principals who were sipping exotic cocktails garnished with little umbrellas. Although Lucy hadn't seen the show from the beginning, she was able to infer that the actors were portraying lovers reconciling after a spat.

She shook her head in disbelief at the ease with which they spoke their hearts. They were only performers enacting a script, of course, but still, she found it amazing that people—even fictional characters—could verbalize their feelings so unflinchingly, face-to-face. She couldn't imagine ever giving voice to the feelings she'd shared electronically with Loverboy that morning. Without the buffer of the computer between them, she would never have spoken so candidly. The scene on the television struck her as laughably phony.

At the end of the scene, the camera pulled back to a long shot of the cruise ship floating in a calm blue sea, and a man's voice crooned unctuously about the "Love Boat." Lucy vaguely recalled a popular series of that name from when she'd been a child. She'd never actually seen it, though; her father had been strict about television consumption.

When a commercial for vegetarian pet food came on, Lucy turned to take her sandwich, then filled a glass with citrus-blend. When she reached the cashier, she pulled her cash-card from her pocket.

"My treat," came a man's voice from behind her. Jim Kazan's voice.

She glanced over her shoulder. Finding him standing so close to her, she stiffened. Loverboy might tell her she was wonderful, but in Jim's presence, she felt foolish and exploited. "No, thank you," she said tersely.

He had already handed his cash-card to the cashier, who eyed Lucy inquiringly. Resigned, Lucy shrugged, helped herself to a napkin and lifted her tray. By the time Jim was pocketing his card, she'd started toward the no-TV lounge.

"Wait, sweet beets," he called after her. "Please wait for me."

She stopped and took a deep breath. When she'd seen him yesterday, she had been outraged. Today, she seemed unable to feel much anger. She was in no condition to discuss Smart-Town with him, however.

Since eluding him seemed impossible, she figured her best strategy would be to sit silently and eat her sandwich while he raved about promotional gambits and big splashes for the project. As it was, she should probably be grateful that he was willing to talk to her instead of sneaking off to the men's room to confer with Artie Bauman.

As long as Jim didn't raise any personal issues, she'd be okay.

He had retrieved his tray from a nearby table, and they walked together to the no-TV lounge. Jim closed the door behind them, shutting out the canned laughter that bubbled from the television's quadraphonic speakers. The silence of the empty lounge wrapped around her, soothing her nerves yet at the same time making her wary.

She and Jim sat on a couch and placed their trays on the coffee table in front of them. Lucy tried not to let Jim's nearness distract her; she tried to ignore the faint woodsy scent of his after-shave and the muscular solidity of his thigh just inches from hers on the cushions. She tried not to remember the way his mouth had possessed hers Friday night, the way his kiss had ignited a billowing warmth within her.

She occupied herself by spreading her napkin across her lap and sipping demurely from her drink. She fussed with her sandwich and waited for him to say something.

"Do you want me to quit Smart-Town?" he asked.

Startled, she twisted on the sofa to view him. "Leave the project, you mean?"

He nodded. She had never seen him so solemn before. His eyes were clear and unwavering, his lips pressed into a straight line, his dimples nowhere in evidence.

Her first thought was that if Jim did remove himself from Smart-Town, her life would be a whole lot less complicated. She would no longer have to waste precious energy trying to psyche out his motives, whether he was mutilating her files or taking her out for dinner—or kissing her. If he left the project, he would probably never kiss her again.

Which would be for the best, she tried to convince herself. She might have enjoyed kissing him last Friday, but she certainly didn't love him. He lacked the sensitivity and selflessness she hoped to find in a man—the sensitivity and selflessness she had already found in Loverboy.

But what about Smart-Town itself? Much as it galled her to admit it, Jim's alterations to the water-system design made a great deal of sense. His predictions of increased funding for the project based on a high-profile debut of the system at WEC-II made sense, too.

The fact was, Jim was good for Smart-Town. If Lucy intended to be an effective manager in Emilio's absence, she had to do what was best for the project, regardless of the cost to her emotional equilibrium.

"I'd like you to stay on," she said quietly, lowering her gaze.

She could feel his eyes on her, examining her down-turned profile when she refused to look at him. "Are you sure?"

"No, I'm not sure," she snapped.

"Hey, Lucy..." His voice was as hushed as hers, as subdued and tentative. He slid his thumb under her chin and tipped her face up so she was forced to look at him. "I think we can work together, don't you?"

His eyes were so blue it hurt to gaze directly into them, but he refused her the freedom to turn away. His lips curved in a diffident smile. Despite the light tone of his voice, he seemed deadly serious.

She wasn't sure whether he was saying they could work together professionally or in some other way. She decided not to ask him for clarification. "I can't work with someone I can't trust," she told him.

"You can trust me."

"Oh, of course," she scoffed. "I can trust you to prowl around behind my back, invade my files and foul up my designs." She saw the protest taking shape on his lips and quickly cut him off. "You improved the water system, Jim. I'm not going to deny that. The work you did was excellent. But the way you went about it was so sneaky—"

"It wasn't sneaky," he argued. "I came in and worked on it during the weekend because I couldn't stand being home alone."

"I'm sure you could have found someone to spend the weekend with you," she said caustically. "I'm sure half the women here at Access—if not half the women in Kansas—would have been happy to keep you company."

"I didn't want half the women in Kansas," he said, his tone quiet but sharp. "I wanted you."

His words resounded in the small, otherwise silent room. Lucy drew in a deep breath. It was too tempting to believe him, too tempting to interpret his words as some sort of serious declaration.

Anyone sneaky enough to break into her files couldn't be taken seriously, she reminded herself. "Look," she said, swallowing the tremor in her voice. "Just because we happened to have a pleasant time over dinner Friday night—"

"Pleasant? We had a sensational time," he said grandly. "And dinner was the least of it. Out in the parking lot, in case you've forgotten—"

"I haven't forgotten," she interrupted. She wished with all her heart she could have forgotten, but she couldn't.

He tactfully refrained from mentioning the kiss. "In case you've forgotten," he said, "I asked to see you over the weekend, and you turned me down."

"So you took your revenge by coming here and—"

"Revenge? What the hell is wrong with you?" His fingers tightened into a fist; his eyes darkened with rage. For a long moment, he wrestled with his temper; apparently it subsided, because when he next spoke, his voice was low again, taut but controlled. "I came to Access over the weekend to distract myself. I was disappointed that you wouldn't see me, and I came here because I thought playing on a computer would make me feel better. You rejected me, Lucy, and I came here to lick my wounds."

"Rejected!" As if she were a heartbreaker, desirable and in demand, treating men with cavalier insouciance.

"That's what I call it when I ask a woman out and she says no. And when I've gotten my ego kicked in, it sometimes helps if I sit down and bang on my computer for a while. It's therapeutic. If anyone should be able to understand that, you should."

Averting her eyes, she gave a tiny nod. Frank used to charge that she used her computer as the ultimate sublimation. Whenever they fought, she would exorcise her emotions on her PC.

Apparently, Jim operated the same way.

Even so, it was one thing to exorcise one's emotions and another to decipher someone else's passkey and burglarize her files. "I've seen the way you operate, Jim. You join a project, take it over, perform a bit of wizardry and then walk away. I'm not going to let you do that with Smart-Town."

"Damn Smart-Town!" he exploded. "We aren't talking about Smart-Town, Lucy. We're talking about *us.*"

"*Us?* What on earth makes you think that word applies to you and me?"

"The way we kissed," he said, abandoning discretion. "The way I kissed you. The way you kissed me." Saying it aloud seemed to defuse his anger in some way. When he continued, his tone was muted. "I keep telling you, Lucy, I like you. I don't know why you can't deal with that."

"I can deal with it," she mumbled, aware that that wasn't entirely the truth. "I can deal with it just fine. You like everyone with two X chromosomes."

"I like people with an X and a Y, too," he said, his patience beginning to fray once more. "We're not talking about like. We're talking about *like.* What do you think— I kiss every woman I meet the way I kissed you the other night?"

"I have no idea whom you kiss or how you kiss them," she said edgily.

He reached for her face again, pinching her chin between his thumb and forefinger and forcing her face back to his. "Then let me set you straight, Dr. B. I don't kiss other women the way I kissed you. I'm not interested in other women the way I'm interested in you. I don't *like* other women the way I *like* you. Cripes," he groaned, shaking his head. "You're supposed to be smart. So be smart, Lucy. Pay attention. Take notes. *I like you.*"

In the soundproof lounge, his words had nowhere to go. They reverberated in the air, palpable, demanding acceptance. To acknowledge them, however, would mean acknowledging her own feelings. What had happened in the parking lot Friday night *had* been sensational. And while she wasn't sure she *liked* Jim, what she felt for him was strong and real.

His gaze held hers. Even as his hand relaxed along her jaw, she couldn't look away. Staring into his eyes, she saw no duplicity or deception, no tricks or schemes. What she saw, to her amazement, was doubt and hope and yearning—a mirror image of her own feelings.

"Do we understand each other?" he asked.

She opened her mouth, but her voice didn't seem functional. She answered with a nod.

"Good."

He looked away then, his expression more thoughtful than triumphant, and reached for his pita-pocket sandwich. Lucy had no appetite, but she gamely took a bite of her own sandwich and labored hard to swallow it.

They ate in silence, avoiding each other's eyes, yet Lucy was acutely attuned to him. She noticed the grace of his fingers and felt their lingering warmth on her chin, where he'd touched her. She noticed the strength of his legs stretched out in front of him, the rugged shape of his jaw, the athletic contours of his chest beneath his shirt. His presence permeated the room, permeated her consciousness. What insane impulse had led her to believe she could resist him?

"There's some business we need to discuss," he said at last, sounding reluctant about it.

She was still reeling from the intensity of what they'd already discussed. She couldn't imagine how they could talk shop now.

"Why don't we go up to my office?" he suggested, as if he, too, needed a change of scenery. "Would you like to bring your sandwich?"

She shook her head. "I'm not really hungry," she mumbled, rising to her feet.

"Not for this, anyway," he joked, stacking her plate onto his empty one. "I bet you'd get hungry real fast if I bought you a hot-fudge sundae."

She managed a feeble smile. His joke was intended to ease the tension, and she appreciated his effort.

They traveled in silence down the hall and up the stairs to the third floor. Lucy desperately wanted to be able to converse sedately about work with him, and she groped for an appropriate overture. When she hadn't been fuming over his destruction of her files the previous day, she'd been thinking of ways to improve on his new design.

"Here's an idea," she said as he unlocked his office door. "If we could rig the water shunts with microgenerators, when rainwater passed through them it could produce electricity."

His hand on the doorknob, he turned to her. "That's a fantastic idea! Harnessing the water power—I love it. Let's play around with it." He swung open the door and ushered her inside.

She had never been inside Jim's office before, and her initial reaction to it was astonishment. Compared to her prim and orderly office, his was bedlam. His bookshelves held fewer books than playthings—a yo-yo, a Frisbee, an antique metal Slinky, a lap-top video-game set, a chess set in which the pieces were based on characters from the original Tenniel drawings for *Alice's Adventures in Won-*

derland, a deck of cards and a wooden three-dimensional puzzle. Along one wall stretched a massive floor cushion shaped like a whale. A framed copy of the *Newsweek* cover on which Jim had appeared hung above his desk; a Velcro dart board hung on the opposite wall. Against the far wall, below the windows, stood a pinball machine.

Lucy headed straight for the pinball machine, her eyes shining in awe. It was old-fashioned, its sloped playing table cluttered with lights and cylindrical obstacles, bumpers and flippers. The vertical back wall held a bright rendering of a cartoon figure with spider webs drawn all over him, accompanied by the title Spider-Man printed in block letters in retro-style grandiosity.

Lucy had vague memories of the few pinball machines she'd seen in the vestibules of family restaurants and bowling alleys when she'd been a child. She was sure she must have played pinball once or twice, but it was so long ago, she could scarcely recall what the game was like. By the time she had reached high school, the classic machines had all been replaced by video games, which faded in popularity by the end of the last decade as people purchased their own personal video games and the arcades went out of business.

"Would you like to play?" Jim asked, moving around her and groping along the underside of the playing table. He pressed a switch and the machine exploded into action, flashing its lights and feeding a heavy silver ball into the starting position.

Lucy ran her fingers along the chrome edge of the table, barely able to take in the display. "I've never done this before," she confessed.

"Ah," Jim said slyly, "a pinball virgin. Well, the first time can be rough, but I'll try to make it as good for you as I can."

Her cheeks flushed, but she refused him the satisfaction of knowing he'd rattled her. "Thanks," she said dryly.

"That's what I like—gratitude." He guided her hands to the buttons on either side of the playing table. "Push these and see what happens."

She did. The flippers whipped back and forth. "Oh!" she gasped, then let out a nervous laugh and pressed the buttons again.

"A light touch will do it," he assured her. "They can be very responsive if you touch them the right way." She pressed them yet again, more gently this time. "That's it," he encouraged her, "nice and easy. You use them to whack the ball back into play. You want to keep the ball alive for as long as you can."

"I'm supposed to keep the ball alive by whacking it," she summarized uncertainly.

"See this hole at the bottom?" He pointed it out to her. "You want to keep the ball from rolling in. Once it's in there, you can't score anymore with it."

"And the goal is to get a—a good score?" she half-asked, feeling another wave of heat creep over her cheeks.

"It's one of the best goals there is," he agreed with a sly smile. "You want it to last as long as it can."

Doing her best to rouse herself from this game of innuendo, she cleared her head with a nod. Jim went on to explain the game's features—the gates, the little flags that increased the point value of certain passages, the various obstacles and the extra-ball light—and she gave the playing table a sober evaluation. She had never yet encountered a computer that could get the better of her; she'd be damned if she'd let herself be conquered by this elaborate toy.

"Now remember, these are double flippers—top and bottom. The same buttons operate both sets. To keep the ball in play takes timing, quick left-right action. The right rhythm is very important.''

Lucy cleared her throat. "I—I'll do my best."

"It takes practice," he said huskily. "Like all good things."

Ignoring the suggestive laughter that colored his voice, she pressed the buttons and watched the flippers jerk back and forth. "This springy knob here gets the ball into play, I take it?"

"Try it and see."

She shot him a quick look, then yanked back the knob with her right hand and watched the silver ball fly up the chute.

Bells chimed. Lights flashed. She was so stunned, she forgot to press the flipper buttons. The ball rapidly skidded to the bottom of the table and vanished into the hole.

She frowned. "Did I do something wrong?"

"You didn't do anything at all." Jim positioned himself behind her, extended his arms along hers and covered her hands with his. "Okay—try another ball. I'll help you with the flippers."

He felt strong and solid, his chest pressing lightly into her back and his large hands easily covering hers. The slight calluses on his fingertips and the leathery smoothness of his palms rubbed her knuckles; his breath brushed her ear as he angled his head around her to see the table.

How on earth was she supposed to concentrate on the game when he was standing so close? How was she supposed to pay attention to the balls and lights and flippers when her entire nervous system zeroed in on him, absorbing his proximity, his height and strength and the agile motions of his fingers on hers?

He sent a new ball into play, and before she knew what was happening, his body was driving rhythmically against hers, manipulating the table and the flippers in a lively dance that kept the ball zooming. More bells chimed, flags rose and fell, bumpers vibrated and the scoreboard clicked incessantly as he accumulated hundreds and hundreds of points. "Don't fight me," he exhorted her as her fingers tangled clumsily with his. "Get loose, Lucy—go with it."

She started to giggle.

"Lucy," he chided, though he succumbed to a laugh, as well. "You're never going to learn if you don't pay attention."

She sank against him, dissolved in laughter. "Well—all that flashing and clanging—how am I supposed to think with such a commotion going on?"

"You're not supposed to think," Jim explained. "There *are* a few things you don't do with your mind, Lucy." He pulled her hands away from the buttons. "Just feel it and go with it." He turned her in his arms until she was facing him. "After a while," he said gently, "it comes naturally."

Her laughter faded as she studied him. His gaze was warm as it roamed her face, his lips less than an inch from hers, his eyes intense. His smile waned and he closed his arms around her, drawing her to him.

It comes naturally, she thought the instant before his mouth found hers. She heard the words in Jim's sensuous voice: *Just feel it and go with it.* His voice echoed dreamily through her mind, speaking other words: *I like you. You are wonderful....*

Jim hadn't said she was wonderful, though. Loverboy had been the one to tell her that. Why were the words reaching her in Jim's voice?

Because he was the one kissing her. He was the one caressing her lips with his, teasing her teeth with his tongue and then stealing inside. He was the one holding her, plunging one of his hands into the thick tumble of black waves at the nape of her neck and sliding the other down to her waist, tracing circles against her skin through her blouse and then venturing farther down, to the small of her back, to her hips.

You are wonderful.... The sentiment came not from Loverboy but from Lucy herself, directed at Jim. Anyone who could awaken such heavenly sensations in her had to be wonderful. Anyone who could make her laugh until her eyes filled with tears, and who could kiss her until her soul filled with the same joyful tears, anyone who could make her feel so womanly and appealing and downright sexy was wonderful beyond description.

His tongue lured hers, tantalized it, dueled with it, then surged past it with an aggression that shook her to her toes. Sensing the trembling in her knees, he gathered her even closer to himself, rocking his hips to hers until she felt his hardness, until she began to move instinctively against him, seeking, yearning.

Hesitantly, she lifted her hands to his broad shoulders. She ran her palms along their breadth, then swept her hands up into the long golden locks of hair that fell past his collar in back. When she combed her fingers through the silky strands to his neck, he groaned.

His skin felt warm against the tips of her fingers. It wasn't like her to be so forward, but she couldn't keep herself from venturing beneath his collar, tracing the chain of his Whole Earth amulet, imagining how he would look shirtless with that beautiful gold pendant lying against the hair of his chest. Imagining how he would look wearing the amulet and nothing else.

That she could be entertaining such a blatantly erotic vision shocked her. She had been living alone for too long—that must be it. She hadn't been with a man in the two years since she'd left Boston, and before she'd left, her relations with Frank hadn't exactly been wild and wanton. Back in '94 she'd gotten a five-year time-release contraceptive surgically implanted in her forearm, although, as things turned out, she'd hardly needed it.

Now, for the first time since she'd left her husband, she found herself thrilled that the implant was still viable. Amazing how with one simple kiss, a man could inspire all sorts of absurd fantasies.

Except that this wasn't a simple kiss and this wasn't just a man. This was James Kazan, Sexiest Felon of 1988, skimming his hand up her side and under her arm, then along her ribs to the underside of her breast. This was James Kazan, once considered the nation's most dangerous hacker, curving his hand over the soft mound of flesh and massaging, causing her nipple to grow hard and her breath to grow short, igniting a sharp spasm of longing deep in her abdomen.

This was James Kazan, hotshot wizard and media darling, making a pass at her. He'd made passes at her before, and she'd rejected him before. Why should she be so receptive to him now? What had changed?

Everything, she realized. Everything had changed.

With a sigh, she turned her head to end the kiss. He brought both of his hands back to her waist and hugged her tightly, nuzzling her hair with his lips. "I guess you haven't heard about the aphrodisiac quality of pinball," he whispered.

She smiled and rested her head in the hollow of his shoulder. "You should have warned me."

His hips moved again, allowing her to feel his swollen flesh, sending his erotic message through her body. "My house is closer than yours, I think," he murmured, his voice hoarse, his arms still locked around her.

"No," she mumbled, as much to her own inflamed soul as to him.

"Yours is closer than mine?"

"No—I mean—" She took a deep, ragged breath and leaned away, unable to put much room between her body and his with the pinball machine pressing into her back. "We're supposed to be working, Jim."

He gave her the space she so desperately wanted, loosening his hold and edging back. He coiled a dark tendril of her hair around his finger, then let his hand wander behind her ear, igniting a shimmering heat that spread down through her entire body. "Do you really want to talk about microgenerators right now?" he asked.

That was the last thing she wanted to talk about, and he knew it. "I—I'm..." She sighed again, determined to speak honestly, yet unable to shape her muddled thoughts into coherent sentences. "I haven't exactly been dating a lot since my divorce, and..." She let her voice drift off, wishing she could come up with some clever quip to sum up the peculiar combination of desire and apprehension gnawing at her.

"Lucy." He cupped her cheeks with his hands and held her head steady, peering into her eyes. She sensed no mockery in him, no amusement at her vulnerability. "I haven't exactly been dating a lot lately, either."

"Why not?"

He smiled. She observed the sexy laugh lines at the outer corners of his eyes, the deep dimples scoring his cheeks, the unwavering solemnity that seemed to lurk just behind his grin. "I've been waiting for you, Dr. B."

She wanted to believe him. She wanted to trust him the way she trusted Loverboy.

Maybe she could. Loverboy thought she was wonderful. Was it really so strange to think that Jim thought so, too?

His thumbs moved against her temples, stroking, soothing. "Here's the deal," he proposed. "Either you go out with me this weekend, or I'll spend the entire weekend here at Access, pulverizing all your files. What'll it be?"

She felt her lips curving into a smile to match his. He'd been waiting for her, and in a sense, she'd been waiting for someone like him, too, someone who could arouse her body the way Loverboy aroused her mind. "With an ultimatum like that," she said, "I don't know that I have much choice."

"I'm glad to see you respond well to threats," he joked, giving her a light kiss on the tip of her nose and then releasing her. "Now..." He cleared his throat, ran his fingers through his hair as if to remove any traces of Lucy's touch and marched to his computer table. "Let's get to work and see what happens if we introduce microgenerators into the water system."

"I thought you wanted to streamline Smart-Town for WEC-II," she reminded him, following him to his desk and accepting the swivel chair he chivalrously offered. "That's going to make the system more complicated."

"Yeah, but what the heck," he said with a jovial shrug. He turned on his computer and hoisted himself up to sit on his desk. "It's such a terrific idea. I say, let's run with it for a while and see what happens."

Lucy focused on the monitor, praying for her brain to warm up and fill with logical sequences as the computer did. And gradually, her brain did warm up, following the paths of her emotions, changing directories until she could scroll through the files of her soul.

According to the data, according to every entry she'd ever made, according to the circuitry of her heart, she was able to reach one unwelcome conclusion: as appealing as Jim was, as arousing, as sensual and sensational...as much as she desired him, she didn't love him.

She loved Loverboy—and he was beyond her reach.

Some internal circuit breaker activated itself, shutting off her inquiry. So she didn't love Jim. So what? He wasn't asking her to love him—he was asking her only to go out on a date with him. Love didn't have to be a part of it.

He began to free-associate, coming up with new ideas for the system while he drummed on the monitor frame with the eraser end of a pencil. She nodded vaguely, although one small part of her brain couldn't stop dissecting her feelings about what had happened in the past few minutes, in the past hour, in the past week. What had happened since she'd tried to be a wife and failed, since she'd learned to blame herself for not being good enough or womanly enough or lovable enough—and since Loverboy had attempted to unlearn her of that self-destructive lesson.

She couldn't have Loverboy. But she could have Jim, at least for now, for a while. She might not love him, but she liked him, maybe even *liked* him. And she desired him. She desired him in a way she'd never desired a man before—not even Loverboy.

So she'd see him this weekend. She'd be brave and take a chance. He was asking for a date, not a lifelong commitment, not a promise to forswear all others. Just a date.

She might as well run with it for a while and see what happened.

Chapter Nine

Kissing Lucy Beckwith had been incredible. Brainstorming with her was even better.

True, her work habits tended toward the fastidious. She kept a pen and paper at her elbow and diligently jotted down the name she assigned to every new file. She never had more than two windows open on the screen at one time and was appallingly organized about shifting data from one file to another so nothing got misplaced. She sat primly in the chair, her knees and hips bent at ninety-degree angles, her hands perpetually poised on the keyboard. Unlike her sweet stammering after they'd kissed, now she spoke in crisp, grammatical sentences—sometimes in fully shaped paragraphs.

"What we need here," she orated at one point, "is a loop that will get us back on track fast. You can see what's going to happen if I tack in some arguments." She entered a series of qualifiers, typing faster than Jim could read, defining each step and then postulating on the consequences of each modification in the program.

Listening to her expound on her hypotheses provoked an extremely unintellectual response in his lower abdomen. He couldn't help it—her intelligence turned him on. To ease the strain, he leapt off his desk and paced around the office.

"Please sit down," she scolded without shifting her eyes from the monitor. "It's distracting having you prowling around in circles."

It was distracting watching her perform mental pyrotechnics, too, but she didn't hear him complaining about it, did she? "I can't sit down," he said. "You've got the only comfortable chair in the room."

"You can have it," she offered, rising.

He urged her back into the seat, allowing his hand to linger on her shoulder for a few precious seconds. "No, no, it's okay. I'll survive," he assured her, resuming his perch on his desk and twiddling a couple of pencils as he reviewed the figures on the monitor.

"Please stop doing that with your pencils," she chided in a deceptively gentle tone.

"Doing what?"

"Banging them on your knee."

"Hey, it's *my* knee. I can bang it if I want."

He prowled some more, lobbing ideas at her, admiring the spins she put on them as she lobbed them back. "Could you stop playing with that Slinky, please?" she requested in the middle of a particularly long volley.

"The Slinky helps me think."

"Silence helps *me* think."

"I take it you don't want me to turn on the CD player, then."

She sent him one of her gamma-ray scowls. "How can you concentrate when you're listening to music?"

"How can you concentrate when you're all alone in a room with a sexy guy like me?"

He felt more than saw her flinch and realized that his casual joke struck a nerve. Obviously it wasn't the pencils and Slinky and CD player that distracted her. It was the sexy guy.

He felt warm—not in his groin this time, but in his mind, in his heart. At long last, he'd gotten through to Lucy, gotten through in a positive way. The ice maiden had thawed.

For two years, he had puzzled over her cold veneer. He knew how ice and road slush were created: ice from being frozen, deprived of heat and light, and road slush from being driven over, mixed with the dirt in the road and brutally crushed beneath the treads of tires. He was up on his physics, though; he knew that both ice and slush were water—pure, vital H_2O, solid and semi-solid forms requiring just a touch of entropy to become liquid again.

He reflected on everything Lucy had unwittingly told him that morning about her ex-husband and the brainwashing he'd given her, about how the jerk had somehow convinced her that whatever had gone wrong in the most important relationship in her life—up to now, Jim amended with maybe a bit too much confidence—had been her fault alone. As smart as she was, she ought to have seen through the guy's garbage. But as smart as she was in computers, she wasn't the least bit smart when it came to romance.

Thirty-one years old, and she was still a beginner at the male-female game. She considered flirting a grim business. She thought that just because Jim was friendly with women, he must be enjoying a turbo sex life. She took everything at face value; she was oblivious to nuance and insinuation.

Only when she kissed him did he understand what a responsive woman she was. The way her mouth met his and her tongue challenged his, the way her fingers probed the skin below his collar, the way her body arched to his . . .

He sprang off the desk and paced some more.

"I'm plugging in another argument," she called to him from the computer.

"Well, isn't that just like you."

She gave him a sharp look, then relaxed slightly as his grin registered on her. "I wish you would take this more seriously."

"I wish you would take off your blouse."

She appeared to be miffed, but he detected the amusement in her dark, sparkling eyes. "How do I turn you off?" she asked with a reluctant laugh. "There must be a switch somewhere."

He shouldn't keep goading her, he really shouldn't—but how could he resist when she handed him an opening like that? "I'll show you where the switch is," he offered, sliding his hands along his belt to the buckle and pretending to open it.

She blushed like a schoolgirl and swiveled the chair so she was facing the computer again. "About our seeing each other this weekend," she mumbled. "I just remembered I have to wash my hair."

He smiled. Damn, but she was brave. In over her head with him, and she still fought back. He'd been impressed by the spunk in her dialogues with Loverboy, but now that spunk was beginning to infuse her dealings with him— exactly as he'd hoped it would.

"You wash your hair, and I'll blow it dry for you," he volunteered, coming behind her and pressing his lips to the crown of her head. He felt her shoulders go rigid, but he also heard the tiny sigh that escaped her. His gaze narrowing on the monitor, he frowned. "Hey, why don't we try something like this, instead?" He reached around her, nudged her hands away from the keyboard, and typed in a different argument. They watched as the computer assessed this new command and came back with a series of options. And then Jim and Lucy were off and running once more, calculating together, traveling on the same wavelength, charging through the data in perfect tandem.

God, it was good, his mind and hers coming together. It was orgasmic.

"Attention, folks," a metallic-sounding voice squawked through the intercom box on the desk, interrupting the cerebral orgy Jim had been reveling in. "This is Sophie Dexter in the Social Concerns Department. We have a young lady from Los Angeles visiting with us today who's trying to raise money to restore the Watts Towers. If anyone would like to meet with her, she'll be in the dining room discussing her charity and accepting donations until four-thirty. Ante up, boys and girls—help save this symbol of L.A.'s Watts neighborhood. Thanks."

Lucy glared at the box and then over her shoulder at Jim. "Dara-Lyn Pennybopper."

He shrugged innocently. "I passed her name along to Sophie, okay?"

Lucy scowled. "Great. Now you've got Sophie waxing euphoric over the Watts Towers."

"Why not? They're terrific sculptures—or at least they used to be, before they came tumbling down."

"How many children will be fed if we give money to rebuild them? How many babies will get inoculated? How many new classrooms will be constructed? How many orphans will find homes?"

"One, maybe," he mumbled under his breath. "Come on, Lucy, be nice. Let's go downstairs, get some coffee and say hello to Dara-Lyn."

Lucy pursed her lips and shook her head. "That girl has a crush on you."

"That girl," he said with mock arrogance and a wink, "has outstanding taste."

WHAT WAS IT ABOUT DARA-LYN that set Lucy's teeth on edge? Was it her inarguable cuteness, the spiky appeal of her clothing and her hatchet hairdo? Was it that she was petite, the way Lucy had always longed to be, blond and bubbly and chipper despite the losses she'd endured? Was it not so much that she had a crush on Jim Kazan as that he so manifestly enjoyed her adulation?

There was no doubt that he enjoyed it. As soon as he and Lucy entered the dining room, Dara-Lyn broke off from the two patent attorneys she'd been talking to and waved exuberantly at him. Waving back, he stranded Lucy by the door and strode across the room to Dara-Lyn. She favored Lucy with a bogus smile and then directed the full power of her grin to Jim, who soaked it in like an old-time beach bum soaking in the sun.

Why should Lucy be surprised? He thrived in the public eye. If Lucy were to get involved with him, she would have to tolerate the always-in-the-spotlight part of him. She would have to accept that strange young girls would fawn all over him and that he would do nothing to discourage their devotion. She would have to accustom herself to his being shadowed by the media whenever he did California and to having his name bandied about in the national press.

To someone like Lucy, Jim's zeal for publicity was a major drawback. Of course, she didn't love him, so the fact that he wasn't perfect shouldn't have bothered her all that much. Still, she wished he would exercise some restraint. Did his ego truly require a smitten teenage groupie to inflate it even larger than it already was?

She remained near the doorway, watching as Jim greeted Dara-Lyn. Debating whether to wait for him or go back to her office alone, she surveyed the dining room. Sophie Dexter sat at a table near Dara-Lyn, looking official. A few of the stockroom staff were gathered around another table, enjoying frozen fruit pops and watching the Love Channel's late-afternoon talk show, on which two couples were debating the benefits of outdoor sex. The new woman from personnel stood with the patent attorneys, listening to Dara-Lyn's melodramatic description of the demolished towers, and a few more Access employees trickled in behind Lucy to hear what Dara-Lyn had to say. A good-looking young man clad in summerweight coveralls loitered beside the coffee machine, turning a key ring around and around in his hand.

He looked curiously familiar to Lucy. Where had she seen him before? The ID badge fastened to the chest pocket of his coveralls identified him as an NVS worker. Perhaps he had accosted her at the mall recently, soliciting funds.

The mall, yes—that was where she'd seen him. Lucy suddenly remembered Dara-Lyn waving at him through the glass wall of the restaurant the night she'd disrupted Lucy and Jim's dinner at the Art House. "He's my ride back to the hostel," Dara-Lyn had said.

Whether from distrust or just plain orneriness, Lucy refused to become a party to Dara-Lyn's Watts Towers pitch. She gravitated toward the coffee machine instead, and acknowledged the young man with a nod before she inserted her cash-card into the machine and pressed the button for black decaf.

"How's it going?" he asked pleasantly.

"All right, I suppose. Are you collecting for Watts Towers, too?"

"No. I'm just a friend of Dara-Lyn's. We're both living at the hostel. She needed a ride over here, and I was happy to oblige."

"That was kind of you."

He shrugged. "She's such a cutie, you know? And a Big One orphan, too. I'd do anything to help her."

Lucy angled her head toward Dara-Lyn. "So why aren't you over there, helping her?"

He chuckled. "She doesn't need my help, at least not when it comes to raking in the money for the Watts Towers. Look at her—she's already charmed checks out of two of your associates."

Lucy spun around and experienced relief when she saw that Jim wasn't among those writing checks. Yet.

She turned back to the young man, who continued to watch Dara-Lyn as she addressed the small crowd with the aplomb of a professional fund-raiser. His gaze brimmed with respect and fondness for the girl. Just like Jim's, Lucy comprehended unhappily when she glanced back toward Dara-Lyn.

Lucy swore to herself that she wasn't jealous. How could she be jealous of a mere child? Just because Dara-Lyn exuded youth and vitality, just because she had hair the color of the sun that she could wear in an outrageous style without looking silly, just because her skin was smooth despite her apparent unconcern about overexposing it, and her eyes were wide and animated, and her wrists looked so delicate in contrast to the clunky chain bracelets encircling them, just because she was slight enough to stir the protective instincts lurking within the souls of otherwise evolved men . . .

The young man broke into Lucy's thoughts. "That guy she's talking to—that's James Kazan, isn't it?"

"Yes."

The young man shook his head, his admiration extending to Jim. "Dara-Lyn talks about him a lot. She just thinks the world of him."

"Obviously," Lucy muttered.

"He's a pretty special guy," the young man observed. "I remember hearing about his exploits when I was just a kid. For a while, there, all I could think of was becoming a wizard like him when I grew up. Only they weren't called wizards back then." He frowned. "What were they called?"

"Hackers," Lucy answered. "Hackers and nerds."

"Nerds had a negative connotation, though," the young man noted. "I think James Kazan had more to do with changing the image of wizards than anyone else. He made computer work glamorous."

Another fan. "Why don't you go over and ask him for his autograph?" she suggested wryly.

The young man gave her a sheepish grin. "I haven't got the nerve. Not like Dara-Lyn. I've got to hand it to her—nothing stops her. She wants something and she just takes a deep breath and plunges in."

Abruptly Lucy realized that that was what she was jealous of: Dara-Lyn's ability to figure out what she wanted and then go after it without hesitation or self-doubt. If Dara-Lyn wanted to raise money for a restoration project, she did whatever was necessary to raise money. If she wanted to worship Jim Kazan, she worshipped him. She was a child, an orphan, a survivor of a natural disaster of unprecedented magnitude—and nothing stopped her from going after what she wanted.

Perhaps the reason Lucy couldn't act with such brashness was that she didn't know what she wanted. She was beginning to develop some ideas, though. She wanted Loverboy's charm—and Jim's. She wanted Loverboy's electronic lovemaking—and Jim's lips, his hands, the sensual motions of his body against hers. She wanted a combination of the two men, a fusion, the best of both, rolled into one.

She wanted the impossible.

You're not supposed to think, Jim had told her earlier in his office, when she'd botched her attempt at pinball. *Just feel it and go with it.* She would go with what she had: communications with Loverboy for the rest of the week and a date with Jim Saturday night. As compromises went, it wasn't bad.

THE TROUBLE WAS, SHE HEARD nothing from Loverboy. More than once, anxious to hear from him, she'd tried to summon him through her computer. Stalled in one or another aspect of the Smart-Town design, she had opened a second window on her monitor and, feeling weird about it, sent a message into the electronic unknown: *A > Loverboy? Are you there?*

He'd had to be *there,* somewhere, wherever. But he hadn't been on line, in her circuit. He hadn't responded.

A > Loverboy? Send me a sign.

Nothing.

If he was upset about her impending dinner date with Jim, he could at least have allowed her a chance to explain, to assure him that Jim was by no means his rival and in no way capable of supplanting Loverboy in her affections. If he'd had to travel out of town, he could have still left her a note informing her that he was incommunicado, as he had the last time.

They had always been honest with each other, hadn't they? His very last words to her had been: *That's the honest truth, Lucy. You are wonderful.*

What if he hadn't been telling the honest truth? What if she wasn't wonderful? What if he'd gotten sick of her lack of romanticism and decided to move on, leaving her to the questionable mercies of James Kazan?

Her panic about Loverboy compounded her panic about Jim. Logically, she knew Jim's interest in Dara-Lyn was nothing more complicated than the interest a Californian might take in the plight of an unfortunate young fellow Californian. But when it came to matters of romance, logic tended to fall short. Which was why Lucy shied away from romance.

So why wasn't her logic sufficient when it came to Jim?

He'd said he liked her, and she tried to convince herself that that was enough. She liked him, too. If he wanted to shower attention on a teenage survivor of the Big One, so be it. If he wanted to flirt and tease and relish his fame, let him. If he still thought Lucy had a significant personality problem, as he'd remarked not long ago, well, he was entitled to his opinion.

If he didn't like her, he wouldn't have asked her out. He wouldn't have kissed her. He wouldn't have spent the last several days at Access sending her meaningful looks and secret smiles, invading her office through the intercom box and spinning out high-cholesterol fantasies about the Saturday-night dinner reservation he'd made for them at The Court. "Shrimp dripping in butter sauce," his voice would emerge from the box in a sultry murmur. "Fettuccine Alfredo, topped with prosciuto. Filet mignon *au poivre*. Chocolate mousse with whipped cream..." Nor would he have stopped her in the hall Friday afternoon and whispered, "If I pick you up at seven, the sun will be pretty close to having set. So dress dark."

She owned little in the way of dark clothing. But a Saturday-night dinner at The Court was a special occasion worthy of new clothes. As soon as she got home Friday, she settled at her personal computer and tapped into the home-consumer net. She booted up Apparel, Ladies, then skimmed the options and requested Evening Wear. She reviewed the styles available in her price range and decided on an elegant tunic-and-slacks outfit in midnight-blue silk. She typed in her name and address, her measurements and her cash-card number, and requested next-day delivery.

Saturday morning, after a five-mile bike ride along the Kansas River, she paid a visit to the Montega house, where she found Emilio and Dolores even more exhausted than they'd been the previous week, and little Isabella even more lovely. When Lucy returned home around lunchtime, a parcel from one of the mall boutiques was waiting on the front porch. Bristling with anxiety and anticipation, she tore open the package and unfolded the silk outfit. Would such a stylish ensemble look ridiculous on her? Too fancy, too chic, too *it?* Would Jim think she was trying too hard to impress him?

Sighing, she carried the outfit upstairs, spread it out on her bed and then went back down to the living room and spent thirty minutes on her Nordic-Track. As soon as she'd caught her breath, she headed back outdoors, mounted her bike and took another long bike ride along the river. The sun passed its noontime height, leaving in its wake a scorching heat. She was dripping with sweat by the time she got home.

Too edgy to eat anything, she unwound with a fruit shake and some mindless TV viewing. Deliberately avoiding the Love Channel, she tuned in to the Video-Kix network, where she watched an advertisement for Pepsi-Seltzer and one for Sasagami Rice Chips, "the Asian treat—no meat, no sweet." Then a two-minute joke clip featuring a rather wizened Robin Williams, and then another ad, this one for Harley Mopeds, "Solar Wheels For Folks Who Mean Business." Then a rap video by Lloyd Droid:

> "Get yer head in gear, duh-DEE-duh-DEE, dear
> Gotta use yer brain, gotta make it gain
> Cuz I love you—get smart, get yer gray matter clear
> Cuz I love you—I'm the wizard in an info-blizzard
> Duh-duh-DEE-duh-duh-DEE-duh-DEE-duh-DEE, smart
> That's my art part, baby, that's the smart art part…"

Her head pounding in time to the rigid percussion, Lucy dragged her weary body off the couch and trudged back to the kitchen for another fruit shake. Lloyd Droid was gone from the screen by the time she returned, and the vacuously handsome veejay gave a plastic smile and said, "Hey, kids, call your parents to the tube. This one's an oldie, just for them."

The screen filled with a provocatively attired woman with platinum hair and a totally unspontaneous-looking pout. She started to sing a song about being a material girl, one Lucy remembered well from her teenage years. "Madonna," a caption at the bottom of the screen identified her.

Do you smoke after sex? Lucy choked on her drink and sat up straight as the sight of Madonna jarred her memory. Way back at the beginning of her affair—if that was the word for it—with Loverboy, he'd used that joke and she'd had to invent her own punchline for it because all she could remember was that it had been a classic line associated with a blond bombshell from a previous era. Definitely not Madonna, Lucy decided as she watched the writhing, bleach-headed singer. Someone else. She wished she could remember who—or at least could recall the punchline.

It didn't matter. Lucy watched the whining, slithering singer with her cottony hair and decided she wasn't the least bit sexy. Lloyd Droid, on the other hand, with his driving lyrics about intelligence...

Suddenly invigorated, Lucy turned off the television and headed to her home computer, back in the kitchen. She yanked a stool over from the breakfast bar and switched on the machine.

A > Do you smoke after sex? she entered once the monitor had warmed up.

The computer purred. She stared at the screen, combed her memory, recited the words to herself again and again, lowered her hands to the keys and typed, *A > I don't know, I never looked.*

Opening her eyes, she let out a triumphant hoot. That was it, the classic punchline to a classic joke. A Mae West joke, she remembered now. She read the question and its gag answer out loud, smiling with relief that she'd finally solved the mystery.

Abruptly, the cursor jumped down a line and spelled out a message: *A > I liked your first answer better.*

Loverboy. Loverboy was back. What was more, he was *here,* in her house. *A > Where are you?* she typed, unsure of how she felt about his invasion of her home. *How did you find me here? Who are you?*

A > I'm with you, love. I found you by looking—and kind of by accident. And I've really got to go.

A > Who are you?

A > I'm someone who shouldn't have broken into your house. Forgive me my weakness. I adore you.

She again demanded to know who he was, and then, when that received no response, to know how he'd found her, why he hadn't been in touch all week, why she should be prohibited from initiating their contacts, when she would meet him. . . .

Her fingers gradually slowed as she comprehended that he was gone.

He must know where she lived or at least what sort of equipment she owned. It had to have been pure luck that he'd attempted to reach her while she'd had her machine on. But how could he have broken into her home circuit? She wasn't hooked up to any central network at the moment.

Puzzled, she studied the screen with its few lines of text. How could an outsider break in?

The same way an outsider would break into her house, she reasoned: through force or manipulation. She couldn't think of any scientifically sound way someone could force her computer to accept his input without her being linked with a network. He must have manipulated his way in. But how?

Her heart pounded as she assessed what Loverboy's latest message meant: she made him weak. He was with her. He adored her. And he'd performed a feat of incomprehensible technical legerdemain just to tell her so.

So she wasn't cute and blond. So she wasn't romantic. Loverboy adored her anyway.

Her confidence renewed, she lifted her shake in a silent toast to the computer monitor and drained the glass. Everything was going to be fine tonight. Loverboy adored her. He thought she was wonderful; he craved her body; he was convinced she was a romantic.

She danced up the stairs, infused with Loverboy's spirit. From the door of her bedroom, she gazed at the new silk outfit spread across her bed, dark and fine and just a bit daring.

She was a woman, she was smart and she was adored. She was going to have a wonderful time tonight.

Lloyd Droid's rhythmic rap filled her head: *That's the smart art part.* Grinning, she chanted the words, imagining them in Loverboy's nonexistent voice and then in Jim's husky baritone as she pulled off her sweatband and headed to the bathroom for a shower: *Cuz I love you—I'm the wizard in an info-blizzard. That's the smart part, DEE-duh-DEE-duh-DEE, smart.*

Chapter Ten

All right, so he was a louse. So maybe there was something just a tiny bit unethical about having devised a skeleton key that would unlock a route from a compatible terminal through the town's power lines to Lucy's private home computer. He hadn't set out to break and enter; he'd just meant to indulge in a little innocent voyeurism. Was that a crime?

Well, yes. But it wasn't as if he'd actually intended to commit larceny. He'd had only the purest of motives when he'd turned on his own home computer after work on Friday.

He'd gotten home to find his fax machine laden with material from Louise Taylor, the Home-Ties volunteer in Minneapolis. Everything appeared to be in order regarding the Coker family, Louise had informed him. The Cokers were excellent prospects for a Home-Ties adoption. The sooner Jim could send them a Big One orphan, the happier they'd be.

He turned on his computer and booted up Home-Ties, searching the data base for preteen girls and then winnowing down the possibilities. This one was afraid of animals. That one needed to live within fifty miles of her grandmother, who was too frail to take care of her but wanted her nearby. This one had two brothers, and Jim refused to split up siblings. That one was allergic to just about every known pollen on the planet—definitely not a good candidate for farm life.

Dara-Lyn. A vision of her crystallized in his mind, her compact physique and mop-framed face, her bright eyes and indomitable personality, her voice as she told him she was willing to leave California and she'd very much like to be adopted.

She was too old for the Cokers; they didn't want a teenager. Yet Jim could easily see her living on a farm, surrounded by open space and fresh air, applying her boundless energy to the rewarding job of creating a new family with a decent, solid couple like Alice and Dennis Coker. Jim could picture it.

He ran through the data base again, looking for alternate candidates. But Dara-Lyn insistently popped up in his mind, demanding his consideration. She wasn't what the Cokers asked for—not quite. She had never mentioned any interest in living on a family farm in southern Minnesota—not specifically. But it could be a match. It could just work.

Determined not to reach a hasty resolution on such a crucial matter, Jim procrastinated by opening a second window on the monitor and doodling. He played Laser Go for a few minutes, got bored, and decided to see what was cooking on one of the central nets.

What he found cooking was Lucy's computer. Wandering into the consumer net, he spied a clothing order being placed by Lucinda Beckwith of Birch Lane. Before she could leave the net, he inserted a placemark, then paralleled her out into her home computer, storing on his hard disk every signpost along the way so he'd be able to trace the route through to her computer again and again as long as she and he were both drawing electricity through Horizon's east-end power station.

So it wasn't exactly legal. So what? At least he hadn't paid attention to her measurements when she'd placed her order.

Except for her bust: thirty-four gorgeous inches.

All right. He was a lawbreaker, he was a lecher, he was a louse. None of that was as bad as being a fool, and when he programmed his skeleton key to unlock her computer on Saturday, scanned her entry about smoking after sex and leapt in with a Loverboy response... now *that* was foolish.

His strategy had been to phase out Loverboy. He'd refrained from sending Lucy any Loverboy messages all week at work. Loverboy had achieved his purpose in getting her to unbend and contemplate romance; the task accomplished, Loverboy's services were no longer needed. As it was, Jim had spent most of the week—at Lucy's behest—away from his computer in meetings with Artie Bauman and the business-development folks on SmartTown's behalf.

The time had come to bump Loverboy off. Jim had Lucy's consent to a Saturday-night date, he had a table for two reserved at The Court, he had the stirring intensity of her kiss to keep him going. A night of high expectation lay before him, and Loverboy was no longer a part of it.

So he'd backslid a little on Saturday afternoon. So he'd permitted Loverboy a brief swan song. So he'd caught Lucy in the act of recollecting the punchline of that hoary old Mae West wisecrack.

So he'd discovered, however deviously, that Lucy had sex on her mind.

One look at her Saturday evening and he'd certainly have been within his rights to infer that she did. She wore a scoop-necked blouse of dark blue silk that displayed the creamy contours of her throat and collarbones to dazzling effect, and matching silk trousers that draped loosely to her ankles, hinting at the slender length of her legs. Her hair was held back from her face with silver combs in a style that set off her smooth, pale complexion and drew attention to her eyes. Tantalizing chains of interlocking silver rings dropped from her earlobes nearly to her shoulders and glinted whenever she moved her head.

When she opened her front door to greet him at precisely seven o'clock, he gave her one sweeping glance and very nearly said, "The hell with dinner. Let's go to bed."

Instead, he complimented her appearance, then offered her his arm and escorted her down the walk to his superlight. They drove to the mall through the balmy evening, and splurged on a right-side feast at The Court. They ordered different entrées and traded tastes; for dessert, they split a slice of cheesecake and a portion of strawberry shortcake, and they sipped brandy. All the while, they talked—Jim about his sister and her family, about his adventures at WEC-I, about Artie Bauman's ideas for SmartTown's debut; Lucy about Emilio's new daughter and her plans to return to Mount Palomar in August.

Sated on the rich food and nourishing conversation, they went to the mall's third floor to catch the ten o'clock showing of *Tommy* at the Horizon Art Theater. Instead of *Tommy, Last Tango in Paris* was now playing.

Jim knew enough about that movie's torrid sexual content to give him pause. Lucy apparently knew nothing about *Last Tango*. "It's a real oldie, isn't it?" she recollected as they loitered outside the theater, discussing their options. "Do you know anything about it?"

"It's kind of racy," Jim told her, unsure of how Lucy would respond to such a steamy film.

She gave him an adventurous smile and said, "Why don't we check it out? I'm game if you are."

Hoping for the best, Jim inserted his cash-card into the turnstile, watched as it ticked off the twenty-dollar admission price for two, and then withdrew the card and ushered Lucy inside.

At around midnight, with the sound of the movie's concluding gunshot resounding in their ears, they left the theater. Most of the stores were closed for the night and the interior lights of the mall had been dimmed, but after the pitch darkness of the theater, Jim's eyes took a few seconds to adjust. Once he could see clearly, he gave Lucy a long, measuring look, trying in vain to read her reaction to the film.

"What did you think?" he asked as they took the escalator down.

She ruminated for a moment. "It was interesting. It offered some astute insights on the human psyche."

"What insights?" he asked.

"The idea that sometimes it's easier to love a person when you don't know too much about him. The lovers in the movie never really knew each other, and that heightened their love. When you don't actually know someone, you can imagine that person to be everything you need or want...." She drifted off, her smile becoming distant. "What did you think of the film?"

He sorted his thoughts as they strolled to the escalators. What he'd thought was that none of the sexual activity on the screen was anywhere near as exciting as merely kissing Lucy in his office had been. Seated beside her in the dark theater, he'd been much more captivated by her rapt profile, by the slenderness of her fingers woven through his, by her alluring scent. He'd spent the whole time wondering what the hell he was doing in the Art Theater with her,

watching two actors making love, when they could have
been making love themselves.

"It was okay," he mumbled, ushering her down to the
first floor. He wondered if she knew what he was really
thinking, if she could detect his mood in the pressure of his
hand around hers. He was trying hard to remain composed, but the mere feel of her palm against his was doing
all sorts of delightfully uncomfortable things to his con-
stitution.

Would she respond to him the way she had in his office? Would she welcome him into her bed? Or would she
prefer to spend the next several hours dissecting the movie?
If he didn't kiss her soon, he might go crazy—but if he
kissed her *too* soon, she might be furious.

Cripes. Here they were, within shouting distance of the
twenty-first century, and men and women still operated on
parallel lines when it came to this sort of thing. They might
be traveling in the same direction, but were they moving at
the same speed? How did one get parallel lines to inter-
sect?

Neither of them spoke on the ride to her town house.
Lucy seemed reflective, gazing out at the passing night, not
fussing when the wind tugged several strands of her hair
free of the combs. The silver light of the quarter moon lent
her skin an ethereal radiance, and her lips curved in a
pensive smile that sent a bolt of desire through him. He
allowed himself a quick peek at her legs and his nervous
system short-circuited.

He had to kiss her. He had to feel her mouth on his, her
body pressed close to his. He had to inhale her fragrance
and run his fingers over her firm thirty-four-inch bosom.

Holding her hand, he walked her to the front door. Once
she'd pulled her key from her purse, she turned to him and
smiled timidly. "Would you like to come in?"

Another bolt zapped along his nerve endings. "You know what will happen if I do."

A faint flush tinged her cheeks, but she bravely held his gaze. "Yes," she whispered. "I know."

He looked at her for a long, aching minute, thinking not about her legs or her bosom but about her keen intelligence and her tender ego, about the compelling mixture of courage and vulnerability revealed in her dark, shimmering eyes. He wanted to reassure her, to tell her she'd made the right decision, to swear to her that he wasn't going to belittle her the way her former husband had. He wanted to promise her that tonight he was going to awaken the romantic in her.

But he wouldn't dare to speak the words that would expose him as Loverboy, so he didn't speak at all. He touched his lips lightly to hers, then took the key from her and unlocked the door.

SHE WAS SUDDENLY EXTREMELY anxious.

The evening had gone well; not a single awkward moment or wrong move had marred it. She'd enjoyed dinner, enjoyed the movie, enjoyed Jim's company. She'd enjoyed the way his eyes glowed when he looked at her, the way they lingered on her in her uncharacteristically sophisticated outfit.

She hadn't felt too tall or too gawky. She hadn't felt like a nerd. She hadn't even felt bashful.

Until now. Until Jim crossed the threshold into her home and closed the door behind him. Until he set her key on the mail table and enveloped her in his arms.

"I'm nervous," she blurted out when his mouth was an instant away from taking hers.

Recoiling, he regarded her with puzzlement that rapidly dissolved into a gentle smile. "So am I, sweet beets. So am

I." And then the kiss came, hard and hungry, raising her nervousness another few notches.

"I just—" Breathless, she turned away and swallowed, hoping to still the tremor in her voice. "I'm not really good at this."

He laughed. "Lucy, it's *me,* Jim. What are you scared of?"

"You—Jim," she muttered, although a small laugh escaped her, as well. "You've got groupies. You've got female fans all around the country, dreaming of you and flocking to you. You're a celebrity."

"Oh, of course!" he snorted. "My fame is based on invasion, penetration and general screwing around, isn't it?" He chuckled and nudged her face back to his. "What do you think, *Newsweek* put me on its cover because of my brilliance in bed?"

"The thought crossed my mind."

Apparently aware of the underlying seriousness of her statement, he stopped smiling. "Lucy. Relax." He rubbed his hands along her spine, attempting to knead out the stress knotting her muscles. "Do you want this to happen?"

"Yes," she admitted, her voice barely audible. She wanted Jim, wanted to make love with him, wanted his hands to keep moving on her. Her fear was that she would disappoint him, that he'd turn on her afterward and make some snide remark about how she performed better with a computer than with a man.

"Are you worried about birth control?" he inquired. "We're safe on that account. I've got a temporary fix."

What a rare, thoughtful man, she thought. Even her own husband, who'd been opposed to <u>having</u> children, had refused to submit to the reversible vasectomy procedure doctors had perfected a few years ago. The temporary fix was deemed safer than the hormone implants devised for women, but few men bothered to undergo the surgery. Even in 1998, most men believed that contraception was the woman's burden.

Not Jim, though. The happy-go-lucky wizard with his toys and his fame was more mature and sensitive than she'd given him credit for being. At least when it came to sex, he displayed the kind of responsibility she might have expected of Loverboy.

Loverboy wasn't here. Loverboy wasn't standing in the front hall of her town house, just inches from the stairway that led up to her bedroom. Loverboy wasn't gazing at her with the most beautiful blue eyes she had ever seen and smiling at her with the most sensuous mouth. Impulsively, she wrapped her arms around Jim and covered that smile with a kiss that began in gratitude but swiftly transformed into something much more passionate. His lips urged hers apart, his tongue mated with hers, and his arms pinned her to him, holding her steady as he flexed his hips in an insinuating rhythm against hers.

"If we don't get to a bed soon," he murmured, his lips brushing hers with each word he uttered, "I'm going to make love to you right here."

"The bed's upstairs," she managed.

Navigating the stairs wasn't easy, given her overheated condition, but with Jim beside her, propelling her upward, she somehow made it to her bedroom. As soon as she adjusted the dimmer switch by the door to imbue the room with a soft amber light, he gathered her into his arms again. His lips covered hers, nibbled them, teased and tasted and excited her as much with subtle playfulness as he had earlier with sheer aggression.

He slipped one hand under the edge of her tunic, journeyed up along her spine to her brassiere and flicked open the clasp. Then he roamed forward, brushing the lacy undergarment aside, cupping his hand around her breast.

She moaned. If she could be this insanely aroused when she was clothed, what would it be like to lie naked with Jim? To see his hands on her instead of merely feeling them? To touch him as intimately as he was touching her?

Inspired, she groped for the buttons of his shirt and tugged them open, then pushed the shirt out of her way. His chest was lean and hard, covered by a wedge of hair. She plowed her fingers through the golden curls and up to the amulet. She fingered it gently. "How did you get this?" she asked. It was something she'd wanted to ask him for a long time, but the question had always seemed too personal. "The president has to nominate you for a Whole Earth award, right?"

Jim nodded. "I won it for helping the Big One victims."

"Really? For cleaning beaches?" Lucy wondered why clearing refuse from the Southern California coastline should be worth more than repairing telescopes—or why Jim should receive such a prestigious award when dozens of other people who'd also cleaned beaches hadn't received them.

He considered his reply. "I don't know," he finally said. "I'm kind of a high-profile person, I guess. Maybe I got it because I'm such a shining example for other felons trying to rehabilitate themselves."

Lucy detected a trace of sarcasm in his tone and backed off. Whatever he'd done to win the medallion, it was something he clearly didn't wish to discuss. And as her hands continued to rove across his chest, journeying over the springy golden hair and watching in fascination as his muscles flexed beneath his skin, she realized that she didn't much feel like talking about the necklace, either.

Filling her hands with the green linen, she tugged his shirttail free from the waistband of his slacks. Although he let go of her to slide his arms from the sleeves, his lips continued to dance with hers. If he hadn't had to pull Lucy's top over her head, he might never have ended the kiss at all.

Removing the tunic loosened the silver combs, and she yanked them out of her hair. With exquisite care, Jim opened her earrings, plucking each one off and then kissing the lobes. He placed the earrings on her dresser, then turned his attention to her slacks, and then his own. As soon as they were naked, he pulled her down onto the bed.

He kissed her soundly, tangling her tongue with his, twining his legs through hers. His body was warm and hard against hers, his muscles sleek, his limbs lightly covered with pale hair, and his stomach flat. Touching him was more exciting than she had imagined it would be; her hands skimmed over his back, over his chest, down to his narrow hips and then up to his taut pink nipples. Everywhere she caressed him seemed to please him. He sighed, smiled, groaned and smiled again, shifting beneath her questing fingers and returning her bold exploration stroke for stroke.

His lips roamed over her face and throat. His hands traveled over her breasts and ribs and down to her waist, behind her to the roundness of her bottom and forward with a provocative whisper of friction between her thighs, up across her belly, across the sensitive flesh of her breasts again and deep into the dense black tumble of her hair.

She let one hand drift down to his buttocks and he shuddered. "I've got news for you, Dr. B.," he whispered, struggling for breath. "You are really, really good at this."

She almost refuted him. She almost pointed out that it was only because Jim's body was so beautiful that she couldn't stop touching it, only because his kisses burned through her that she was ablaze with passion. If she'd been good at it so far, it had been due to luck, not skill, and luck was a finite blessing. Sooner or later, it would run out.

If she loved Jim, though, perhaps it wouldn't run out. Perhaps love would supplant luck or bring about more luck or make her luck last longer.

She gazed up at him, at his ruggedly handsome, dimpled face, his wild blond hair and his hypnotic eyes. She felt the rise and fall of his chest against hers and the rise and fall of his hips as he pressed his arousal against her. She tried to envision herself loving him, swapping off-color jokes with him and confessing her insecurities to him, being elated by the merest contact from him and sinking into near despondence at his absence.

No. Only with Loverboy did such whirlwind impulses seize her. Only with Loverboy—a being she loved blindly, in a vacuum, like the lovers in *Last Tango in Paris*. Only with a man she loved and didn't know—a man she loved *because* she didn't know him—did she experience such feelings.

She ordered herself not to think about Loverboy. She was with Jim now, and that was enough. Jim was the one exploring her chin and the underside of her jaw with his lips, then grazing a path to her breast and sucking the swollen red tip into his mouth. Jim was the one reaching down between her legs and sliding his fingers through the soft thatch of hair to the dampness below. Her hips writhed; her body arched beneath his skillful touch. She moaned, thinking she should beg him to stop before it was too late—and wanting to beg him never, never to stop.

Of their own volition, her hands mimicked his, moving down his body to arouse him as he aroused her. He felt hard and powerful, lunging against her palm in a way that made her abdomen tighten with yearning. His hand left her, then curved around her wrist and drew her hand from him.

Every muscle in her body clenched in abject pleasure as he poised himself above her, as he found her, as he bound himself fully to her. Pausing for a moment, he lifted his head to gaze at her. She saw the strain in his face, the tension in his jaw and the consummate joy illuminating his eyes. Her heart told her she could love this man, love him as much as she loved Loverboy. Her heart and her soul and her body... definitely her body.

Only her mind stubbornly held back.

He withdrew and thrust again, fierce and possessive, moving in a slow, inexorable rhythm. Ringing her arms about his back, she closed her eyes and pictured shooting stars. She heard a lilting rhyme: *You were in my bed, visions of ecstasy in my head*... She imagined two bodies coming together, uniting, *2HRT-BT1*. And then the words: *I dream of having your long, lovely legs wrapped around my waist, holding me deep inside....*

Without thinking, she wrapped her legs around Jim's narrow waist. He surged deeper. "Yes," he murmured, his voice a gravelly rasp of sound as his body filled hers in a building crescendo of desire. "Oh, God, yes...."

She struggled to maintain her equilibrium, her sanity, her control. But the driving force of his hips pushed her over the edge. She felt herself slipping, then tumbling into a bottomless pool of sensation, her consciousness dissolving into pulsing echoes of bliss.

Her mind vanished. There was only her body and her soul and her heart. There was only love for Jim.

A LONG TIME LATER, HE WAS still out of breath, still sweating, still holding her. In time, his respiration would return to normal and his skin would cool off. He wasn't going to stop holding her, though.

He rolled onto his back, bringing her with him, cushioning her head with his shoulder and savoring the texture of her hair as it spilled over his upper arm. Her knees brushed against his thighs and he reached down to pull one of her legs across him, taking the time to appreciate the smooth muscles of her calf. Three cheers for the Nordic-Track, he thought with a smile.

Opening his eyes, he looked around. Lucy's bedroom was small and, not surprisingly, neat. Except for the items he'd tossed on it when he'd been tearing off her clothing and his own, the top of her dresser was clear. A Shaker-style chair occupied one corner of the room, a small TV frame was mounted on the wall across from the bed, and a Mondrian print adorned another wall. Through the open door to the hallway, he saw a shadow sliding repeatedly over the wall in an arcing pattern; apparently it was cast by the ceiling fan circulating cool air up through the town house. The night table on his side of the bed held a phone, a halogen reading lamp and a dog-eared copy of a Douglas Adams fantasy novel with a bookmark protruding from a point about a third of the way through the text.

Jim grinned. He had read every Douglas Adams book at least twice. That Lucy should share his literary taste was just one more bit of proof that he belonged in her bed.

Cuddled against him, she seemed to doze. He permitted his hand another gentle excursion along her leg, this time exploring not just her calf but the lovely oval of her knee and the satin skin of her thigh. She sighed and snuggled closer. Her eyes remained closed.

"Are you asleep?" he asked in a whisper.

"No."

He lifted his hand to her head and swept away the tresses that obscured his view of her face. "Are you in love?" he asked.

She blinked her eyes open. Her expression was a lot less euphoric than he had hoped. "Jim..." Her voice was low and husky, provoking both desire and concern. She drew a meandering line across his chest with her index finger, provoking more desire while her delay in answering his question provoked more concern. "I'm... I'm divorced. You know that."

He knew much more than that, but he kept his mouth shut.

"I haven't..." She sighed. "I haven't made love with anyone since my divorce. I mean, until now. What's happened here..." She sighed again. "I don't take it lightly."

He didn't like this. He didn't like it at all. "Well, that's a relief," he grumbled.

She propped herself up on her elbow and peered down at him. "I'm trying to be honest, Jim," she said. "I don't know if I'm in love or not. You mean a lot to me, and this..." Her hand molded to his chest. He wondered if she could feel the beat of his heart, if she could tell from its ferocious pounding that he was really not thrilled with her halting answer.

"What?" he prompted her when she didn't continue.

"Well, I—I'm kind of involved with someone else."

Oh, God. It was worse than he'd thought. He withdrew his arm from her and let his head drop heavily onto the pillow. He stared at the ceiling and wrestled with his thoughts, fighting off bitterness in his search for a way to salvage the situation.

Whoever she was involved with, she hadn't made love with him yet. If she ever did, Jim couldn't believe it would be anything at all like what they had shared tonight. They'd been sublime together. Nothing in Jim's past came close to comparing with it, and he was self-confident enough to believe the same true for her.

Okay. He had fantastic sex going for him. And fantastic collaboration at work—this past week, at least. He and Lucy had known each other for a long time—granted, they hadn't been friends for long, although he'd certainly tried to forge a relationship with her practically from the moment she'd set foot in Kansas.

What ammunition might his rival have? Was the guy handsome? Intelligent in a way Jim wasn't? Was he shy, like Lucy? Did she feel more comfortable with someone who wasn't so extroverted?

She was waiting for him to say something. He let out a long breath and kept his eyes trained on the textured ceiling above him. "What exactly are we talking about, Lucy? Do you want me to back off? Do you want me to bow out of your life?"

"No."

"You want to date both of us simultaneously?"

"I'm not . . . I'm not exactly dating him," she confessed.

He frowned and twisted to look at her. She was staring at his amulet, running her fingertip lightly over its circular edge. "What kind of involvement do you and he have?" he asked.

"It's . . . an affair of the mind, I guess."

"Wow. It sounds kinky."

She shot him a quick, angry look. "I don't expect you to understand, Jim. You're a very . . . physical person. You wouldn't understand that some relationships operate on a different level."

"An affair of the mind, huh?" he said, striving with all his might to keep his anxiety at bay.

"That's right."

"And does this affair of the mind light your fire?"

"Don't make fun of me," she snapped, pushing away from him.

He easily caught her in his arm and drew her back down beside him. "I'm not making fun of you, sweet beets. You said I wouldn't understand, but I'm trying to. You're having an affair of the mind with someone, but you're willing to have an affair of the flesh with me. Is that right?"

"You make it sound tawdry."

"Which part—the mind or the flesh?"

He felt her tensing up within the curve of his arm, but he refused to let her go. "I should have known better than to confide in you," she complained.

"You should have known better than to let me make love with you. Now that I have, Dr. B., we're operating on a new level. I'm entitled to know certain things about my competition. His name, for instance."

She grunted something unintelligible against his chest.

"What?"

"I don't know."

"You don't know if I'm entitled?"

"I don't know his name," she said, obviously exasperated.

A bemused smile crept across his lips. She hadn't slept with the guy and she didn't even know his name. "What do you call him when you're having this affair of the mind?"

Her cheeks darkened to a pretty pink, and she buried her face against her arm. "Loverboy," she mumbled.

He heard her. His smile grew, his heartbeat resumed its healthy tempo, his muscles relaxed as he reveled in the identity of his alleged rival. But the past few minutes had been so painful for him, he'd be damned if he wouldn't torment her just a bit longer. "I'm sorry, Lucy—I didn't hear you. What did you say you call him?"

Again she lifted her face, her eyes ablaze with anger and cheeks burning with embarrassment. "Loverboy. Okay? That's the way he introduced himself."

"Loverboy," Jim enunciated. "Lov-er-boy. What an evocative nickname. Loverboy. And this love manifests itself how? Cerebral copulation?"

"You can go home," Lucy retorted, shoving him for emphasis. "I refuse to let you stay here and make fun of me—or him."

He'd mocked her long enough. Gathering her to him in a crushing embrace, he murmured, "I'm sorry. No more teasing." He buried a kiss in her hair and felt her subside against him. "Can you blame me for being jealous?"

A faint laugh escaped her. "No one has ever been jealous over me in my life," she admitted. "I don't know why you're attracted to me—or why he is, for that matter. I'm not exactly a femme fatale."

"You're brainy and beautiful," he told her, cupping his hand under her chin and angling her face to his. "What's more, you're as sexy as hell. I don't know what your definition of a femme fatale is, but honest to God, woman, I *am* attracted." He kissed her deeply, drinking her in, feeling her tremble and shift restlessly against him. Arousal spread down through his body, engorging him, heating his blood. He lifted her onto himself and pulled her down, needing her around him, hot and damp and pulsing with life.

She responded. Lord, how she responded. No matter how much she thought she was involved with Loverboy, this was what counted. This was where the love was. Right here. With Jim.

Chapter Eleven

"I think you ought to meet him," Jim said.

They were seated in Lucy's living room, sipping the last of their coffee and viewing the electronic newspaper on her television. In the olden days of real Sunday papers, they could each have retired with a section and read in silence. Despite the eye strain of reading the text on a TV screen, however, Jim preferred the electronic newspaper. Not only did it spare acres of forest land, but it kept Lucy from hiding behind a broad page of newsprint.

She sat beside him on the sofa, clad in a long, white bathrobe held shut by a sash tied at her waist. His shameless gaze strayed again and again to the knot in the sash. No matter how many times he'd made love with her last night, no matter how weary his body was, he wanted her again.

He suspected, however, that if he gave the knot a tug, she would give his hand a slap. She seemed subdued in the morning light, remote from him even as she lounged in the curve of his arm, her eyes dutifully scanning the lines of print that scrolled across the TV screen. He hoped what was bothering her was nothing more than fatigue.

His life might have undergone a splendid, cataclysmic transformation last night, but according to the electronic newspaper, the world in general seemed not to have changed much. The president had hosted a gala in honor of the prime minister of the People's Democratic Republic of China-Taiwan. An oil tanker had run aground near Vancouver, but thanks to the ship's double-hull design, no oil had spilled into Puget Sound. A hologram production of *A Chorus Line* had opened to good reviews in Kansas City. Rap star Lloyd Droid had escorted the glamorous, if significantly older, Joan Collins to the grand reopening of Disneyland. Economists were predicting that the price of gasoline would fall below three dollars by summer's end. In Boston, a deranged Red Sox fan had manacled himself to a seat in Fenway Park and refused to unshackle his wrists until the team won the World Series.

Reading that item, Lucy had let out a laugh and said, "He'll be there well into the next century." It had been her only genuine laugh of the morning, her only real smile.

Jim tried to make sense of the melancholia that had settled around her since they'd arisen from bed an hour ago. All night long, she'd been vibrant, uninhibited in her passion. Even asleep, she'd been inseparable from him, her head nestled into the hollow at the base of his neck, one pale, graceful arm slung across his chest, one leg trapped between his thighs.

But now, as they sat together on the couch, switching from the news to the science section, and then to sports and finally to the comics, he sensed a schism widening between them. Lucy seemed to be wrestling with some inner demon. Despite her apparent warmth toward Jim, her occasional comments regarding the news and her polite offer to refill his coffee cup, he knew something was troubling her.

Loverboy. She had made love with Jim, but she thought she was in love with Loverboy.

He considered telling her the truth, putting her mind at rest, reassuring her that the man she loved and the man she'd made love with were one and the same.

Yet he couldn't bring himself to do it. Not here in her living room, with her long, slim body curled up next to his on the sofa and her head resting against his shoulder. If he was going to make a confession, it should be somewhere else, in some neutral place where they were both fully clothed and the atmosphere wasn't fraught with intimacy. Someplace like Access, maybe.

"I really think you should meet him," he repeated.

Shifting in the curve of his arm, she glanced at him. "Meet whom?"

"Loverboy."

She frowned and looked back at the TV. In the *Doonesbury* strip occupying the screen, Honey was explaining cryogenics to an aging Uncle Duke, whose only concern was whether he'd be able to bring a shaker of martinis with him into the freezing chamber.

Lucy stared at the comic strip with vacant eyes. She wasn't reading; she was puzzling over Jim's suggestion. "Why do you think I ought to do that?" she asked.

"So you'll be able to make an informed choice between him and me."

"You must be confident I'll choose you."

"After last night—" he gave her a squeeze and kissed the hair at her temple when she didn't turn her face to him "—yeah, I'm pretty confident."

She continued to gaze blindly at the screen. "I'd like to meet him," she admitted. "But he won't let me."

"How do you know that?"

"I keep asking him who he is, and he never gives me a straight answer."

Guilty as charged. But if Jim couldn't bump off Lover-boy one way, he'd do it another. If he couldn't make Lucy forget about her make-believe electronic-lover, he could reveal the truth about him. Either way, she'd be forced to recognize that Jim was the man of her dreams.

"Why don't you tell him you've met someone else?" he proposed with spurious innocence. "If he hasn't got the guts to step forward, you can kiss him off."

"I don't know." Lucy lowered her gaze to her lap and fidgeted with the edge of her bathrobe sash. "What if he steps forward and I think he's wonderful?"

"I could handle that," Jim replied, then winced at the flippancy in his tone. He was supposed to be worried about his competition. "What I mean," he hastened to explain, "is that if you discover he's the man you want, I'd rather know right from the start. I don't want to have to share you with someone else, and I don't want you torn be-tween two guys. I'm exercising the wisdom of Solomon here, Lucy. If you want to be with him, I'll let you go."

She lifted her eyes to his and he saw they were glisten-ing with tears. "Oh, Jim . . . I want to choose you, I really do. But . . . I'd never be able to live with myself if I didn't find out first, if I didn't meet him. You're right, I've got to find out." She slid her hand around to the back of his head and pulled him to her for a deep kiss. "I hope it's you, Jim," she whispered, then kissed him again.

He responded—he couldn't help but respond. His mouth opened against hers and he let her guide him down onto the cushions, let her run her fingers over his chest beneath the unbuttoned flaps of his shirt, let her draw his hand to the knotted sash he'd been contemplating all morning. He untied it, pushed back the robe and moved his hand over her soft, bare skin.

But a part of his brain detached itself from the marvels of Lucy's body and nagged him, chastising him for his penchant for taking things too far. Years ago, he had invaded the Pentagon computer network for fun and wound up with a suspended sentence and a criminal record. And here he was, over a decade older and supposedly wiser, going too far again, aiming only to apply a little playful heat to Lucinda Beckwith's chilly soul and instead creating what to her was a heartbreaking dilemma.

She was more than melancholic about having to choose between Jim and Loverboy. She was anguished and miserable.

As he scattered tender kisses across her face, he tasted the tears that seeped through her thick dark lashes and ran down her cheeks. In her woeful eyes and possessive embrace, he discerned a desperate poignancy, as if she believed this was the last time they would ever make love, as if she were preparing to say goodbye to him. As if she already knew that, when forced to make a choice, she would wind up choosing Loverboy.

For once, his brain failed him. He couldn't come up with an easy answer, a brilliant solution, an obvious remedy for the mess. The golden-boy wizard, the sexiest felon of '88, the savior of defense security systems, the designer of *2HRT-BT1* and lover of Lucinda Beckwith, Ph.D., didn't know how to program his way out of this one.

So he kissed away her tears and loved her and hoped that when she finally found out who Loverboy was, she'd be able to laugh about it.

A > Why, all of a sudden, do you want to meet me?

A > It's not all of a sudden, Lucy entered into the computer. *I've been asking to meet you right from the start.*

A > No, you haven't. You've been asking me who I am.
A > Okay. Who are you?

The hum of the motor seemed magnified in her austere office, echoing off the stark white walls. No, it was magnified by her nerves, echoing in her soul. Never before had a conversation with Loverboy carried such weight. Never before had a computer chat with him threatened such dire consequences.

A > You broke into my home computer this weekend, she typed when he didn't respond to her demand that he identify himself.

A > I couldn't help myself.
A > How did you do it?
A > I'm a wizard.
A > Will you meet me?

Silence. She counted the blinks of her cursor.

A > Only if you promise you won't be angry with me.

Angry? Why would she be angry with him? In his own bizarre way, Loverboy had done wonders for her. He had made her think about love and smile about sex. He had made her care about the impression she made and the way she expressed herself. He had drawn her out of her self-protective shell.

Ironically, he had enabled her to view Jim Kazan as a friend and a lover. If anything, Loverboy ought to be angry with her for taking the humor and compassion he had instilled within her and giving it all to Jim.

A > I won't be angry with you if you won't be angry with me.

A > I could never be angry with you. I love you, Loverboy wrote.

Tears welled up in her eyes, blurring her vision. She couldn't believe how weepy she'd become in the past twenty-four hours. Ever since she'd awakened next to Jim

Sunday morning, she'd felt her fate pressing down on her, reminding her that if she chose between Jim and Loverboy, she would hurt one of them—and herself at least as much. Yet she couldn't *not* choose. It wouldn't be fair to deepen her involvement with both men. It wouldn't be fair to continue a physical love with Jim and a mental love with Loverboy and never commit her heart to either.

It wouldn't be fair to them—or to her.

In all the years she had known Frank, she had never wept over him—not when he was courting her, not when he married her, not when he criticized her and not when he agreed with her that a legal separation was in order. Not even when she held the final divorce decree in her hands. She'd been sad, demoralized, lonely and frightened, but she had never been reduced to tears.

Was weepiness a symptom of a romantic nature? she wondered.

She reread Loverboy's last statement and fought against a fresh surge of tears. *A > We have to meet,* she insisted. *Name a time and a place. If you love me, you'll do this.*

The computer hummed. The cursor blinked. *A > After work today. Five o'clock in the parking lot outside Access.*

She swallowed. This was it, then, the encounter she'd been aching for. Excitement battled with dread in her heart. *A > How will I know you?* she asked.

A > I'll be the one in love with you.

She swallowed again, closed her eyes and turned off her computer. Her hands trembled against the keys; her shoulders shook. Fantasy time was over. She was going to meet him.

Before she could collect her wits, Jim's voice blared through the intercom box on her desk. "Lucy?"

She mopped her damp cheeks with her palms. "I can't talk now," she said.

"I had some questions about the microgenerator water-power system—"

"Not now," she said.

"Are you okay?"

She pulled a tissue from the box she kept in a side drawer, blew her nose and cleared her throat. "Yes, I'm okay."

"Can we meet for lunch today?"

"I don't think so. I'm going to skip lunch." Merely thinking about food made her queasy.

"You don't sound good. What's up?"

She could tell him it was none of his business, which wouldn't quite be true. She could tell him she was feeling uneasy about having their office affair become public knowledge at Access, which would definitely be true.

Or she could tell him the truth. "I'm meeting Loverboy after work today."

"Oh." He fell silent for a minute, then said, "Well, good luck. Good luck to him, too. Most of all, good luck to me. I think I'll need it."

Despite the hint of pessimism in his words, she heard a humorous lilt in his voice. It bolstered her. She wanted to apologize to him for ever having thought he was egotistical or superficial. She wanted to assure him that, whatever the outcome of her meeting with Loverboy, James Kazan would always lay claim to a part of her heart.

She held her silence. To say such things now might sound like a farewell—and perhaps a farewell wouldn't be necessary. Perhaps she would discover that Loverboy wasn't the man of her dreams. Perhaps he was nothing at all like what she expected.

She wanted to know. She *had* to know. But as excited as she was about meeting him, she was frightened, too.

She was frightened by the possibility that he *would* be everything she'd ever dreamed of. If he was ... she would have to say goodbye to Jim.

AT TEN MINUTES TO FIVE, she left the building. She hadn't gotten any work done all day; there was no point in remaining in her office. She stepped outside into the late-afternoon sunshine and positioned herself near the row of hedges that bordered the lot to watch and wait.

Access workers paraded out of the broad glass double doors, exchanging farewells and adjusting their sun-jackets. She noticed Victor, the visor of his sun hat pulled low over his eyes and his lips curled in an everpresent scowl. She spotted two of the dining room servers, plump and maternal, chattering nonstop as they ambled to their superlights. She watched Patricia stride directly to the moped idling at the curb and climb into the sidecar. Her husband leaned down from the driver's seat to kiss her, then handed her a helmet, revved the engine and coasted down the driveway and away.

Lucy saw Jim exit the building, strolling side by side with the new woman from personnel. The woman said something and Jim threw back his head and laughed.

He *was* confident, wasn't he. He was so confident he would emerge victorious in a contest with Loverboy that he could actually be laughing and flirting with a young lady while Lucy waited to meet the one person who jeopardized his place in her heart.

She wasn't jealous about his easy camaraderie with the pretty young employee. Rather, she felt resentment that he could be so damned self-assured, so offensively certain of the outcome of her rendezvous with Loverboy.

She watched as he accompanied the young woman to the curb, waved and sent her on her way into the lot. He began to walk back to the building, then halted and rotated, scanning the grounds until he saw Lucy. A slow, beguiling grin spread across his face and he sauntered toward her.

She shrank back until the hedges stopped her, and she tried to ward him off with a forbidding glower. When he came within earshot, she muttered through gritted teeth, "Get out of here."

Her stern command took him aback. He hesitated and arched his eyebrows in surprise. "Well, isn't that a lovely welcome," he said, resuming his approach.

She retreated another step and felt the spindly branches of a bush poking her back. Great. She'd really dazzle Loverboy if she greeted him with leaves and twigs tangled in her tresses.

Jim slowed his pace as he closed in on her. "Why are you hiding?"

"I'm not hiding," she retorted. It occurred to her that she had no right to lash out at him, and she sighed plaintively. "I'm sorry, Jim, but... could you please leave?"

He shoved his hands into his pockets and regarded her quizzically. Above him, the sky was an endless blue, punctuated by a few delicate wind-tossed clouds. The sun glanced off his face, emphasizing his ruggedly handsome features. His hair was tossed by a warm gust of air, and the longer strands got caught in the collar of his sun-jacket.

She recalled the way he'd looked in her bed, the way his eyes had shimmered with desire as he'd held himself above her, as he'd joined himself to her. She recalled the potent grace of his limbs, the supple strength of his torso, the astonishing sensitivity of his touch.

She shouldn't be thinking such things when her meeting with Loverboy was just minutes away. "Please," she implored him, her voice breaking. "Please don't stay, Jim—I'm begging you."

He frowned. "Why?"

"I'm meeting him," she confessed.

Obviously, Jim knew whom she was referring to. "Here? In the hedges?"

"In the parking lot. He said he'd meet me here. Please, Jim. I'm really nervous."

"Don't be."

"I don't want you here," she said, to which he responded by moving even closer to her, close enough to reach out and unravel a tiny leaf from her hair. "Please, Jim—I promise, I'll phone you and tell you what happened as soon as I get home."

"You don't have to phone me," he insisted, taking yet another step closer.

"I don't want you here."

"It's too late."

"It's *not* too late. If you go right now, everything will be fine."

"You want to meet Loverboy, don't you?"

"Yes, but . . ." Her eyes met his and a shiver rippled the length of her spine. An idea flickered across her brain and she dismissed it as too appalling to contemplate. "Please go," she said firmly, raising her chin defiantly.

"Lucy." He tendered a slight smile and reached for her again, this time to stroke her cheek.

She flinched. "Jim—if he sees you here with me—"

"He already does," Jim said quietly.

Lucy peered past him. "Is he here?" she asked, breathless with anxiety. "Do you know who he is?"

"Oh, God, yes." Jim closed his eyes for a moment, engaging in a moment of private communication with himself. Then he opened them again and presented Lucy with a strangely bright smile. "Yes. I know who Loverboy is."

She swallowed and flexed her fingers, which felt cold, nearly numb. "Point him out to me," she whispered, surveying the flow of people leaving the building.

Jim folded his hand around her shoulder and forced her to look at him. "Okay."

She searched his face. He gazed steadily at her, his eyes intolerably blue, his smile gone. "Jim?"

"'I crave your body,'" he quoted. "But you already know that, Lucy, love."

"No." She tried to twist away.

"'Last night I dreamed you were in my bed, visions of ecstasy in my head—'"

"Stop it." She was shivering uncontrollably, despite the warmth of his hand on her shoulder.

"Come on, Dr. B. You've got to admit that wasn't a bad poem."

It had been an astonishing poem, making up in visceral impact for what it lacked in artistry. She still had the piece of paper she'd written it down on, tucked into a drawer of her night table, beside her bed.

Jim had composed it. He'd been behind the whole thing. The truth struck her with incontrovertible force, like a fist to her solar plexus. Gasping for breath, she stared at the man who had spent the weekend making love to her, stared at him with horror. "You bastard!"

"Hey, Lucy." He plied her with one of his adorable grins. "Don't be angry. It was only a joke."

"A joke!" Her cheeks flared with color; her stomach twisted in a strangling knot of rage. "What is this, some sleazy technique of yours? A shortcut for getting a woman into bed? You find some way to sneak past her defenses and scan her psyche—"

"Now, Lucy, you know I—"

"Or was it simply a ploy to undermine me at work? First you use your computer to distract me, and then in person, you seduce me, and meanwhile, you get more and more of a voice in Smart-Town. Was that it?"

"Lucy." He appeared affronted that she would accuse him of such deceit.

"Was it that you wanted to take over the project, or just that you wanted to knock me down a peg?"

"I didn't want to do anything to you!"

"Well then, you really botched things. Because you did do something to me, Jim. You made me feel like an idiot."

"I don't think you're an idiot. I think you're a genius."

"Right—a genius who talks to a computer because she doesn't know how to talk to a man. It almost sounds perverted, doesn't it?"

"No," he asserted. "It was a game, Lucy. A lover's game."

"Except for the fact that one of us didn't know the rules. One of us was playing blind. One of us—" Her voice faltered and she swallowed a sob. "One of us didn't realize we were only playing."

"It was a serious game," he murmured in an ameliorating tone. "I mean, I took your Loverboy messages to heart."

"Wonderful. I was telling Loverboy things I would never tell you."

"I know," he muttered, frustration creeping into his voice. "I wish you would have told me, but you never would."

"Because I didn't trust you. Rightly, as it turns out."

"Lucy..." He reached for her and she recoiled, stumbling against the hedge. Obviously he could read the rampant hostility in her face because he fell back, allowing her the room to move clear to the shrubbery. "What did you tell Loverboy that you would never tell me?" he asked gently.

She had told him about her failure as a romantic and her failure as a wife. She had exchanged bawdy wisecracks with him. She'd ventured into discussions that evolved from political debates to steamy intimacies. She'd let Loverboy distract her from her work.

"You tricked me," she whispered, mortified as she recalled the deeply personal nature of her dialogues with Loverboy. "You cheated."

"Ah, Lucy..." He sighed. "I tried the traditional route with you, and you never gave me a chance. Everything I ever told you as Loverboy goes for me as Jim Kazan. The poems, the graphics, everything. That was just me talking. Loverboy was just a part of me."

The safe part, Lucy thought morosely. The part she could deal with because it existed only in a computer.

Frank had been right: she dealt with computers better than with humans. Now that she knew Jim had read every word, every confession, every secret confidence she'd entered into her computer, she felt betrayed, defiled— violated.

"I hate you," she said, her voice taut with fury. "You think you can trespass wherever you damned well please— whether it's the Pentagon or my mind. You think if you're clever enough to find a way inside, then you deserve to be there. You break in, take what you want, wink and smile and say, 'Hey, it's only a joke'. Well, it doesn't work that way, James Kazan. When all is said and done, you're a thug."

She was too angry to continue, and too humiliated. Jim already knew far too much about her. If she continued ranting, she would reveal even more of her tattered ego to his prying blue eyes.

Pushing past him, she raced along the hedges to where they ended at the building's main entry. Out into the parking lot she ran, brushing past fellow workers, mumbling her apologies but not slowing her pace until she reached her bicycle. She straddled it and pushed off, pedaling as hard as she could.

If Jim chose to, he could easily overtake her with his superlight. But she prayed he wouldn't follow her. She couldn't bear to face him right now. She couldn't bear to face anyone.

She wanted only to be alone, away from the thief who had broken in and stolen her soul—and called the whole thing a joke.

Chapter Twelve

Well, Jim thought, *that went spectacularly badly, didn't it?*

In his worst-case scenario, he had imagined that Lucy would chew him out, maybe scold him for fooling around a bit too much. Outside chance—she'd accuse him of having had a laugh at her expense. He'd never laughed at her, of course—not as Loverboy, anyway—but, all right, she might toss an inflated charge or two at him.

He'd never expected her to *hate* him.

Had he only dreamed last weekend? Was he crazy to think they'd begun to build something good together? Hadn't she at least *started* to fall in love with him?

She probably had, he concluded glumly. If she hadn't, she wouldn't have been so infuriated by what he'd done.

In time, he hoped, she would cool off. She would realize, upon calm reflection, that he had absolutely no interest in taking over her project or making fun of her, that his only motivation had been to win her love. She would regain her mental faculties and see the thing for what it was.

A joke.

A really, really stupid joke.

Still zonked by her lacerating anger, he wandered back into the building. He needed to cool off, too. He needed to unwind, sort his thoughts, do some mental doodling and scope a way out of this disaster.

He climbed the stairs to the third floor, walked down the silent, empty hallway to his office and let himself inside. He moved directly to the pinball machine, switched it on and waited while it flashed and clanged to life. Then he sent the first ball into play and settled in for some heavy-duty analysis of the situation with Lucy.

She *did* have a sense of humor. In his Loverboy guise, he'd seen ample evidence of it. Why couldn't she have a sense of humor with the flesh-and-blood Jim? Why couldn't she see the comical side of his Loverboy gambit?

Same reason the federal government had been unable to see the comical side of his adventures inside the Pentagon computer network. They hadn't found much to laugh about when Jim had gained access to information regarding the number of missile silos in Siberia, the location of Lybia's desert arsenals, the sub-rosa research on chemical weapons being performed at several extremely reputable institutes of higher learning in the United States. Back in the eighties, before the Iron Curtain had been drawn open and the Wall had come tumbling down, the Department of Defense hadn't reacted with tolerant good humor to the discovery that a twenty-three-year-old graduate student from the Bay Area had psyched out the code for issuing attack orders to a Strategic Air Command post in South Dakota.

What a bunch of duds, he thought as he hammered away at the pinball machine's buttons, shaking the table, scoring on two flags and winning himself an extra ball. The Pentagon and Lucy Beckwith—two of a kind.

Of course, he hadn't wanted to sleep with the Pentagon.

He still wanted to sleep with Lucy. No matter how furious she was with him, no matter what venomous feelings she harbored toward him, he wanted her. Especially after the past weekend, when he'd discovered how attuned their bodies were, how sweet and responsive she could be, how pleasurable it was to wake up and find her beside him.

He enjoyed discussing cinema with her and gorging on right-side food with her. He enjoyed collaborating with her on Smart-Town. He enjoyed her company, her intellect, her principles. He held in high esteem anyone who did California. How could he not desire a woman who had so much in common with him?

Last weekend, he'd had the chance to satisfy that desire—and it only made him want her more. When they'd made love and she'd wrapped her legs around him, exactly as he'd once described as Loverboy, he'd felt completely, blissfully overcome. And afterward, when he'd held her trembling body to his and allowed himself to believe they could be this close forever—

Damn. He loved her. Crabby, cranky, bitchy, aloof, moody, sanctimonious, staid, defensive, unbelievably difficult... He loved her.

Why couldn't he love someone easy? Why couldn't he love someone who giggled at his jokes and agreed with his every utterance? How had Lucy Beckwith gotten under his skin in such a crazy way? Was it because she was the only intelligence he hadn't been able to crack?

He pounded on the pinball machine and rolled up points at an unprecedented rate—three hundred fifty thousand... three-eighty... four hundred thousand—and still two balls left. Abruptly, he turned off the machine. Who cared if he was close to setting a new Spider-Man record? Making up with Lucy was more important.

He would call her, he decided. He would drive home at a leisurely RPM, giving both of them a little more time to compose themselves, and then he would give her a call and—well, if he had to, he'd apologize. He wasn't sorry he'd invented Loverboy, but he was sorry his ploy had backfired. He'd never meant to hurt her. What he'd done *shouldn't* have hurt her. But when it came to love, even intelligent people weren't always rational and things that shouldn't hurt sometimes did.

The wide blue Kansas sky failed to buoy him. The rush of wind past his ears didn't soothe him as it usually did. Once he'd reached the main intersection in downtown Horizon, he very nearly pointed the superlight in the direction of Lucy's town house, but he exercised tact and cruised straight to his own house. Better to soften her up on the phone before he attempted a face-to-face with her, he figured. If he showed up at her door unexpectedly, she might greet him with a punch in the nose.

He drove to his own street, forcing himself to wave at a neighbor who shouted a hello to him from behind his solar-powered mower-mulcher, forcing himself to smile and nod at Rosie Titus as she wheeled a load of fresh laundry from the line in her sunny side yard. How ironic, he thought, that as recently as five years ago, clothes lines were deemed irredeemably archaic, but now they were viewed as just one more efficient application of solar energy.

He neared his own driveway and slowed down when he spotted the compact figure of a woman seated on his front step, a bulky backpack propped against the step next to her. Even from a distance, he couldn't help but notice her unevenly chopped blond hair and her gaudy attire. He steered into the driveway, pressed the button for the automatic door opener and coasted into the garage. Vaulting out of his superlight, he pulled off his sunglasses and strode outside, up the front walk to Dara-Lyn Penny-bopper.

"Hi," she said, rising to her feet and giving him an entreating smile.

He was in no condition to entertain her. Yet it occurred to him that her presence might not be such a bad thing. She might be able to distract him the way his pinball machine hadn't. He could talk to her in concrete terms about a possible adoption, get an idea of whether she would be amenable to living on a farm like the Cokers', see if there was, in fact, a match. After the wretchedness of the past hour, he was eager to accomplish something positive before the day was done.

"What are you doing here?" he asked, then cringed inwardly at his lack of courtesy. He compensated by presenting her with a big smile that felt strained.

"Bobby brought me here," she said, her own smile looking just as strained. "I got your address from the directory."

"Well, okay," said Jim. His gaze strayed to her pack. "Are you planning to stay awhile?"

"I hope you don't mind," she said anxiously.

He frowned. "I...uh...it's not that I mind, Dara-Lyn, but..." She was an orphan, for crying out loud. He couldn't just send her away, could he? "Aren't you staying at the youth hostel?"

"I'd rather stay with you."

Sure she would. He was famous. Hackers and wizards and other assorted aficionados would all love to stay with him, too, but that didn't mean he had to open his home to them.

On the other hand, she was a Big One orphan, and if Jim had a soft spot, it was for Big One orphans.

"Umm...why don't you come in for a few minutes and we'll work this out over some iced herbal tea?"

"Okay," she agreed, her smile taking on an unnervingly confident quality as she hoisted her pack off the ground.

Jim unlocked the front door and ushered Dara-Lyn inside. As she romped down the entry hall, swinging her oversized pack and crowing over how happy she was to be here, he stared after her, trying to fend off a creeping apprehension.

When Lucy had told him she didn't trust Dara-Lyn, he'd laughed off her warnings. But now, as he observed Dara-Lyn commenting on his framed photographs of Big Sur, on the sleek chrome of the stairway railing, on the polished laminate of the floor and the panoramic view of the Kansas River from his living room windows, he wasn't laughing at all.

Something, some eerie, undefinable intuition, told him that letting Dara-Lyn into his house had been a major mistake.

SHE WAS *HERE*, REALLY, truly here, in James Kazan's actual house, and the excitement of it was enough to overcome her disappointment in the place. She had thought his house would be bigger, given how famous he was and all. Big houses weren't considered *it*, but she didn't know of anyone who deep down inside would prefer to live in a smaller house over a bigger one.

Not only was his house modest in size, but it was awfully Great Plainsy, bland in color and kind of cluttered. The cushions of his living room sofa were rumpled, and the walls were covered with yawn-worthy landscape photos. Assorted retro toys—a couple of yo-yos, a radio-controlled Jeep and a stuffed Grover doll wearing a black sash embroidered with the words I miss Jim Henson—collected dust atop various shelves and tables. The rugs scattered across the floor were icky brown.

Well, no matter. Once she was all settled in, she would do some redecorating. Her mother had taught her lots about colors and visual impacts; here in her father's house, she would have plenty of opportunity to apply that knowledge. She would hang some prisms in the windows to catch the sun and replace the brown rugs with orange-and-green ones, and get a pet dog. Like Toto from *The Wizard of Oz*. That would be a real Kansas thing to do.

"I've got to check my phone messages," Jim said from the doorway, "and then I'll get us some iced tea and we'll talk."

"Okay." She sent him off with a smile, then turned to gaze out the windows at the prettiest scenery she'd seen since arriving in Horizon. Not that the drowsy Kansas River could compare with the great rolling waves of the Pacific at high tide, not that the flat green acreage beyond the river could compare with the majestic peaks of the coastal range, but—

No, she mustn't think like that. That part of her life was over with. California, her mother...all that was history. Horizon was her home now, James Kazan was her family, and she'd better get used to it.

She wandered around the room, investigating his home entertainment center, his chrome-and-leather rowing machine, a shelf full of computer mags and science-fiction books, a framed photograph of a blond woman and an Asian man with two adorable little girls perched on their knees, and another framed photograph of an older couple with whitish-blond hair, standing in front of a hedge of lilacs.

Relatives, Dara-Lyn guessed. Family. *My family,* she thought, her heart pounding as she gazed at the photograph of the older couple. *My grandparents.*

The sound of footsteps startled her and she sprang back from the photograph. James Kazan entered the room carrying two tumblers of iced tea and a small brown bottle. "Here," he said, setting the glasses on the table in front of the couch and indicating that she should sit. Then he handed her the bottle. "This is for you. My sister sent me a case of the stuff."

She read the label: Blond Block.

"It's a high-density sunscreen specifically designed for blondes," he said.

"Oh." Dara-Lyn folded her fingers tightly around the bottle. It was the second thing James had ever given her. The first thing was his business card, which right this very minute was tucked into her breast pocket, just inches from her heart.

He sat next to her on the couch and gave her a benign smile. "So, I think it's time for you to explain what you're doing here."

She swallowed. She glanced at her glass of iced tea. She clung to the bottle of sunscreen. She moistened her lips. "I'm . . . here," she began, then winced at the hesitant quality of her voice, "because this is where I belong."

James quirked an eyebrow.

She wished he would say something, but he just stared at her, waiting for her to continue. She inhaled, then said, "I'm not just talking about Horizon." Her fingers began to go numb from her bloodless grip on the sunscreen bottle, and she forced herself to put it down on the table. She took another deep breath and tried to pretend she was doing a pitch for Watts Towers. If she could approach total strangers and ask for money, she could certainly approach James Kazan and ask for his acknowledgement. "I mean *here*. I'd like to stay *here*."

"Here?" He looked bemused. "In my house?"

"Well, yeah."

He digested this. To Dara-Lyn's relief, he didn't look repulsed by the idea. He didn't go into a temper meltdown or anything. He remained on the far end of the couch, scrutinizing her, mulling over her statement. "You're talking about adoption, aren't you?" he asked.

He'd figured it out. He knew why she'd come, what she wanted from him. She wouldn't have to knock herself out putting everything into words. "Yeah," she said brightly, suppressing the urge to fling her arms around him and call him Dad.

"When we discussed adoption last week at Access, Dara-Lyn..." He hesitated, struggling to express himself precisely. "I didn't mean that *I* would adopt you."

Her smile faded. Her hope dimmed a few watts. "Why not you?" she asked.

"I'm not married. I live here by myself. I work odd hours. I can't provide you with a stable family life."

"I wouldn't know what a stable family life was if I stepped in it."

He conceded with a wry smile. "I know you want to be adopted, and I think it's a wonderful idea. But you should be adopted by a real family, with two parents. I'm a single man—"

"My mom was a single woman and she was a great mother."

"Yes, but she was your mother."

"And you're my father."

It blurted out before Dara-Lyn could stop herself, and in retrospect, she was kind of glad. Why try to be smooth about it? There was no simple way to tell a man he was your father. "You're my dad, James Kazan, and I'm your daughter," she announced, giving him what she hoped was her winningest smile. Then, because she couldn't help it, she uttered the brief, wondrous phrase she'd been dreaming of saying ever since she boarded the maglev in Los Angeles nineteen days ago.

"Hi, Dad."

HE GAPED AT HER. HE TOOK IN her big, imploring eyes and her petite body, her weirdly manicured nails and the sundarkened insteps of her sandaled feet. This girl, this child, this—for God's sake, *teenager*—was his daughter?

He exerted himself to keep breathing. He supposed what he was going through was some sort of universal male nightmare: the stranger blowing into your life to announce that you fathered her during some casual, longforgotten fling. But Jim had never been casual about sex, and he'd never been careless. He'd even had a temporary fix, just because he felt so strongly about avoiding accidental parenthood.

After what felt like an hour, he realized he had to say something. "What on earth makes you think I'm your father?" he asked in a rusty voice.

"Well, my mother—"

"I never knew your mother, Dara-Lyn."

"I know," she hastened to assure him. "You never met her. It's not your fault."

"What's not my fault?" he asked weakly, unable to stop staring at the girl even though the sight of her continued to exert a paralyzing effect on his lungs.

"Well, you see..." Dara-Lyn stood and crossed to her back pack. She opened it, rummaged inside and pulled out a large brown envelope, which she carried back to the sofa. She lifted the flap and slid out what appeared to be some faded newspaper and magazine clippings. "My mother saved these. I found them in our house before it was wrecker-balled." She passed the clippings to him.

He handled them gingerly, not so much because they were brittle with age as because he assumed they contained something so incendiary they would leave third-degree burns on his fingertips. What they contained, he discovered, was his infamous past.

He scanned the articles, pausing to peruse a few, his brow furrowing as he relived his long-ago moment of glory. His parents kept a scrapbook containing the same assortment of clippings, but he hadn't looked at the scrapbook in years. "This is—this is all stuff about me," he muttered.

"My mother saved them. She went to the Mensa Sperm Bank because she wanted a perfect baby. She was so pretty—I wish you could have known her. She was beautiful, but she always thought maybe she wasn't so smart, so she figured if she went to the Mensa Sperm Bank, there would be a fifty-fifty chance her baby would be smart."

"A sperm bank? I thought—Dara-Lyn, you told me you had a father." He wasn't exactly positive she'd told him that, but he had a vague recollection of her saying something like it and he clung to that recollection with all his might.

"I do have a father," she said with a beatific smile. "You."

"No! I'm not your father. If you were conceived at a sperm bank—"

"I still have a father," she insisted, speaking slowly, as if she considered him mentally impaired. "Someone had to supply the sperm, right?"

"Well, it sure as hell wasn't me!"

Dara-Lyn slid closer to him so she could review the clippings on his lap. She lifted one, read it silently and then waved it in front of his face. "Here. This article says you said you paid a call at the Mensa Sperm Bank in 1982. I was conceived in August of 1982. And look at me," she continued quickly, before he could protest. "I've got your exact coloring. We look enough alike that you want me to use your sunscreen. And I know I'm not very tall, but my mother was short, so I guess I inherited her build. She had brown hair, though, and brown eyes, and look at me. Blond hair, blue eyes, just like you. And my chin, see? We both have square chins. I know I'm not as smart as you, but the Mensa Sperm Bank doesn't offer guarantees. And I've got to admit, I'm a whole lot smarter than my mom was."

He opened his mouth and shut it. His forehead ached from his frown. He was remembering something, remembering a name. "Dulcie," he murmured as it came back to him. "Dulcie Pennybopper. Oh, God."

Dara-Lyn leaned forward expectantly. "You did know my mother?"

"I got a letter from her," he groaned, turning away and shaking his head. There had been so many letters. Even today, years later, he still received letters from wannabee hackers and genuine wizards and occasionally a woman with something to offer. But back then, after his arrest, so very many letters... And one had come from a woman with the peculiar name of Dulcie Pennybopper. He'd known it had sounded familiar the first time Dara-Lyn had mentioned her mother's name. Now he understood why.

"She wrote to you?" Apparently Dara-Lyn hadn't been aware of that. "My mom wrote to you?"

"Dara-Lyn..." He turned back to her. He had to put this as gently as he could. It was the child's mother he was talking about. "When you're famous, Dara-Lyn—and I *was* famous for quite a while—"

"You still are," she said reverently.

He ignored the compliment. "The thing is, I got letters from people. I got—" he chose each word with great care "—letters from women. Some of them were kind of... brazen. Do you understand what I'm saying?"

"Ladies sent you their undies," Dara-Lyn said calmly.

He let out a mirthless laugh. "Yes. That about sums it up." He shook his head again. "I don't remember the names of the women who wrote to me, but your mother's name was so unusual. Dulcie Pennybopper. I remember getting a letter from her. She said I'd fathered her child, and I—" He abruptly fell silent.

"You what?"

"I passed the letter along to my lawyer. I assumed the woman was..."

"After your money," Dara-Lyn concluded.

"After *something*. I've never been particularly rich. The Pentagon doesn't pay you for burglarizing their computer system." Another laugh escaped him, this one sympathetic. One obvious fact would exonerate him, and while he hated having to disillusion Dara-Lyn about her mother and her past, he had to tell her. "Dara-Lyn, I never made a donation to the Mensa Sperm Bank."

"But the article—" She jabbed a finger at the pile of clippings in his lap. "You're quoted as saying—"

He handed her the article so she could see for herself. "I'm quoted as saying I paid a call at the Mensa Sperm Bank. And that's true, I did pay a call. I was a freshman at Stanford University, just across town, and a few of my classmates and I went there as a gag. They turned me down."

"You?" She seemed shocked. "You're so—so *it*. How could they turn you down?"

"I was seventeen years old," he explained. "I was too young."

"Seventeen isn't too young," she argued. "I mean, I've known kids in school..."

"Seventeen was too young for the Mensa Sperm Bank," he clarified. "They're very selective."

"Only as far as IQ, I thought."

"Well, now you know. They turned me away."

"Then—" She appeared bewildered. "Then why did you say that in the newspaper? Why would you lie about something like that?"

"I didn't lie. I said I paid a call, and that's all I did."

"But you *implied*—"

"Because I was tired of being asked the same questions over and over. Because when I said that, I'd been asked too many times by too many people whether I was smart, and I just got a little too clever with my answer. Because..." He felt weary all of a sudden, drained, racked with remorse. "Because I have a tendency to take a joke too far sometimes."

Dara-Lyn appeared to be on the verge of tears. Good God, what had she expected when she'd come here? That he'd open his arms and cry, "At last! My long-lost daughter!"?

He almost wished he *could* do that. She was so forlorn, so desperate for a father.

"Listen," he said gently, sliding her cherished articles back into their envelope and placing it on the table. "What you need, Dara-Lyn, is a real family, one that can adopt you. I can help you with that, if you'll let me."

She lifted her tear-filled eyes to him. "I don't believe you," she said.

"I *can* help you—"

"No. About being my father. I don't believe you."

He sighed. "I'm telling you the truth."

"I don't believe you!" She started to sob.

What now? Had a hex been placed on him so that he was fated to make women despise him forever? He was almost willing to concede that, in Lucy's case, he might be partly to blame for incurring her wrath. But he was blameless here. He'd done nothing to Dara-Lyn, nothing to her mother. All he'd done was sound off to the wrong reporter at the wrong time with the wrong words.

All he'd done was to make a joke when restraint would have been the wiser course.

"Dara-Lyn, I know of a family that might like to adopt you—a mother, a father, an older sister and a farm. But we can only explore an adoption if you're willing to believe me about this other stuff."

"Well, I don't," she snapped, fury mixing with her sorrow.

"I'll prove it to you, then. Come with me." He stood, took her hand and led her into the kitchen. Locating the chrome tissue dispenser under one of the cabinets, she yanked out a tissue to wipe her eyes and nose. A simulated soprano announced, "The tissue dispenser is low."

"Thanks, Bambi," Jim muttered reflexively, moving to one of the telephones.

"Who's Bambi?" Dara-Lyn asked.

Not bothering to answer, he turned on his PC, typed in a tele-directory command, and then *Palo Alto*. When the screen filled with listings, he issued a search command for *Mensa Sperm Bank*. The cursor blinked for several seconds, and then the telephone number appeared on the screen. He lifted the receiver of his personal phone, placed it in the interface cradle and waited as the computer dialed the number for him.

Once the call was connected, he turned off his computer and switched on the phone's speaker attachment. "I want you to hear this for yourself," he whispered. "I don't want you to think I'm hiding anything from you."

Through the speaker, they heard a click, and then a woman's pleasant voice: "Mensa Sperm Bank, good afternoon."

"Hello," Jim said. "This is James Kazan. I'm calling to get confirmation from you that I never made a donation to your sperm bank. Could you please confirm that for me?"

She hesitated before speaking. "Don't you *know* whether you donated?"

"*I* know I didn't. It's someone else who needs to hear it from you." Man, did this sound idiotic.

"Well, I'm sorry, but I can't help you out."

"Why not?"

"What you're asking is confidential. We give out no information on our donors."

"But I'm *not* a donor! I never was. And your records can prove it."

"I'm sorry. We can neither confirm nor deny any information on our donors. We ensure all donors absolute privacy."

"I'm not asking you to identify donors," he explained, his patience wearing thin. "All I'm asking is for you to confirm that I'm *not* a donor."

"I'm sorry. I can't give out that information."

Jim cursed under his breath. Into the phone, he said, "How about if I can prove I'm James Kazan and not an imposter?"

"And how could you prove that?"

Good question. "I could fax you my birth certificate."

"You could fax us a forged birth certificate," the woman responded.

"My social-security number?" he attempted.

"An imposter could find out James Kazan's social-security number without much difficulty."

"Would a little gift of some sort make it easier for you to bend the rules?" he cajoled.

"If you're suggesting a bribe, you're suggesting breaking the law. Goodbye." She disconnected the call with an emphatic click.

Groaning, Jim turned off his speaker. How was he going to be able to substantiate that he wasn't Dara-Lyn Penny-bopper's father? Genetic testing would offer definitive proof, but to subject Dara-Lyn and himself to the test would invite unwelcome publicity—which, he suspected, he could cope with better than she could. She was just a child, alone and grief stricken. To have her hopes dashed in public view might demolish her.

Maybe he could travel with her to Los Angeles. If her birth records hadn't been lost, they might prove something.

But he couldn't leave for Los Angeles now, not when there was so much work to be done on Smart-Town before WEC-II. Not when there was so much work to be done on Smart-Town's chief designer.

"Listen," he said to Dara-Lyn. "I'll figure something out. I'll get the proof you need. But first, I've got to make a personal call."

Dara-Lyn glowered at him, her lower lip poked forward in a pout. "I'm hungry."

"Help yourself," he said, indicating the pantry with a wave of his hand. He removed a beer from the refrigerator for himself, popped it open and waited until Dara-Lyn had pulled a snack from the cabinet. She sent him a suspicious look. "It's a *personal* call," he stressed.

Reluctantly, she trudged into the living room.

Jim dialed Lucy's number. She answered on the second ring. "Hi, Lucy," he said with as much cheer as he could manufacture. "It's me."

A pause, and then she muttered, "Which you? The real one or the computer one?"

Great. This call promised to be even more fruitless than the one to the sperm bank. "I called to say I'm sorry," he told her, keeping his voice down so Dara-Lyn couldn't eavesdrop from the adjacent room. "I know you're angry, and I deserve it, but please—"

"You're right," she said cutting him off. "I'm angry."

"I was hoping that by now you would have come to your senses."

"Oh, my senses," she sneered.

"It was supposed to be a joke," he said for what felt like the hundredth time. "I thought you'd be amused."

"Unfortunately, I have an underdeveloped sense of humor. Ask my ex-husband. I don't know how to laugh at jokes when I'm the butt of them."

"You weren't the butt of it, Lucy. You were the target of my affection. Remember the love poem Loverboy sent you? *I* wrote it. Those words came from *my* heart."

"Then you should have signed your own name to the poem," Lucy retorted. "Instead, you disguised yourself. You were probably winking and smirking behind your mask, and—"

A deafening blast of rock music shook the house. "Dara-Lyn!" Jim hollered, wondering if she could hear him through the cacophony. "Turn if off!"

The music decreased in volume, and Dara-Lyn appeared in the doorway, looking sheepish. "Sorry, I just wanted to watch Video-Kix."

"Not now," he snapped. "Now go back in there and eat." He hounded her out of the kitchen with his angry glare, then took a deep breath and directed his attention back to Lucy. "I'm sorry, I—"

"You have company," she said in an ominously cool voice. "Dara-Lyn Pennybopper is visiting, I take it."

"Yeah. It's a long story, Lucy, and I don't want to go into it right now."

"I'm sure you don't."

He couldn't miss her sarcastic undertone. "I'll explain it when I can. She's an orphan and I'm trying to save her life, all right?"

"That sounds like a worthwhile endeavor. Don't let me keep you, Jim."

"No, wait!" he shouted, sensing she was about to hang up. "I called you to apologize. I called you to say your sense of humor does need some work, but I love you anyway. Okay?"

Silence.

"Lucy?"

The line was dead.

Had she heard what he'd said? Had she hung up after he'd confessed that he loved her or before?

He hoped before; he hoped she hadn't heard. If she was going to behave like road slush when he openly declared that he loved her, she didn't deserve his love at all.

He really hoped she hadn't heard.

Taking a deep draught of beer, he collapsed onto the chair in front of his computer screen. *One crisis at a time,* he cautioned himself. *One crisis at a time.*

Ideally, solving the Dara-Lyn crisis wouldn't take more than a few hours. Solving the Lucy crisis might take a lifetime. The best strategy would be to start simple and save the tough one for last.

When he offered the sperm-bank receptionist a bribe, she'd said he was suggesting something illegal. Well, there was more than one illegal way to find out information. And when you were James Kazan the illegality of choice was obvious.

He turned the computer back on, listened to it warm up and began his electronic journey to Palo Alto.

Chapter Thirteen

"Wake up," the synthesized voice purred. "Wake up."

Lucy bolted upright in bed. For her new home in Horizon, she had bought a state-of-the-art bedroom phone with a built-in timer that switched from a nerve-rattling electronic bleat to a gently whispered "Wake up" if a call came late at night. But this was the first time anyone had telephoned her after ten-thirty, the hour at which she'd set the switch. Being roused out of a dreamless slumber by a strange voice was, in its own way, as nerve-rattling as the old-fashioned bleating.

She waited until her heart stopped pounding, then eyed the luminous digits on her alarm clock. Twelve-fifteen. She lifted the receiver. "Hello?"

"Lucy, it's Jim. Don't hang up."

She groaned and sank against the pillow. She was so tired, so very tired. She'd spent well over an hour and a half tossing and turning in bed, trying without success to unravel her hopelessly tangled thoughts about Jim and Loverboy and her own dreary shortcomings and insecurities. At long last, unable to reach any conclusions, she'd emptied her mind and relaxed into sleep, only to be shocked awake by a call from the subject of all those insomnia-producing thoughts.

Just two nights ago, he had shared this bed with her. Although he'd returned to his own home Sunday night, his scent had lingered in the sheets, on the pillow. She'd felt his presence and reveled in her memory of his body snuggled under the blanket with hers, his arms holding her. She had hoped that once she'd worked things out with Loverboy, Jim would return to her bed again and again.

She'd worked things out with Loverboy, all right. She'd worked out that Jim, in collusion with his computerized alter ego, had made her the patsy of an extravagant practical joke.

She was still infuriated with Jim when she'd stumbled into bed several hours ago. His high-powered smile and his hypnotic eyes haunted her, and her heart continued to echo the words she wasn't sure she'd heard him say on the phone the last time they'd spoken—that her sense of humor needed work.

That he loved her.

Whenever his resonant final words threatened to melt her steely resolve, she recalled the rest of what she'd heard on the telephone—most particularly, Dara-Lyn's high-decibel rock music. Lucy would bet the quart of rocky-road ice cream she had stashed in her freezer that Jim would never ridicule his favorite Big One orphan the way he'd ridiculed Lucy. Just because Lucy hadn't been a victim of the earthquake didn't mean she was imperturbable and unbruisable, fair game for his perverse pranks.

But I love you anyway, his voice lulled her.

She held the receiver to her ear and debated whether, despite his plea, she should hang up on him.

"Are you still there?" he asked.

"For the moment."

"I've been arrested."

She sat upright again. "What?"

"I'm calling from the police station. I've been brought in on a federal charge—interstate hacking."

"What?"

"They told me I could make my one call. I probably should have called my lawyer, but I called you instead."

"Interstate hacking? Jim! What did you do?"

"Hey, I can't exactly chat right now, Lucy. Can you come downtown? I know it's late and you hate me. But I couldn't imagine calling anyone but you."

She cupped her hand around the phone, tenderly, as if it had become very precious. He couldn't imagine calling anyone but her. He was in trouble and he needed her.

All of sudden, she couldn't imagine doing anything but going downtown to bail him out.

"I'll be there," she promised, then hung up the phone, shoved her disheveled hair out of her face, swung her legs over the side of the bed and headed for the bathroom to wash. By the time she doused her face with hot and then cold water to sharpen her brain, she remembered that she hadn't yet forgiven him—that perhaps she *couldn't* forgive him.

The chance to see him in dire straits was worth a midnight bike ride downtown, she convinced herself. If any dreamy, affectionate reasons existed for going downtown to spring him from police custody, she refused to consider them. She wasn't a romantic, after all.

The street was dark, only a few scattered mercury lamps shedding a peach-hued glow on the roadway and turning the neatly planted trees into eerie silhouettes. The brisk wind forced Lucy to pump hard on the pedals as she journeyed past the sleeping houses, along the empty avenues and out of her residential neighborhood.

At this late hour, downtown Horizon wasn't much brighter than her neighborhood. In ways both good and bad, Horizon was a small town. Lucy had no interest in late-night carousing; the town's tendency to shut down at eleven o'clock didn't bother her. But riding through the tranquil darkness was a little unnerving.

Nearing the community garden, she heard the ghostly hiss of the overnight irrigation system spraying misty arcs of water across the acres of carrots and cabbage, tomatoes and cucumbers planted by residents who, like Lucy, lacked private yards large enough to accommodate a garden. A superlight coasted past her in the opposite direction, its motor humming. Then silence again as she pedaled north of the garden, past the Unitarian church, past the Catholic church, past the Horizon Municipal Building to the one downtown building with its windows ablaze with light. She parked her bike and locked it—an old habit from her Boston youth, she acknowledged, since no one in this somnolent Kansas town was likely to steal a bike from the rack in front of the police station at half-past midnight.

Even after her swift, windy ride, she wasn't quite awake enough to tolerate the glaring lights and liveliness inside the police station. She stood in the entry, blinking and waiting until she had grown accustomed to the bustle. Then she approached a bright-eyed, uniformed woman behind the front counter. "I'm here to see James Kazan," she announced.

"And you're . . . ?"

"Lucinda Beckwith. A—" she almost said friend "—colleague of Jim's at Access Computer Systems."

The woman appeared to recognize Lucy's name. "Right this way," she said as she emerged from behind the counter and strolled down a corridor.

Lucy followed the officer past a vacant, surprisingly pristine holding cell and down a hallway, where she indicated the door Lucy should go through.

Lucy found herself inside a small, uninhabited lounge with sturdy-looking furnishings—plastic Parsons tables, upholstered chairs, a couch and a wall television. The television was on, broadcasting a show Lucy couldn't identify. It involved a man wearing a tuxedo, holding a microphone and standing between two giddy women in scant bikinis. "For our next stunt," the man blathered, "our two contestants are going to dive into this huge vat of butterscotch pudding. Somewhere in that pudding is a genuine one-karat diamond ring set in eighteen-karat gold. Now, Mindy and Sushi can swim in the pudding, eat the pudding, paw through the pudding, roll in the pudding or shovel the pudding out of the vat with their bare hands in their search for the ring. Whoever finds it first wins the stunt. Are you ready, ladies?"

Lucy closed her eyes. She wasn't even ready to *watch* such a nauseating activity.

"Hi," Jim's voice reached her from behind. She spun around in time to see him enter the room.

She stared at him, momentarily speechless. He looked fatigued, his hair mussed and his jaw shadowed by a stubble of beard, the sleeves of his dark gray shirt rolled up and the top two buttons undone, displaying his Whole Earth amulet in a fleeting glint of gold. His trousers were wrinkled, and the laces on one of his green sneakers were untied.

Evidently, he had followed her gaze down to his feet, where he noticed the untied laces. He squatted and made quick work of tying them, then straightened and smiled tenuously. "Thanks for coming."

He smelled like sleep and warmth and masculinity. She swiftly averted her eyes and issued a stern mental reminder that she despised him. "What happened?" she asked.

"They let me call a lawyer, after all," he said. "I just got off the phone with him. The police have been very nice to me. The only thing I can't get them to do is turn off that damned TV." He jabbed a finger at the wall screen. Lucy glanced up to see the two nubile women flailing and wallowing in the enormous tub of pudding. Shuddering, she turned her back on the broadcast.

"Maybe you should ask them to put you in the holding cell," she suggested dryly. "I didn't notice a TV in there."

"There's one in there, all right," he informed her. "I think this is the way they break their prisoners—they make them watch the Love Channel late at night. It's pure torture." He gathered her hand in his, and the heat of his grip made her aware of how icy her fingers were. "Lucy, does the fact that you're here mean we can get beyond the Loverboy stuff?"

"I didn't come downtown to get beyond anything," she insisted, reminding herself as much as him. "I'm here because you're in trouble. But since your lawyer is on the way—"

He tightened his grip on her, as if afraid she was about to flee—which, she had to admit, was a possibility. "My lawyer is in California," he explained. "I haven't got a local attorney. But that's all right because the hacking occurred in a California computer. I'm hoping he'll be able to negotiate a settlement on that end before this goes much further."

"Then what do you want me for? To post bail?"

His thumb moved gently over her wrist, sending a tingling heat up through her arm. She hardened herself against it as best she could. "I think they're going to release me on my own recognizance," he said. "I wanted you here for moral support—"

She snorted.

"—and also to take Dara-Lyn."

"Take her where?"

"Back to your house for the night."

"Why should I do that?"

He regarded Lucy for a minute, then led her to the couch. Sitting, she tried to ignore the raucous shrieks and laughter spilling from the television set.

Jim sat beside her, his hand still closed tightly around hers. "I was arrested for hacking into the donor files of the Mensa Sperm Bank."

She intended to snort again, but a laugh emerged instead. "The Mensa Sperm Bank?"

"Yes. Dara-Lyn was conceived with their sperm, and for some reason, she became obsessed with the idea that I was the man behind her sperm."

"What?" Jim was under arrest. Dara-Lyn Pennybopper was preoccupied with sperm. This was serious—and all Lucy could do was laugh.

"Lucy...it isn't funny," Jim reproached.

"I know," she said, then convulsed in fresh gales of laughter. Her eyes grew moist and her breath came in great, wheezing gasps. "Oh, Jim—a sperm bank?"

"Not just any sperm bank. The Mensa Sperm Bank," he emphasized. "That's not to say I ever had anything to do with the place or with Dara-Lyn's birth or anything. It's just something she got hung up on, something her mother apparently believed, too. Dara-Lyn thought I was her father. She came to Horizon to find me because she was convinced of it."

Lucy had sensed from the first time she'd seen Dara-Lyn that the girl wasn't totally trustworthy. She recalled how Dara-Lyn had spotted her Access ID one late afternoon at the mall, how Dara-Lyn had zeroed in on her, how a few days later, she'd interrupted Lucy's dinner with Jim, how she'd finessed her way into Access, how she'd constantly wooed Jim with her pretty blue eyes and her spurious innocence.

Knowing the reason for the girl's behavior made Lucy a great deal more willing to excuse it. Dara-Lyn hadn't been a gaga groupie trying to worm her way into her idol's life. She'd been a motherless child searching desperately for a nonexistent father.

Lucy grew solemn. "So, you want me to take her home with me?"

"Just for tonight," he requested. "She refused to go back to the hostel, but I thought maybe tomorrow, we could talk to her friend Bobby and he might be able to persuade her to go back there."

Lucy nodded, recalling the amiable young man who had accompanied Dara-Lyn to Access when she'd visited the company.

"I'd like to see Dara-Lyn adopted," Jim went on. "I think a real family is what she needs."

"Aim high, why don't you," Lucy muttered. Of course Dara-Lyn needed a family, of course an adoption would be ideal. But Lucy and Jim were in no position to bring about such a thing.

Jim studied her for a minute. The noise level decreased as the TV cut to a commercial for Catch-the-Wind domestic windmill generators. "Lucy...have you ever heard of Home-Ties?"

She nodded again. Who hadn't heard of it? Despite Home-Ties' low profile, its success in arranging adoptions had received numerous plaudits. "Can we get in touch with them?" she asked.

"We already are in touch with them," Jim said slowly. "*I'm* Home-Ties."

Lucy frowned. "What do you mean, *you're* Home-Ties?"

"I founded it," he told her. "I run the program out of my home. I have volunteers around the country who do assessments of the adopting families, and I've got another group of volunteers in the L.A. area who keep me updated on how many adoptable children they've got. I feed everything into the computer and look for matches."

"You're kidding." It wasn't that she didn't believe him or that she thought what he'd described was impossible to achieve. What she didn't believe was that he could have established it without turning it into a publicity circus. The man couldn't even clear rubble from a beach without courting the attention of the national media.

Perhaps he could read what she was thinking. "I'd rather not let it get around that I'm the person behind Home-Ties. So please don't tell anyone," he said.

"Why don't you want it to get around?"

"Because..." He gazed straight into her eyes, as if he could see right through them and into her soul. "Because you're right—I'm a show-off and I enjoy my fame. But Home-Ties is really important to me. I'm not doing it for the print space. I'm not doing it to score points with the media. I'm not doing it for myself, and I don't want the program to be overshadowed by me."

"But *some* people must know you're in charge."

"My parents do," he acknowledged. "My sister and her family. A few people in the Department of Health and Human Services, because I had to get certain licenses and clearances to run the program."

Her gaze fell to his chest, to the beautiful gold amulet shining against the soft blond curls. "The president?" she asked, understanding now why he had received the medallion.

"Someone leaked it to her," Jim said with a modest smile that quickly faded. "And I've leaked it to you. Don't tell anyone, okay?"

"If you don't want me to, I won't," Lucy promised. Her fingers had become cold again without the protective warmth of his hand around them. She reached for his arm and he instantly enveloped her hands in his again.

"I have a family I think will make a good match for Dara-Lyn," he said. "Decent people, rock solid, and I think that's what Dara-Lyn needs. The only problem was that before I could get her interested in an adoption, I had to convince her I wasn't her father. And when the Mensa Sperm Bank refused to say unequivocally that I'd never made a donation, I hacked into their files in search of the proof I needed. I found it, too. I checked their alphabetical listings, their date-of-deposit listings, even their genetic-traits listing. I wasn't anywhere in it." A wicked smile teased her lips as he added, "Actually, some pretty interesting folks *were* in it—a couple of Nobel Prize winners, two of my professors from Stanford.... There were some real surprises. Thank God Dara-Lyn didn't recognize any of those names. All she saw was that my name wasn't in there."

"How did she take the news?"

He shrugged. "It could have been worse. It could have been better."

"I'll bring her home with me," Lucy said. She had little confidence in her ability to nurse Dara-Lyn through what must have been one of the most traumatic nights of the girl's life since the earthquake that had orphaned her. Someone more maternal, more empathic would be better.

But Jim had asked for Lucy. He needed her help. She would do the best she could.

"The police have her down at the other end of the building somewhere," he said. "When they first brought us in, they tried to give her a candy bar, but she wouldn't take it. Too right-side, she said."

"Do you want me to feed her dinner?" The thought of having to prepare a meal at this hour didn't thrill Lucy.

He shook his head. "She ate at my house. Just give her a place to sleep—and maybe a hand to hold."

Lucy glanced down at her own hands enveloped in Jim's, resting in his lap. She was still angry about his having romanced her under false pretenses. It didn't compute that the same man who had treated her so insensitively could be so charitable toward Big One orphans. She simply couldn't make sense of it.

She shoved her confusion aside for the time being. Right now, helping Dara-Lyn was her top priority.

Rising, she plunged her hands into the pockets of her slacks and eyed the door. "I guess I'll go find her, then."

Jim stood when she did. He accompanied her to the doorway, then leaned toward her, as if about to kiss her cheek. He must have read the churning distrust in her eyes because he pulled back before his lips could brush her cheek. "Thanks," he said.

With a faint nod, she turned and left the room.

A LIGHT TAPPING ON HER DOOR awakened Lucy. She sat up and squinted at her clock: a few minutes past six.

She heard the tapping sound again. "What?" she mumbled.

"Lucy?" The door cracked open and Dara-Lyn peeked in. "Can I turn on the TV downstairs in the living room? I would've just done it, but James got really mad at me yesterday when I turned on his TV without asking first."

Jim. Dara-Lyn. Fractured memories of the previous night began to fit together in Lucy's bleary mind. His arrest. Her trip to the police station. His revealing that he was the intelligence behind Home-Ties. Her co-operation in housing Dara-Lyn for the night.

His claim that he loved her.

She was too tired to make sense of the large picture, so she focused on the trivia. "Why on earth do you want to watch TV at this hour?" she asked Dara-Lyn.

"I thought maybe he'd be on the news," Dara-Lyn explained, opening the door wider.

Lucy rubbed her eyes, yawned, turned on her bedside lamp and lifted the remote control from her night table. "Come on in—we'll watch the news together."

Dara-Lyn opened the door fully. She had on an ankle-length sleepshirt, and her blond hair looked even more tousled than usual. With a shy smile, she crossed to the bed and climbed on next to Lucy.

Lucy punched the buttons until she got a local station. "In Lebanon yesterday," the female half of a two-person newsreading team declared, "Moslems and Christians poured into the streets in a spontaneous celebration to mark the fifth anniversary of the cease-fire." The screen filled with images of swarms of people chanting and prancing through the narrow streets of the Lebanese capital. Lucy was as pleased as anyone at the continuing peace in the Middle East, but this wasn't the news story she was anxious to hear.

She glanced at the girl on the bed beside her. Dara-Lyn traced the stitches on Lucy's blanket with her index finger. The lightning bolt she'd painted onto her nail had begun to fade. Just like her dreams of being Jim's daughter, Lucy thought.

They hadn't talked much last night. Dara-Lyn had been withdrawn, immersed in a dark depression. Lucy had thought Dara-Lyn might feel better if she vented her feelings, but she'd had no idea how to get a conversation started. Lucy had felt helpless to combat the girl's misery, so she'd offered what she could: a bed made with clean linens and all the privacy Dara-Lyn needed.

Now, with Dara-Lyn seated next to her, her head propped against a pillow and her legs extending halfway down the bed, Lucy felt just as inept as she had last night. "Did you sleep well?" she asked, then castigated herself for resorting to polite drivel.

Dara-Lyn sent her a quick, nervous smile, conveying that Lucy wasn't the only one who felt awkward and bashful. "Yeah. Your futon is more comfortable than the beds at the hostel."

The newsreaders continued to report the world's important events, but neither Lucy nor Dara-Lyn listened.

"Do you think he's still in jail?" Dara-Lyn asked, finally.

Lucy shrugged. Before she could conjecture on Jim's current status, the story they were waiting for came on. "Closer to home," the male newsreader said, "out in Horizon, a local hero has found himself in legal hot water again."

Dara-Lyn leaned forward and clutched Lucy's arm. Jim appeared on the screen, standing on the steps outside the Horizon Police Station, looking even scruffier and more haggard than he had last night. And sexier, Lucy added, taking in his rumpled shirt, his stubble of beard and his sleepy, deep-set eyes.

"James Kazan," the newsreader continued, "who gained international fame over a decade ago when he used a personal computer to break into the Pentagon's top-secret security network, was charged last night with a new hacking crime. According to authorities, Dr. Kazan broke into the private files of the Mensa Sperm Bank of Palo Alto. Our reporter Alison Lambert was on the scene when Dr. Kazan was released from police custody.''

Alison Lambert was one of six reporters crowding around Jim on the front steps of the building. Microphones were thrust at his face; questions were shouted at him. ''Why did you do it, Kazan?'' someone asked.

''Because it was there,'' he shot back.

''Why a sperm bank?''

''Well, I was looking for a savings bank, but I made a wrong turn somewhere.''

''Jim, is it true that the charges against you have been dropped?''

Jim nodded. ''My lawyer has negotiated a settlement. In return for having the charges against me dropped, I will be providing the sperm bank with technical advice.''

''What sort of advice, Dr. Kazan?'' asked Alison Lambert.

He gave the reporter a wink. ''Use your imagination.''

Lucy grinned. In spite of his exhaustion, in spite of the legal hassles he'd just endured, his wit didn't fail him. Nor did his dimples.

''He's so *it*,'' Dara-Lyn murmured with an appreciative sigh.

The newscast went on to other stories, and Lucy turned off the television. Then she twisted on the bed and scrutinized her young charge. She saw past Dara-Lyn's idol worship to something inside the girl, something sad and afraid, something that tugged at Lucy and made her want to gather Dara-Lyn into her arms.

To smother the girl in a protective hug would be totally out of character for Lucy. Instead, she asked, "Are you all right?"

Dara-Lyn stared intently at the fading lightning bolt on her nail. "Yeah," she said softly. "I guess."

"I wish I didn't have to go to work today," Lucy said. "I wish I could stay here all day with you. But I can't."

"That's all right," Dara-Lyn told her. "I'll just call Bobby and he can come and get me."

"And then, maybe Jim can work things out and you'll have a real home with two parents who'll love you and take care of you. A real home, Dara-Lyn, not a group home, not a hostel. It'll be wonderful, you'll see."

Dara-Lyn nodded again.

Even with her face angled away, Lucy noticed the tears spilling down her cheeks. "Dara-Lyn...I'm sorry it didn't work out the way you wanted it to."

"It's okay," Dara-Lyn mumbled, wiping futilely at her cheeks. "I mean, about James and all. I mean, if he isn't my father, I can't make him be my father. I just wish I had my mother," she said, no longer bothering to contain her tears. "I never cared about who my father was until I lost her. I miss her so much!"

Impulsively, Lucy reached out and pulled Dara-Lyn into her embrace. She massaged her trembling shoulders and rocked her gently. "I know," she whispered, absorbing Dara-Lyn's wrenching sobs. "I know. It hurts."

Dara-Lyn clung to her. Lucy tightened her hold, accepting Dara-Lyn's weight on her lap and the fierce weight of emotion in her heart. At that moment, nothing mattered more to Lucy than to make Dara-Lyn feel better, to comfort her in any way she could.

"It's all right," she whispered, cradling Dara-Lyn. "It's all right to cry. It hurts, I know. I lost my mother, too."

Dara-Lyn peered up at Lucy with overflowing eyes. "Really?" she asked. "In the Big One?"

"No. She died in an auto accident years ago."

"Does it ever stop hurting?" Dara-Lyn asked in a tremulous voice.

"No," Lucy answered honestly, wiping away a few tears of her own. "But in time, the pain is easier to bear. I promise you, Dara-Lyn, in time, it will be easier."

"I want a mother," Dara-Lyn murmured tremulously.

And I want a child, Lucy almost responded. She drew in a deep breath, recalling the delicious experience of holding little Isabella in her arms. That memory was replaced by a more recent memory, of Jim gazing earnestly at her in the police lounge. *Home-Ties is really important to me. I'm not doing it for myself....*

He was doing it for children like Dara-Lyn. He was doing it because children mattered, and babies and families. They mattered more than fame or notoriety or professional success. They were the most important thing in the world.

"Think of it this way," Lucy said, still cuddling Dara-Lyn, still stroking her quaking shoulders. "You had, what? Twelve or thirteen years with your mother, right?"

"Thirteen," Dara-Lyn mumbled.

"And no one can ever take that away from you. No earthquake can destroy it. Those years will be yours forever."

Dara-Lyn rested her head against Lucy's shoulder and wept. Lucy ruffled her hair and then closed her arms snugly around the girl once more, amazed at how deeply she shared Dara-Lyn's grief, how intimately tied to her she felt, how natural it seemed to hug her. Her eyes stung with tears, as well, tears for the mother she'd lost and the years she'd spent foolishly believing that just because she hadn't had a mother, she couldn't be a mother.

She could—with the right man, a man who considered children as indispensable as she did. A man who would do everything in his power to help a child without expecting gratitude or courting glory. A man, Lucy reluctantly admitted, with a sense of humor to ease her over the rough patches and push her past her own insecurities.

A man who thought she was wonderful and said so in writing—on a computer.

After a while, Dara-Lyn wound down. Her body grew quiescent and her breathing became more regular. "Thanks," she mumbled in a shaky voice.

"Thank *you*," Lucy whispered, so softly Dara-Lyn couldn't hear her. Louder, Lucy said, "Let's call Jim and tell him how he looked on TV." That wasn't what she really wanted to tell him, but it was all she could comfortably say in front of Dara-Lyn.

"Let's," Dara-Lyn agreed, cheering slightly. As Lucy lifted the telephone and punched in Jim's number, Dara-Lyn coached her. "Tell him he looked really *wow*. Tell him he looks better on TV than Suzette O'Rourke's father on *Sizzle-Vids*. Tell him—"

Lucy waved Dara-Lyn silent as the call was connected. Jim's phone rang four times and then his answering machine clicked on.

"Jim?" she shouted over the tape. "Are you there?"

"...Come to the phone right now, but if I'm not in jail, I'll call you back," the recorded message droned.

Not funny, she thought. After the beep, she said, "Hello, Jim—it's Lucy, and I—" She scrambled to think of what to say.

"Tell him he looked *it*," Dara-Lyn cued her.

"Dara-Lyn told me to tell you you looked *it* on TV. And I—"

"He looked *wow*."

She shot Dara-Lyn an impatient look, then obediently said into the phone, "Dara-Lyn says you looked *wow*. And I—" *love you,* her brain completed the sentence "—I need to talk to you. Please call me."

He didn't call, not while she and Dara-Lyn got dressed, ate breakfast, phoned the hostel and waited for Bobby to come and pick Dara-Lyn up. After hugging her goodbye and promising to see her that evening—maybe with news about a new family for her, a new home—Lucy went back inside and stared at her silent telephone.

If he'd wanted to talk to her, he would have contacted her. Still, she couldn't stop herself from dialing his number again. She listened. "... if I'm not in jail, I'll call..."

Maybe he *was* in jail. Or maybe he was being interviewed by *USA Today* or *Newsweek*. Maybe hearing Lucy tell him she loved him wasn't that important to him right now—or maybe he thought she had something else to tell him, something he didn't want to hear.

"This is Lucy again," she said once his message ended. "I'll be at work if you want to talk." With a sigh, she hung up.

And prayed he would want to talk.

A > KNOCK, KNOCK.

Lucy stared at the newly opened window filling the lower half of her monitor and reread the message that appeared above the blinking cursor. There was no doubt in her mind who had sent it. Although it was nearly noon, Jim hadn't yet arrived at Access, but that didn't matter. He'd already proved—more than once—that he could break into any computer from anywhere in the world.

Her heart began to race. Wherever he'd been, whatever he'd been thinking, he must have gotten her messages on his answering machine. He must be willing to hear what she had to say.

She stared at the *A > Knock, knock* for a moment, then dutifully typed, *A > Who's there?*

A > Canoe.

A > Canoe who?

A > Canoe believe I've got a family lined up for Dara-Lyn?

Lucy spontaneously clapped her hands and let out a cheer. *A > Oh, Jim, that's wonderful!* she typed.

He didn't respond for several seconds. Then, *A > Can I be Jim now?*

She wasn't sure exactly what he was asking. *A > Why shouldn't you be Jim?*

A > Because he's on your Z list. Because you're mega-mad at him. Because you think he used Loverboy to win your heart. And you're right. He did.

Lucy sighed, then entered *A > It worked.*

A > It did?

A > To my utter horror, yes. It did.

The cursor flashed. No message appeared.

A > I love you, Jim.

Typing that sentence had to have been the bravest, most difficult thing she had ever done. She held her breath, anxious, waiting.

The cursor began to jump, to fly as his words spilled out. *A > Oh, Lucy, Lucy, I love you, too. I'm really zonked—I just got back from the police station and I was going to try and get some rest before I went to work, but I got home and there were your messages. If I had known this was what you wanted to talk about, I wouldn't have bothered coming home. I would have come straight to Access.*

A > That's all right. If you're tired, get some rest. We can talk later.

A > I don't want to wait. I could shower and change my clothes and be there in less than a half hour.

A > You'd be better off staying home. If you come in I might make you work on Smart-Town.

A > You're cruel, sweet beets. Cruel.

A > But a little romantic. Sometimes. When my defenses are down.

Jim's house was over a mile away from Access, but she felt as if the circuits were carrying him to her, connecting them, merging their minds at the speed of electricity. She could hear his laughter. She could picture his smile. She could almost feel his arms around her.

A > Keep your defenses down, Dr. B. I'll see you in a half hour. Sooner, if I can manage it.

A > Take the day off.

A > Can't. I want to see you. I want to hear you say you love me. In the flesh.

A > Access is not the place to do anything in the flesh.

A > That's a matter of opinion. Did you know that I crave your body?

A > I thought that was Loverboy's line.

A > Okay. He craves your body. I crave your mind. And your soul. And your heart. I'm a pretty "craven" guy.

She laughed. *A > I love you—both of you. Shave and shower and come on in so I can tell you.*

A > In the flesh, he asserted. Then he typed in a command *2HRT-BT1.*

Lucy smiled and watched as the two lovers Jim had programmed glided into view on her monitor, moved toward each other, reached each other and absorbed each other. She watched as their red hearts met, united and grew, pulsing together, living and loving together.

    2HRT-BT1.
    2HRT-BT1.
    2HRT-BT1.

Epilogue

Fireworks were banned in the Middle East—the residents of that healing region had seen enough explosions in their skies before the cease-fire in 1993. In Northern Ireland, a committee of Catholic priests and Protestant ministers issued a joint prayer for peace. Along the Amazon, ceremonies were held to honor the Rain Forest Protection Acts signed during WEC-I and WEC-II. In Moscow, despite blizzard conditions, people threw open their windows and invited the police officers patrolling the snow-covered sidewalks to come inside and warm up, to share in the music and vodka.

Along the Riviera, cruise ships sent off bright red flares. In Tokyo, families dressed in traditional garb and performed the tea ceremony. In Calcutta, hundreds of pilgrims marched through the balmy night, bringing food and flowers to the patients at the Mother Teresa Hospice. In midtown Manhattan, no fewer than one and a half million celebrants poured into Times Square to watch a specially designed spherical hologram ride down a laser cable to the roof of a skyscraper, while Dick Clark, at long last showing a hint of gray hair at this temples, led the singing of "Auld Lang Syne." Inside the New World Space

Consortium's International Space Lab, the astronauts drank champagne through straws.

In Horizon, it snowed.

LUCY HALF SAT, HALF LAY IN the bed, gazing out the window at the delicate white flakes that swirled gently over the boulevard and drifted across the school fields. The tree branches were adorned with cottony tufts of snow, and the river was locked beneath a thin layer of ice.

She was warm, though, safe and warm in this softly lit room, with her daughter at her breast. Once Jim got back, her life would be complete.

He hadn't wanted to go home, but she'd insisted. He needed some rest, a shower and a fresh change of clothing, and although he'd called his parents and her father from the medical center, there were other calls to be made: his sister, her brother, Emilio and Dolores, whose New Year's Eve party they'd been at when Lucy had gone into labor.

"What a night," she murmured, feathering her fingers tenderly over the baby's smooth cheek.

It really hadn't been bad, not with Jim beside her every step of the way, squeezing her hand, wiping her face with a wet cloth, encouraging her and cracking jokes whenever things became too intense. "Come on, sweet beets," he would exhort when she grew weary and cross. "You're so pushy, this ought to be easy for you. Don't let Wizard, Junior get the better of you. You're bigger than he is."

"He" turned out to be a she. She weighed seven pounds, six ounces. Her scalp was covered with thin black wisps of hair and her eyes were a pale grayish blue. She was twenty-four and a half inches long. "That's very tall," the obstetrician observed with a smile. "Given who she's got for parents, this isn't surprising."

She was tall and she was ravenous. In the eight hours since she'd been born, she had already nursed three times and was starting in on her fourth feeding.

Lucy ran her fingers over the baby's cheek once more, then stroked her back through the receiving blanket. The baby punched at the swaddling, pushing and clawing until one of her hands was free of the tightly wrapped cloth. She used it to cling to Lucy's swollen breast.

"Don't worry," Lucy whispered. "Nobody's going to steal your food." Before the baby could pinch her, she lifted the hand away. Everything about the newborn was so perfect: the dainty fingers, the hairline creases across the palm, the fingernails as beautiful as tiny pink pearls. Lucy placed her thumb against the curve of the baby's palm and the baby reflexively closed her fingers tight around it.

"I love you," Lucy murmured, watching the peaceful flexing of her daughter's lips and cheeks as she suckled. "I hope to God I'll be a good mother. You picked yourself a wonderful father, at least. And I promise to do the best I can."

For the moment, the baby seemed to have no complaints.

Lucy heard the door opening and looked up as Jim entered the room. The shoulders of his parka were dusted with snow, but he didn't bother to remove it before hurrying across the room to Lucy's side. He leaned over, careful not to crush the baby as he gave Lucy a deep, loving kiss that lasted much longer than Lucy had been prepared for. By the time he drew back, she was flushed and out of breath.

"You shouldn't do that in front of the child," she scolded, although she was smiling.

Peering at the little baby busily nursing, he laughed. "I don't think she noticed," he said, bowing and touching his lips to the knitted white cap covering her head. His eyes glistened with moisture as he gazed at his daughter. "I didn't dream her, Lucy. She's real."

"You're getting mushy-gushy," Lucy teased.

"Indeed I am," he agreed without a trace of remorse. "My sister told me century children are supposed to be endowed with magical powers."

"Century children?"

"Children born during the first year of a century. I wonder what it means when a child is born during the first *hour* of the century."

"In this case, it means she came three days early."

"Mmm. Emilio's envious. He thinks all babies should arrive three weeks late, just like Isabella did, so all new parents get to sweat it out the way he had to."

"Emilio's just vexed because he won't have both of us at work for eight months."

"Well, he's lucky he'll get at least one of us. I think it'll work out well with us alternating weeks of leave." He unzipped his parka and removed it. "I brought you a present."

"What?" she asked with childlike glee.

He fished in one of his jacket pockets and pulled out a bag of chocolate kisses. "Here," he whispered, secreting the bag under her blanket. "Don't let the doctors find out I smuggled in junk food."

"You're incorrigible," Lucy scolded, pulling the bag back out. "Give me a kiss!"

Pretending to misunderstand her, be bowed and covered her mouth with his. Lucy didn't bother to correct him. When at last they parted, she moaned contentedly. "After that, a chocolate kiss is going to seem anticlimactic."

Grinning, he pulled a candy from the bag, tore off the foil wrapper and popped the chocolate in her mouth. Then he unwrapped another one for himself.

"So, who else did you call?" she asked once she had swallowed. "Your sister, Emilio—"

"Your brother, of course, and I called Dara-Lyn in Minnesota. She was very excited. She said she'd like to come down and visit again this summer."

"Will the Cokers let her?"

"I think so. They let her visit last year and it worked out well." He traced the baby's slender arm through the pink fleece of her sleeper, then loosened the receiving blanket and tucked her arm back inside. "We're going to have to name her, you know."

"You mean, we're not going to call her Hey, You?" Lucy joked.

Jim wrinkled his lip. "I think I liked you better when you had no sense of humor."

"I always had a sense of humor!"

"You're right—you always did. It just needed work. So what are we going to name her?"

"Aurora," Lucy said.

Jim eyed her curiously. "Aurora?"

"It means dawn. And here we are, at the dawn of a new century."

"Aurora," he said experimentally. "Aurora Beckwith Kazan. I like it."

"Then Aurora she shall be."

"Do you think she'll inherit your beauty?"

"No. I think she'll inherit *your* beauty and *my* brains," Lucy declared.

Instead of being insulted, Jim gave her a warm smile. "Given her background, the poor kid's probably doomed to become a wizard when she grows up."

Lucy cradled Aurora snugly in her arms. "Maybe she'll surprise us. Maybe she'll grow up to be an artist. Or a dancer."

"A basketball star," Jim suggested.

"An astronaut."

"A pinball champ."

"A pudding wrestler on the Love Channel."

Jim laughed. Lucy laughed. They kissed again, but this time little Aurora expressed her displeasure by shoving away from Lucy's depleted breast and letting out a howl. With an expertise Lucy hadn't known she possessed, she burped the baby, then turned her around and offered her the other breast. Aurora latched on and relaxed, consuming her seconds with great relish.

Jim gazed down at Aurora, his blue eyes once again filling with tears. "I think I'm going to like this century," he murmured. "Nine hours old, and so far it's sensational."

Lucy smiled at him, then turned to admire their child, this miraculous creature who had come to life with the new millenium, who would grow with it and contribute to it and be a part of it. For Aurora, there would be a radiant future, a world better than the one her parents had been born into. A world of clean air and clear skies, of peace and human kindness.

This precious century child did possess a powerful magic: the magic of love and family, of intelligence and humor and a lifetime of tomorrows to explore. Lucy could imagine no greater happiness.

HARLEQUIN
American Romance®

ABOUT THE AUTHOR

Judith Arnold is a first-generation American whose parents hail from Eastern Europe. (As a young boy, her father landed in America on Valentine's Day.) Consequently, she says, "I found American history interesting, but it wasn't *my* history." The decision to write about the 1990s—what is to come—was a natural choice. Besides, Judith has a personal stake in the future of the world—her two young sons, Freddy and Greg. "I spend a lot of time thinking about what the world will be like for my children," she says.

It was especially challenging for Judith to create her version of the nineties' society—a challenge to which she rose admirably. "I'm amazed how many of my predictions have already come true," she says, "including the California earthquake, the end of the Cold War and even the Velcro diapers."

With twenty-two American Romance novels to her credit, Judith Arnold is one of the series's premier authors. Her versatility and an uncanny ability to make us laugh and cry have become her hallmarks. She and her family, including husband Ted, make their home in Massachusetts.

JA

HARLEQUIN

Romance

**This June, travel to Turkey
with Harlequin Romance's**

**THE JEWELS OF HELEN
by Jane Donnelly**

She was a spoiled brat who liked her own way.

Eight years ago Max Torba thought Anni was self-centered—
and that she didn't care if her demands made life impossible
for those who loved her.

Now, meeting again at Max's home in Turkey, it was clear he
still held the same opinion, no matter how hard she tried to
make a good impression. "You haven't changed much, have
you?" he said. "You still don't give a damn for the trouble you
cause."

But did Max's opinion really matter? After all, Anni had no
intention of adding herself to his admiring band of female
followers....

Back by Popular Demand

Janet Dailey
Americana

A romantic tour of America through fifty favorite Harlequin Presents® novels, each set in a different state researched by Janet and her husband, Bill. A journey of a lifetime in one cherished collection.

In June, don't miss the sultry states featured in:

Title # 9 - FLORIDA
          Southern Nights
    #10 - GEORGIA
          Night of the Cotillion

Available wherever Harlequin books are sold.

JD-JR

**THIS JULY, HARLEQUIN OFFERS YOU
THE PERFECT SUMMER READ!**

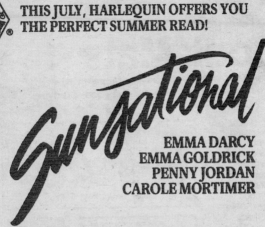

**EMMA DARCY
EMMA GOLDRICK
PENNY JORDAN
CAROLE MORTIMER**

From top authors of Harlequin Presents comes
HARLEQUIN SUNSATIONAL, a four-stories-in-one
book with 768 pages of romantic reading.

Written by such prolific Harlequin authors as Emma Darcy,
Emma Goldrick, Penny Jordan and Carole Mortimer,
HARLEQUIN SUNSATIONAL is the perfect summer
companion to take along to the beach, cottage, on your
dream destination or just for reading at home in the warm
sunshine!

Don't miss this unique reading opportunity.

Available wherever Harlequin books are sold.